Not in the Calendar

By Margaret Kennedy

Troy Chimneys
The Midas Touch
Jane Austen
Lucy Carmichael
Act of God
The Constant Nymph
Escape Me Never
Outlaws on Parnassus
A Night in Cold Harbor
The Forgotten Smile
Not in the Calendar
and others

NOT IN THE
CALENDAR

Margaret Kennedy

THE MACMILLAN COMPANY, NEW YORK

Printed in the United States of America

Library of Congress Catalog Card Number: 64-14526

DESIGNED BY RONALD FARBER

The words of "Moonstruck" by Lionel Monckton are reproduced by permission of Messrs. Chappell & Co., Ltd.

The lines of A. E. Housman are from "A Shropshire Lad"—Authorised Edition—from *Complete Poems* by A. E. Housman. Copyright © 1959 by Holt, Rinehart and Winston, Inc. Reprinted by permission of Holt, Rinehart and Winston, Inc.

TO ELUNED

I could not have ventured to write this book without the advice and criticism of Miss Edith Whetnall and of Dr. Pierre Gorman, Librarian to the Royal National Institute for the Deaf. I wish to thank them for their great kindness, and for the trouble which they took to help me.

MARGARET KENNEDY

CONTENTS

PART I

1. Passion Flower Fruit (1883)   3
2. Sometimes It Does (1891)   25
3. The Greco Lark (1896)   49
4. Arrpairr (1898)   77
5. The Aunt Heap (1906)   95
6. Postbag to Washington (1907)   121

PART II

7. A Journey into Silence (1907)   131
8. A Journey out of Silence (1908)   145
9. Trojan Mothers (1914-1919)   163
10. Candidate for a Halo (1921-1922)   173
11. The Wholebine Monkey (1930)   209
12. Recall (1938)   221

Part I

Now—for a breath I tarry
Nor yet disperse apart—
Take my hand quick and tell me
What have you in your heart.

Speak now, and I will answer;
How shall I help you, Say;
Ere to the wind's twelve quarters
I take my endless way.

A. E. HOUSMAN

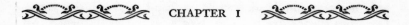

Passion Flower Fruit

1883

ONE

THE MANOR HOUSE at Slane St. Mary's is one of those ancient but nondescript country seats which eventually become private mental homes or preparatory schools after they have been offered to, and refused by, the National Trust. It used to belong to the Knevetts who had a very bad reputation until the early nineteenth century. A virtuous nephew then inherited it from a vicious uncle, having previously amassed a considerable fortune in the Madeira wine trade. He retiled the roof, mended gates, and sent poachers to Botany Bay.

Strive how he might, however, the property never did him credit. Sometimes he could almost believe those who declared that there was a curse upon the place. The people remained a wild, lawless, poaching lot, and saplings from Slane Forest invaded his land as fast as he rooted them up. The Knevetts never enjoyed much consequence in the country. Cut off as they were by the bad forest roads, they remained rustic and awkward, uneasy on any ground save their own. Their neighbors laughed at them behind their backs.

The ghost of wicked Sir Harry gave recurring trouble. Sometimes in the middle of the night the sleep of his blameless nephew would be broken by a tremendous hullabaloo in the dining room. There were yells, thumps, and the crash of broken glass. This evidence of riot ceased as soon as Sir Rich-

[3]

ard, nightcap on head, candle in hand, entered the room. Decorous silence greeted him. Not a chair was disturbed. All the prayer books duly lay in their places for family worship before breakfast.

At length he hit upon a scientific explanation. A vein of rock, running from the house to the village inn, acted as a subterranean reverberator. He had read, in the *Edinburgh Review,* of an invisible coach, somewhere in the South of France, which drove past a gentleman's villa every evening at a quarter past eight. This was, in fact, a stagecoach on a highroad some miles away; the sound was carried by a similar vein of rock. The family were obliged to accept this explanation. The neighbors did not, and young Richard, the heir, had to look outside the county for a wife.

This lady had twelve children who were all still living at home in 1883, although Barbara, the second daughter, was engaged to marry a son of the Bishop of Severnton. These children fell into groups of three. Susan, the eldest, was one and twenty. She, Barbara, and Dick rated as adults. They were followed by three schoolgirls: Flora, Clementina, and Catherine. Then came three boys: Edmund, Robert, and Thomas. Caroline, Grace, and Alice brought up the rear.

It so happened that the six younger girls were, in September, left for a short time in the sole care of their governess, Miss Fitzroy. The boys had gone back to school. Barbara and Susan were spending a week in Severnton choosing wedding clothes. They were recalled, after three days, by a boy on a farm pony. Their brother Dick had fallen off a horse while staying with friends in Devonshire. His parents, misliking the description of his injuries, had set off in a panic to his bedside.

"Though why we should have to fly home, I fail to see," complained Barbara, as they drove through the forest. "What is Fitzy paid for?"

"She doesn't like being alone in the house," said Susan.

"Alone! With six children and ten servants."

"She's afraid of hearing . . . things . . . *you know!*"

"Fiddlesticks. It's only a vein of rock, and nobody does hear it nowadays."

"It never was a vein of rock. It was a trick the servants used to play on Grandpapa."

"What? No! Who says so?"

"Mama told me."

"She told *you?*"

Barbara brooded huffily until curiosity got the better of resentment; she was never disposed to allow any undisputed privileges to her elder sister.

"Well?"

"The first time it happened, after Grandpapa died, Papa dismissed the butler next morning. He'd always wanted to try that, but he couldn't until he was master. And it never happened again."

"But why has all this been kept so dark?"

"It would be disrespectful to Grandpapa's memory. People would laugh if they knew."

"I should have kept my mouth shut."

When did you ever keep your mouth shut? thought Susan, and changed the subject. Had Barbara finally settled on silver gray for the bridesmaids' dresses?

She had not. Silver gray might suit Flo and Kitty, but Clemmie would look a fright in it. The bridesmaids were to wear pink, which would suit none of them, but in which they would all look much of a muchness. Flo? What could Flo do? The material had been ordered.

Flo, according to Susan's experience, might do anything. She might upset a bottle of ink all over the material as soon as it arrived. Since nobody wanted to wear pink, she might act as a public benefactor, and it would be stupid to put Barbara too much upon her guard.

As soon as they reached home the bride marched into the hall proclaiming that she was going to announce her decision on the spot, and get it over. A shrill voice above their heads piped, "Flo says if it's pink she'll frow up in church."

The chubby face of Lallie, the five-year-old darling of the

whole family, peered at them through the banisters. Both sisters flew up to embrace her.

"Where are the others?" demanded Barbara. "Are they all dead?"

"Yeth," said Lallie placidly. "Did you bring me something pretty from Severnton?"

"I hadn't time, dear. We came off in such a hurry. But where are the rest, really?"

"In Heaven. They're dead."

"We don't make jokes like that, Lallie. Where are they?"

The corners of Lallie's mouth went down.

"I don't know. They're gone. They're dead. They poisoned themselves wiv strong poison."

Her sisters stared at her and then at each other.

"Have they eaten something?" exclaimed Susan.

"Passion poison," said Lallie nodding. "It was howwid."

Kitty and Grace, both in floods of tears, now came thundering down the stairs to fling themselves upon their seniors.

"Oh, Barbie . . ."

"Oh, Sue . . ."

"We've eaten poison! We shall die!"

"Agonizing pain and strong convulsions . . ."

"It says in a book. Clemmie has started dying already . . ."

"Flo has crept off to die quietly by herself . . ."

"Stop!" shouted Barbara. "Don't both talk at once. Now, Kitty! What have you been eating?"

"P-passion flower fruit," sobbed Kitty. "We all did. Flo says it is a great delicacy in Persia. But then . . . *then* . . . she found a book in the library that says it's deadly poison . . ."

"You never let Lallie eat it?" interrupted Susan.

"She wouldn't. She didn't like it."

"Oh, thank God! Thank God!"

"Nasty howwid poison," agreed Lallie complacently. "I was good. I wouldn't eat any, and now I won't die, fank God."

"But where's Fitzy?" asked Barbara.

"In the library," said Kitty. "Trying to see what it says in the book Flo found. Clemmie is dying upstairs. We haven't started yet, but we shall . . . we shall . . . any minute."

They all flocked to the library where they found their governess hunting distractedly through volume after volume of a very old-fashioned encyclopedia. She was, as everybody knew, a hopeless fool.

"If I could find Flo to ask her which volume," she wailed, "we might see if there is some antidote. And I've asked for a message to be sent to Dr. Blake. I don't know if it went. The servants don't always take my orders."

"He'll never get here in time," howled Grace. "Death in a few hours, Flo said. Oh, Barbie! Don't let us die! Don't let us!"

Barbara took command.

"An emetic. Ipecacuanha. It's in Mama's medicine cupboard, Sue. Give them a big dose. And then they had better swing head downward in the orchard till they are sick. I'll go and deal with Clemmie."

"It might have been worse," murmured Susan as they ran upstairs. "It might have been Lallie!"

"Oh, yes . . . anybody rather than Lallie. Mama would never get over it if . . . oh, my patience! Just listen to Clemmie!"

Clemmie, stretched upon her bed, and attended by Ida, the schoolroom maid, was screaming at the top of her voice. This, however, was nothing unusual. She had a talent for creating a maximum panic on minimum grounds. In summer it was she who attracted the wasps. In winter it was she who fell through the ice. Nobody had any patience with her.

"Oh, this pain!" she cried, clutching her stomach. "Oh, I'm dying! I'm dying!"

"For the fifty-seventh time," said Barbie brutally. "If you die so often, nobody will notice when you really do. When you've been sick, you'll feel better. It's your own fault for eating the stuff, and no thanks to you Lallie didn't."

"Flo ate it. Oh . . . oh. . . ."

"She does look bad," murmured Ida.

"Really?" said Barbie with heavy sarcasm. "And how many deathbeds have you attended, Ida?"

Ida grew very red, and Barbie pressed the point: "Eh?"

"Three . . . please . . . Miss. . . ."

This was disconcerting since Barbie had not, so far, seen anybody die. Poor people, she remembered, were more frequently exposed to that sort of thing. Ida was a cottage girl and the niece of the kennelman.

Sue came in with the ipecacuanha, and between them they forced a dose down Clemmie's throat.

"So that leaves only Flo," said Barbie, when Ida had been dispatched to dose Grace and Kitty. "I shall give her half the bottle. It's all been her doing. Where can she be?"

"They said she'd crept off to die alone," said Sue.

"Not Flo. She's probably managed to make herself sick on the quiet. But that won't save her. She must take ipecac and be sick again."

They searched the house and garden in vain. Crossing the orchard they came to the swing. Barbie's treatment had been abundantly successful. Kitty and Grace lay limply on the grass. Lallie, who had watched their sufferings with fascinated attention, announced that they had been sick, and been sick, and been sick. . . .

"Then they're all right," decided Barbie. "Where's Ida?"

"Gone back to Clemmie. She thinks Clemmie is very ill."

"Ida is getting rather too big for her boots."

"Here's Flo," piped Lallie.

Flo was the only beauty among the Knevetts. Barbie and Sue, though overtall, were handsome enough with their rosy cheeks, shining hair, and blue eyes—but their hands and feet were clumsy, and they marched through life like a couple of grenadiers. Flo was tall and fair too, but her eyes were dark, and all her movements graceful. Her skin was pale but very delicate. She strolled tranquilly across the orchard and started in surprise at the group by the swing.

"Where have I been? Up in the hayloft, reading *Ivanhoe*. What on earth is the matter with you all?"

"You'll have to take it too," cried Grace, trying to sit up. "You ate passion flower fruit. So now you'll have to swallow ipecac, and swing head downward and be sick."

Flo could scarcely speak for laughing.

"You don't mean to say you believed . . . why . . . you donkeys . . . that was all cram. Barbie too? I'd have thought she had more sense."

"A joke is a joke," said Barbie, scarlet with mortification. "A downright lie is not. We've sent for Dr. Blake."

"Oh, no! Not really? Oh, you'll be the death of me!"

"Clemmie is very ill."

"Oh, I'm sure!"

"But you were so frightened, Flo," pleaded Kitty. "You were shaking with fright when you came and told us what you'd found in that book."

"I'm a first-rate actress. Didn't you know?"

Barbie drew a deep breath, and launched a counterattack.

"All the same, we can't be sure that fruit is not poison. Just to be on the safe side you'd better have some ipecac, like all the others. Hadn't she, Sue?"

"Y-yes . . ." quavered Sue, who was terrified of Flo.

"Me? Take that stuff? Not if I know it."

"You will if we say so. You are in our charge."

"Am I? Not in Fitzy's charge? Where is she, by the way?"

"In the library. Trying to find what book . . ."

"Oh . . . oh . . . if I die of anything it will be with laughing."

"You'll laugh on the other side of your face in half an hour's time. Everybody who ate that fruit has had ipecac and so will you."

"Has Carrie had it?"

There was a sudden silence. They had all, as usual, forgotten Carrie, the tenth and the least conspicuous of the twelve Knevetts.

"I thought not. Go and dose her first, my dears. And you needn't pretend that you don't know where she is. We all know where to find Carrie, on the very few occasions when she's wanted: up in the old kitchen garden, mopping and mowing with the village idiot."

TWO

Sue ran off hastily. Flo would never swallow that dose, and the blame for failure had better rest with Barbie, should trouble ensue.

Discipline for Carrie would be easier. The little girl was gentle and inoffensive, but very slow-witted and a permanent laughingstock among the clever, pugnacious Knevetts. Try as she would, she never seemed able to behave like other people, or even to comprehend what was said to her. This attachment to Winsome Harper, a repulsive cottage child two years younger than herself, was typical. Harper, the kennel-man, was respectable; his daughters, though they were all named after hounds, were clean and well mannered. Had Carrie selected Dainty or Ruby, with whom to nurse dolls or make cowslip balls, no objection could have been raised. Poor Winsome was scarcely human, less attractive than an animal, a mere mournful little lump of flesh. She snorted in a disagreeable way, and was given to fits of wild capers and grimaces. Yet these two had always been close friends, although recently they had taken to hiding from the mockery which their gambols inspired. Hints had often been dropped to Carrie that quiet play would have been more suitable. To copy Winsome's uncouth gestures, her mopping and mowing, was stupid and unkind. Nor was there any point in talking to a person who was obviously stone deaf.

Carrie was unwontedly obstinate in the matter. She prattled away to Winsome as she did to her dolls, and maintained, when reproved, that dolls are deaf too. It was time, perhaps, that such folly should be forbidden. She was no longer a baby. She was eight years old, and must behave herself more seemly.

The old kitchen garden lay at some distance from the house. It had produced no fruit or vegetables for the family since the days of wicked Sir Harry, when it had been allowed to run wild. A new one had been made, by his heir, in a more convenient situation. For some time it was given over to brambles and nettles; then, since the soil was rich, it gradually became a perquisite of cottagers working for the Knevetts. Although never formally made over to them, it was cleared, first by one, then by another, and used for homely crops of beans and cabbages.

Picking her way uphill, among these unofficial allotments, Sue admired the evidence of Harper's industry, nor did she connect a wealth of soft greenery with an earlier crop of asparagus. This delicacy, above Harper's station, must have been raised for the market, and such a practice was not in the bond. Harper might grow food for his family, but had no business to sell his produce. Barbie would have detected such an iniquity and brought it to light. Sue, less observant, panted on up to some heaps of brick and shattered glass which had once been forcing houses.

The two children were, as usual, on a path at the top, beneath a laurel hedge. Absorbed in their play, they did not notice her approach, and she stood watching them for a moment. Carrie's dress was deplorable, far too long and far too narrow. It was evidence both of Fitzy's idiocy and of Carrie's tendency to be forgotten. Ample material for three dresses had been purchased. Fitzy, when cutting it out, had given four deep flounces to Lallie, upon whom she doted, and to Grace, who demanded them. Nothing was left for Carrie save a kind of tubular cassock in which she could scarcely walk with freedom.

They were busy at their clowning, those two. Winsome picked up a piece of glass from the path and gave a broad wink.

"Glass!" said Carrie, also winking and waving her arms about. "Put it in the bird's house."

"Ca-ca-ca-ca-ca!" cried Winsome, trotting off.

Sue stepped forward, and explained her mission, at which Carrie's brown eyes, always a little puzzled, widened.

"But that was a joke about poison. Flo didn't mean it."

"Yes, but we aren't quite sure if that fruit is really wholesome. How did you know it was a joke? Did Flo tell you?"

"No. But she wasn't angry."

This, from anybody else, would have been subtle. One could never be sure that Flo was in earnest unless she was angry. Hence the uneasiness of making up a quarrel with her, although she would eventually declare, in tears, that she had not meant a word that she said. One knew that, for once, she had meant it. Carrie, however, was incapable of subtlety and was told to come along.

"Can't I wait till Winsome gets back? I told her to put something in our old bird's nest. She won't know why I've gone."

"Now, Carrie! Seriously, it's time you stopped making those silly faces and winking and capering. It's not nice."

"But that's her language. She calls glass a wink."

"She has no language. It's all make-believe, and you shouldn't mix it up with truth."

"It is true. Everybody has a language. She can't *say* any word except 'ca.' I've told her that's me. But we have a lot of dumb crambo words. We talk. Really we do."

"Very well. When she comes back tell her you've got to take a dose of ipecac because Flo played a joke on you all."

"Oh, I couldn't. I don't know those words. We only have very few. Just for things round here, that we play with."

"Then tell her to bring some blue and yellow flowers, when she comes back. But I can't wait long. Pick up your chalks. You've left them all over the path."

"Those aren't mine. They're hers."

"Winsome's? Where did she get expensive chalks like these? If you mean you gave her yours, you oughtn't . . ."

"Ida gave them to her. She's Winsome's cousin."

"Oh, dear, yes, So she is. And where did Ida get them, pray?"

"She bought them in Severnton."

"Out of her wages? How silly! They're far too good . . ."

"Ca-ca-ca-ca-ca!"

Winsome had returned. At the sight of Susan she dropped the curtsy which was, in the village, inspired by the sight of any Knevett. Carrie went into a convulsion of capers and grimaces, picked up a stone, dropped it, and said:

"Flowers. Blue. Yellow."

"Ca-ca-ca-ca-ca!" agreed Winsome, trotting off again.

"I hope she won't bring eggs," said Carrie. "It's difficult sometimes. Picking up something and dropping it means yellow in her language, but it means an egg too."

"I can't see why it should mean either."

"Oh, Sue! If you drop an egg, and it breaks, there's all yellow."

"But these chalks! What does she want with chalks?"

"To draw with. I showed her how to draw just as I showed Lallie. She draws better than me. Look. . . ."

After a search under the hedge Carrie produced a queer little book made from old envelopes neatly sewn together. It was filled with pictures in chalk.

"Winsome never drew these!"

"Then who did?"

Who did? Despite their crudity, the pictures displayed a skill and accuracy of line beyond the powers of Lallie, Grace, or Carrie herself. They were all recognizable copies of certain old favorites in the Manor House nursery. Sue could identify several originals—a Kate Greenaway, a Walter Crane, a Randolph Caldecott. Somewhat baffled, she replied with another question, "Where did she get this little book?"

"Ida made it. We have no paper, so she gets the envelopes out of the waste paper baskets, and makes little books for us."

Ida again! This deliberate encouragement of an intimacy disliked by the family smacked of impertinence. The girl did her work well enough, her manners were respectful, but it seemed that her thoughts were insubordinate.

"She should have got leave to do that. It was putting herself forward . . . or else it was rather underhand."

"Winsome has no books or pictures at her house. So she copies mine, and makes her own picture books."

"Ca-ca-ca-ca-ca!" cried Winsome, returning with a bunch of mustard flowers and speedwell.

"There! You see?" cried Carrie in triumph.

"Yes. I see. Now come along."

After a few final flourishes, Carrie came along. As they set off down the hill, Sue asked how long they had been doing this.

"Oh, always."

"No, Carrie. You couldn't have when first you began to play—when you were quite babies."

"I can't remember that time. I can't remember any time when we weren't talking in her language."

"Don't call it her language, as if she had made it up."

"I don't think I made it up," said Carrie, looking puzzled. "We just . . . did. *She* says glass is wink. The sun does make it wink, you know. Anyway, you do see, Sue, that it's real talking? Not what you said?"

Sue hesitated. This uncouth game was more sensible than she had supposed, and she was half inclined to defer an outright prohibition until she had consulted her mother. Irritation swung her the other way. She was the eldest, but they none of them minded her as they should, and Barbie was going to be married first. Carrie at least must submit to her.

"I know," she said at last, "that you only wanted to help poor Winsome . . ."

"No! I talk to her because she's my friend."

"If you do it for your own pleasure, that's selfish. You may have done her harm. You may have excited her, and made her want things she can never have. She'll never change from what she is now, you know."

"But, Sue, she has changed a little. She seems sometimes to understand me when I talk. I think she's begun to hear, perhaps. She might get better and better and better!"

"Nonsense. Grown-up people, able to judge of these things, say she isn't right in the head."

"Did Dr. Blake say? Did he?"

"Don't be silly. Poor people don't have Dr. Blake. They can't afford it. They have that old man from Millthorne, and they only have him for some bad illness they can't cure themselves. I don't suppose they've had him for Winsome. Everybody knows that idiots can't be cured."

"She's not an idiot. She's very clever. She's cleverer than me. They're idiots themselves if they say she is."

"What? You think the whole world, Mama and Papa, and everybody in the village, are idiots because they disagree with you?"

"Winsome is very clever."

"I shan't bother to argue with you. We've never liked your playing with her so much. It must stop. You understand? You mustn't do it any more. From this moment it's forbidden."

Carrie began to howl dismally, tagging along behind Sue in her hideous little buff cassock. It was the final exasperation of a horrible afternoon. To return to the public gaze with a bawling, contumacious Carrie was intolerable.

"Oh, Sue! Sue! P-p-please! I can't even tell her why. We have no words. Ahoo! Ahoo!"

"Stop that! Listen. I'll tell you what you may do."

The howls slackened.

"You must stop that silly dumb crambo. But you may give her some of our old picture books."

"Oh, she'd like that. I'll give her my *Daisy Garden.*"

"No. That's a new book, and Papa gave it to you. There are some torn old ones which are quite good enough . . . there's a *Shock-Headed Peter.*"

"She doesn't like that. I've showed it to her."

"What? All children love *Shock-Headed Peter.*"

"She doesn't like pictures unless she knows what they're meant. She doesn't like the *Alice* pictures. I can't tell her the story, and we haven't got any Mad Hatters or Red Queens in the forest. She didn't even like my farm book at first. But Ida said: Well, when we showed it to Lallie we said *there's a bow-wow,* and *there's a gee-gee.* So Lallie got to know what pictures were supposed to be. People always talk to children when they show them pictures. So I took Winsome to the farmyard with the book, and showed her the hens and the pigs and the cows, when I showed her the pictures, and then she saw what they meant, and liked them. She doesn't like fairies or things she never sees."

"She must be very, very feeble-minded if she can't recognize a picture of a cow unless a cow is pointed out to her."

"Why do you talk to Lallie when you show her pictures?"

"Oh, don't argue, Carrie. Do what you like about *Shock-Headed Peter*. But you're not to play with her any more. I mean it."

"Ahoo! Ahoo! So unkind. I couldn't explain . . ."

"You can tell her it's wrong, can't you? I say it's wrong."

"No. No word . . ."

"If you've got any words, as you call them, at all, you must have got words for right and wrong."

"Ahoo! Ahoo! We don't need them. Ahoo!"

"In that case you've taught her nothing. Nothing at all."

"D-d-don't w-want to t-teach her . . ."

"Oh, look! That's Dr. Blake's trap at the door. He must have got Fitzy's message. Cheer up! Perhaps he will say it's not poison, and you won't have to take that dose after all."

"Ahoo! I hate right. I hate wrong . . . nasty words. . . ."

They became aware of something amiss as soon as they got into the house. Carrie's howls subsided. The silence was sinister. There should have been a bustle and voices if the doctor was upstairs.

Barbie came running down. Her face was chalk-white, and her mouth worked. She stood glaring at them, unable to speak.

"Not really poison?" gasped Sue.

"Have you hit your head?" asked Carrie anxiously. "Like Tom when he fell off the haystack? Have you got con . . . con . . ."

"Shut up, Carrie. Oh, Barbie . . . what is it?"

"Not poison," whispered Barbie at last. "Nothing to do with . . . it's Clemmie . . . very, very ill. He says . . . internal inflammation. He says send for Papa and Mama. He says. . . ."

The sentence remained unfinished, but Sue read the message in Barbie's eyes. This time Clemmie was really dying.

THREE

"I never heard of such a thing! You should ought to have been there! You that waited on the poor thing in the school-room! Not at her graveside because you'd got no black."

Mrs. Harper took a pot of stewed tea from the hob and poured out a cup. Ida's family lived in Slane Bredy, five miles away. She could visit them only on her monthly half day, but she often ran in to see her aunt after church on Sunday evenings.

"I can't stay," she protested. "There's *their* supper. . . . I'm supposed to go straight back. Oh, well, I could do with a cup. It won't kill them to wait a bit. It's only Miss Fitzroy grumbles, and nobody listens to her."

"I should hope not! A governess! Who does she think she is? You don't have to call her *Miss*. Not here."

"Mother said to always call people by the names I'm supposed to, even behind their back. *Miss* Fitzroy and *Miss* Lallie, and never no nicknames. Then she says I won't get caught like she was that time she was in service at Stretton Courtney. Belly Ache they called Him in the hall. She thought it was one of the girls come into the room when she was turning down the bed, and she says: 'Have you got the warming pan for Belly Ache?' and it was Her that had come in. Poor Mother! A warming pan! What she got was a warning pan."

"Better safe than sorry," agreed Mrs. Harper. "But couldn't your mother lend you something for the burying?"

"She'd of lent me her black mantle and bonnet, only she wanted to go herself, see? She says it's a lesson to me, getting blue for Sunday best."

"So it is. A sensible girl gets black, for if there's a death. You're sixteen now, and should behave according. But They ought to give you your blacks. In a proper gentleman's house all the servants gets their blacks when the family does."

"It's an expense. There's ten of us."

"To be sure. But They're rich, aren't they? What it is, They're mean. Can't bear to spend a farthing. Now He's

saying He'll give up the hounds! Says they're an expense."
"No!"

"True as I stand here. What's to happen to us if He does?"
"Won't Uncle go with them?"

"Not if Mr. Aldridge, Stretton Priors, takes them. He got a kennelman already."

"Plenty other gentlemen got kennels. P'r'aps Uncle would do better outside the forest. This isn't much of a place."

"You're right, my girl, it's not. Rain come through the thatch like I don't know what, and down to the spout at the end of the lane for every drop of water. But was you the only one in the house not to go?"

"Jane, she didn't go either. Mrs. Peters said there must be somebody in the kitchen. They left us plenty to do. I had to go down there and help, soon as I'd dressed Miss Lallie. Bread and butter! We cut till we thought our arms'd drop off. And then, when Mrs. Peters come back, of course we'd done it too thick."

"I wonder they let that child go."

"She'd have created if they hadn't. Properly enjoyed herself in her new black dress, if you know what I mean. Of course, she didn't understand, not at her age."

"No, they don't. But wasn't it a dreadful thing? That inflamination! Seems to fly all over a person in no time. Is it true what they say?"

Ida knew this to be a demand for a full account of the whole dreadful business. She could guess what they said: that Miss Fitzroy had failed to summon the doctor in time, or that Miss Barbie had been and gone and administered the wrong medicine. Clemmie's death was a boon to Slane St. Mary's where life was generally as dull as it was hard. Mrs. Harper and her neighbors would have enjoyed it, even had they liked and respected the Knevetts.

Between sips of tea the tale was told, to an accompaniment of horrified clucks from Mrs. Harper. Clemmie had died an hour after her parents, recalled from Devonshire, reached home. Dr. Blake had given up hope as soon as he saw her.

It was The Inflammation. Nothing could have saved her. The grand doctor, fetched from Severnton, he said so too. Yes, all they said about her suffering was nothing but the truth. It was worse than they said.

"Mrs. Dancey told me she was sinking the Monday morning," sighed Mrs. Harper. "But I never thought it would be so quick. When I was bringing my buckets along from the spout I heard the carriage go by, and thought it was Them coming back, but my mind was on my washtub, and you could have knocked me down with a feather when we heard the knell. 'Whoever's dead?' I said to Dainty. We was pegging out the sheets. We counted. Two? A woman. Sixteen? Then it come over me: Miss Clemmie! How did she look?"

"Same as they always do," said Ida glumly.

"They put flowers and that?"

"Yes. I didn't go in there but the once, when we all went. There was a lot to do."

Ida did not fancy all the fuss made over a corpse in a gentleman's house. Everybody had to go about saying Miss Clemmie looked so beautiful. It was a blessing to see her out of her agony, but Ida could see no beauty in death, or in a young creature of her own age, turned into a still, waxen thing waiting to be shoveled into a dirty clay hole and left to rot.

"There was all the sewing," she said, "soon as the stuff come from Severnton. Miss Fitzroy and me, we had to sit up half the night. Good thing we had the machine. Miss Flo! More trouble than all the rest put together. Let this in! Take this out! Even her bonnet had to be trimmed fresh."

"She looked a treat," said Mrs. Harper. "The girls and I all thought so. Very stylish, Miss Flo. Can't think why you have your knife into her like you have. She's a heap better than that Barbie."

"No, Aunty. Miss Barbie aggravates everybody because she thinks it's right. Miss Flo makes mischief, just to amuse herself. But was you there, then? Mother said not."

"Not in church. Harper went in the church, but there wasn't room for half that came. We stood outside, and got a good see. You don't think we'd miss a burying like that? I thought your mother would come in after, but she didn't see fit."

Mrs. Harper, who had gone down in the world when she married, was sensitive to slights from Ida's mother, who had gone up. A carpenter in Slane Bredy, which had a post office, was a better match than a kennelman in Slane St. Mary's.

"She can't have seen you," protested Ida. "I don't suppose she stared around much. It's not nice at a burying. She just run up to the house for a word with me, after, and then she had to go back. Joe Cranton gave her a lift in his trap."

"We saw her. We was all there except Winsome, that we left locked in the cupboard. Didn't dare take her. Couldn't be sure she'd behave."

"I heard . . . but where's she got to?"

"Believe me, or believe me not, she's under that bed. Stops there all the time, these days."

"That's new! Whatever for?"

"How should I know?"

Ida went and knelt beside a bed which took up too much space in the little kitchen, and which accommodated an overflow of Harpers at night. A coiled, inert heap lay there in the darkness. She stroked it gently, whereupon it stirred. A pair of fierce eyes peeped out at her for a moment.

"Can't do nothing with her," lamented Mrs. Harper. "She only comes out when she's hungry. And she's dirty. Wets herself. I'd got her into nice ways, and now she's gone back to nothing but an animal."

"I heard," murmured Ida, her round good-humored face puckered in distress, "that there'd been trouble."

"Trouble! I was never so shamed in my life. The very day after the burying! The governess and the three little girls come past. Out rushes Winsome. Grabs Miss Carrie, and won't let go of her. Of course they haven't been playing these last days, but who's to explain the why of it to Winsome? Miss Carrie, she stood with her eyes tight shut. We dragged Winsome off, kicking, biting, scratching, and making such a terrible noise—cawing like a crow. I said how sorry I was she should behave so bad, and locked her in the cupboard. I suppose I should of whipped her, but I never do. Can't bring myself to it, somehow. It's not her fault she's like she is."

"Well, Aunty, I've got something to tell you about that. It was Miss Sue forbade Miss Carrie to play with Winsome any more. Said it doesn't look nice. And Miss Carrie takes on about it something dreadful. That day, after that set out, she walked on a little way, and then she fainted, dead off!"

"She never!"

"She did. Had to be carried home. *They* thought it was on account of Miss Clemmie. Miss Carrie hadn't properly taken it in before. She's slow, according to Them, but her fainting showed she'd got deeper feelings after all, only a bit late in the day. I had to put her to bed. They were wrong. It was Winsome. She was sobbing her little heart out. She'd been forced to *shut her eyes* to Winsome. She will have it that's Winsome's way of saying: Go away! I don't want you."

"The things children think of!"

"Wanted to ask her mother if they couldn't play again. I said better not trouble Her just now."

"Oh, no. I daresay Miss Sue is right. They can't go on for ever making faces like they do. It looks queer for a young lady."

"Miss Carrie will have it they talk, as you might say. And I do think she managed to learn Winsome something. I believe Winsome is sharper than what you think for. She might get to be more like other people if somebody would take trouble with her."

"No, Ida. You're wrong. She's not all there, and never will be, poor little toad."

"She can't hear. That's all."

"She can see, and doesn't make anything of half she sees. Don't go on at me again about that, Ida." A tear crept down Mrs. Harper's worn cheek. "I lie awake, nights, wondering how she'll do when we're gone. I can't bear to think of her put away somewhere. None of the rest mean to be bothered with her. It's natural. They'll have enough on their plates, likely, without her. It's a hard world for poor people, and you can't say different."

It was. Ida checked an impulse to promise care and protection. She thought of a household in Slane Bredy—a brother and sister saddled, by a promise to their mother, with the life-long care of a drooling, misshapen idiot. Poor Jim and Annie! Neither had married. No husband or wife would take *that* into their home.

The gentle stroking won some response. Winsome rolled out from under the bed, and put her weary, dusty little head in her cousin's lap.

Might it not be better, Ida wondered, if Harper did have to leave the forest? Slane St. Mary's was a dead hole, a hundred years behind the times, so they said in Slane Bredy. Winsome could not be all that half-witted when she drew so nice. In a bigger place some lady or gentleman might take an interest. *They* weren't that sort—not real gentry. Thought no end of themselves, and gave orders, but didn't seem to feel responsible with it. Didn't feel bound to stand between poor people and trouble, as some did. *He* was a hard man, and *She*, poor thing, had plenty on her plate with lying in and miscarriages. Hardly knew more than anybody's name. Miss Barbie, she poked her nose into people's houses all right, but only to read them a lecture.

Winsome turned her head. The fierce eyes were blank now, and the face so white that it recalled the dead girl lying among flowers up at the house—lying now lonely in the grave.

"I believe she's fretting for Miss Carrie."

"If she never has nothing worse to fret over, my girl, her life will be easier than what I think for."

"I ought to be getting back. Come and pet her just a bit, won't you? And . . . she's got a lot of dust in her hair."

Mrs. Harper snatched up a comb and advanced, but Winsome rolled away under the bed again.

It was so late that Ida had to run all the way back to the

house. Her footsteps, thudding up the avenue, seemed to beat out a single word: Sad! Sad! Sad! Sad! Sad!

Miss Clemmie, she's up in Heaven now, singing with the angels. Winsome's worse off. Buried alive! And poor Miss Carrie. . . . You never know, I'll tell her. Things may turn out better than what we look for. We must trust in Providence. It looks after people . . . well . . . sometimes It does.

CHAPTER 2

Sometimes It Does

1891

ONE

THE TREES in the square were all shut in by high hard.
Not like the trees in the wide air at the other house. Ugly
down there, walking with Answer and Bird past trees with
long legs spotted brown and white like those long spotted . . .
giraffes . . . not legs . . . she could not be bothered with words
when she was planning a picture.

Once she had thought that trees were a kind of people standing on one long leg. They moved like people talking. Now she
knew better. Now she knew everything. She could see Bird's
name . . . *Myra* . . . and Answer's name . . . *Miss Maxwell* . . .
called Em up here because it was easier. But she was thinking
in the old way because these trees tasted good. Soft green flut-
tering against high hard. Not quite right to paint. Too much
high hard above green. Downstairs, where Smell had her big
bed, soft green crossed hard just right, with a gap showing
light and sharp dark behind. Better. But that room . . . not!
Never! No! Unless Smell was away. Everywhere downstairs
. . . not! Must paint up here. How paint hard to look hard?
Soft to look soft? How paint moving against stay still?

She turned to get her paint box. Answer was there.

"Wyn! Walk time. You and Myra go with Nellie today. In
the park."

This called for fearful and delicate labor with the muscles

[25]

controlling lungs, larynx, vocal chords, pharynx, palate, tongue, lips, and jawbone. Wyn braced herself:

"Why not you?"

It was not very successfully said. Answer's eyes told her as much, but spared correction out of lesson hours.

"I must go shopping. Buy things for Venice."

Venice! No streets! The sea!

"I hate Nellie."

Wyn explained this in pantomime. First she was Cruel, officiously bustling her deaf charges across the street and making an unnecessary parade of it. Then she was a passerby pausing to stare, puzzled, and to perceive that something must be very wrong with Wyn and Bird.

"I know. But I can't come today."

A bad word, seen only in print. Out with it and make Answer jump.

"Nellie is a harlot."

"Wyn! You must not say that word."

"Bible," suggested Wyn, putting on a holy look.

This time she was not spared. Her speech was corrected. Once again she had stumbled between *m* and *b*.

"Not Mimle. Bible."

"Mible," giggled Wyn, now deliberately careless.

"No. Bible."

"Bimle."

"No. Come and feel my nose."

Fingering noses during an alternated chant of Mumumumumum! and Bububububub! was work for the morning. This was afternoon.

"Not now lessons. I stay. Paint for Mr. God."

She knew quite well that he was not God. Long ago she had really thought so. His name, in Answer's mouth, had that shape and he looked like God, of whom she had seen photographs in an album at the big house. God flew about with a streaming beard and robes, making everything. He whirled one day into the nursery with a streaming beard and a long black cloak. He was terrible and wonderful. He could make a picture of anything. Answer herself was like a little girl in his presence. She did exactly what he told her. She sat meekly with Wyn and Bird and they all drew and painted, and if she did anything wrong he scolded her. Even though he was not God he had to be obeyed.

"Mr. Gordon," said Answer, "will not come again before we go to Venice."

Cruel came bustling in, ready for the walk in her neat black suit and bonnet.

"Now then, Ugly . . . get a move on—do!"

Then she saw Answer. Her face changed. She made her big mouth small.

"It's time she got ready for her walk, Miss Maxwell. Miss Myra is waiting."

"She's just coming, Nellie."

Answer doesn't like Cruel. She looks at Cruel like a cold bath. She looks at us like a warm bath.

"You not there she say Ugly."

A look like a sting from Cruel. A look like a little slap from Answer.

"Go and get ready, Wyn."

Shut eyes tight. Aha! Answer here, and Cruel can't pinch. What will they do now?

Slyly peeping she saw that Bird had come in, pretty and fragile, a creature which might have just fluttered down from the sky. That was why she would always be Bird, just as Em, who knew everything, would always be Answer.

Now, at the sight of their faces, Bird's smile was clouded. She stood looking at them in puzzled grief.

Angry. Fighting. She can't see that. Poor Bird. She can never see bad things, even when they hurt her. Walking all alone with Cruel in the park. No. I go. *A godly righteous and sober life.* Prayer book. Red all round. I must be good.

TWO

Instigated by Wyn, Myra had begged for the trip to Venice; her father would not have consented without the emphatic approval of the governess, and self-interest had played some part in that approval. Christine Maxwell would not have advocated the jaunt unless she thought it beneficial to the children, but she welcomed the prospect for her own sake. Luxurious travel was very much to her taste. Perpetual seclusion, in a large country house or on a top floor in London, could be intolerably monotonous.

In the course of the afternoon she bought a *Baedeker's Guide* and was looking through it, over a cup of tea in Fuller's, when she spied an old friend approaching her table. Instantly she swept the book into her lap. Should Elsie Spender discover that Christine and her charges were just off to Italy, with a courier and a maid, she would sniff.

These two had once learned their trade in a nursery school up north, and had grown fond of each other, although they were always at odds, not only over methods but over matters of principle. For Elsie, the education of deaf mutes was a vocation. She lived for nothing else, thought of nothing else, and she despised women who spent more than five pounds a year upon their clothes.

Christine, an elegant brunette, wanted money. She meant to qualify as governess to some child of very wealthy parents, offering marked skill for an enormous salary. She studied both oral and manual methods, and eventually met Lord Seddon at an International Conference in Milan. He had come there sadly seeking light on the education of his poor little four-year-old Myra. Since he was exactly the kind of employer desired by Christine, they returned to England together, and she had now taught Myra for eleven years.

A conference got up by Italian Roman Catholics was, in Elsie's view, highly suspect, and oral methods were sponsored by quacks. In her struggle to do what she could for very poor children, she had neither time nor opportunity for such flum-

mery. Manual instruction was all that she could achieve in a
no man's land for which the humane thought the State should
be responsible, and which the State was reluctant to recognize.

"What am I doing in London?" she said, sitting down with
a brusque thump at Christine's table. "My sister's wedding.
And I've had to buy a bonnet. What's it like? Like a bonnet, I
suppose. Not much difference between one little bunch of
nonsense on the top of one's head and another."

There would never be much difference between one bonnet
and another on the top of Elsie's head. The face below it
would cancel any frivolity. She had the long upper lip and the
shallow eye sockets of the devotee.

She lost no time in opening fire: "Still in the Belgraves?
Still making faces at the same little Honorable? Can she talk
yet?"

"Not very well," admitted Christine. "But her lip reading
has come on splendidly."

"I always say . . ." began Elsie, but Christine said it
first in a rapid gabble: "That-a-child-with-a-turn-for-lip-
reading-needs-no-help-from-foreigners-and-a-child-with-
no-turn-had-better-stick-to-hands!"

"Sarcastic?" suggested Elsie.

She ordered her tea and launched a second attack.

"Are you really going to spend your whole life teaching
just one child? A child with no living to earn, who could get
along quite well with somebody less clever than you? I've
always said you're a splendid teacher, however much we may
disagree about methods. Good teachers are as rare as hen's teeth.
As many children as possible should be getting what you can
give."

"Not just one, Elsie. How often do I have to tell you that
they adopted another child to learn with Myra? Wyn! I only
had Myra alone for three years; these last eight . . ."

"All right. Two. Two little Honorables."

"Wyn is not a little Honorable. Far from it. She's just the
sort of child you say I ought to be teaching . . . comes from a
very poor home. We ran across her one day, Myra and I, when

we were strolling on Trentstoke Common. A queer little shuffling, snorting creature."

"Snorts, does she?"

"Oh, I soon got her out of that. Their breathing improves doesn't it, very quickly, when once you've taught them to blow up balloons?"

"Yes. If you can afford balloons. Can *she* talk yet?"

"She might talk very well if only she could relax. The harder she tries, the more she tightens up, especially on open vowels. She makes all sorts of discordant noises; she rattles and gugs and clicks. Her 'yes' is pretty well 'Ngeegass.' I can understand her, but nobody else can. I consulted them in Fitzroy Square. They said nothing for it but to get her to loosen up and relax, and I can't. It's nerves really."

These confessions were unpleasant, but Christine could not forego a discussion with a fellow practitioner. Elsie was an inspired teacher. That dour face never discouraged any child. Her experience was vast and her advice worth having.

"Why did they adopt her? She's pretty and pathetic, I suppose?"

"Oh, no. Very plain. Always will be, I'm afraid. Dumpy. Suety skin and sandy hair, and her head is too large for her body. But really alarmingly clever. That first time we met her, she stared at us, and then began to make all sorts of wild grimaces and gestures. I thought she was laughing at Myra, and tried to shoo her off. But she kept following us, with such a piteous look, and began to copy our signs. I'd just begun to suspect the truth when her mother appeared, hunting for her and very cross. They were newcomers. The father worked at some kennels on the other side of the common. They'd just come from somewhere in the West—Slane Forest, I think— because his former employer had given up his kennels. She poured it all out and apologized for the child in a most abject way, explaining that she was feeble-minded. But I wondered if that was so. She reminded me so much of our children at Chelbridge—those who had never had any help at all. It seemed to me that there might never have been a proper diagnosis, and that she might merely be deaf. They weren't Trentstoke people, of course, but I couldn't get her out of my mind, and I called at that cottage a day or two later. I had a long talk with the mother, who seemed to be at her wits' end —complained that the child had become quite unmanageable. Finally I got Myra's doctor to see her, and he agreed with me. It seemed terrible just to do nothing about it. So I asked Lord Seddon if I might try the experiment of teaching her along with Myra. I thought company might be good for Myra, and it couldn't do her any harm, for the child was quite clean, and so forth. I mean . . . there was Myra, with all the help that money could supply, and, only a mile away, this helpless little creature flung away on the rubbish heap."

"You don't have to tell me that. It's what I'm always telling you. I'm glad your conscience pricks you occasionally."

Christine restrained an impulse to hurl the teapot at Elsie's head.

"I only acted as anybody might who had seen the poor child. Why do you think that any ordinary impulse of sympathy and compassion must spring from a bad conscience? Why shouldn't I be sorry for a poor child because I happen to teach a rich one? Anybody not as holy as you are must be a fiend in human shape, I suppose?"

"If your conscience was quite easy," retorted Elsie, "you wouldn't be so touchy. But why did they adopt her? Another ordinary impulse of sympathy and compassion?"

"No, of course not. It was for Myra's sake. The whole experiment worked so well, and Myra got so fond of her. It was quite amazing, the pace at which she caught up with Myra, when she'd never had any teaching before."

"Are you quite sure she hadn't?"

"Her mother swore she hadn't. She just naturally is very clever. She immediately invented a lot of new games to play with Myra, quite unprompted by me. Patterns, for instance, of flowers and pebbles and bits of glass. One had to begin a pattern and the other had to guess how to finish it. But it always had to be played on a path; that was ritual, I don't know why. Preferably a rather inconvenient path in the kitchen garden, near some cold frames. Awful storms if I tried to make them play it on the lawn or the terrace. The stimulant to Myra was remarkable. She made great strides after Wyn came. And then the Harpers moved on to another job in East Anglia, and, sooner than lose Wyn, the Seddons adopted her outright."

"And gave you a chance to show what you could do with a clever child."

The taunt was not completely unjustified. Christine had advocated the adoption of Wyn, just as she had advocated the trip to Venice, partly for Myra's sake, partly for her own. Myra was a sweet, affectionate little creature, but her faculties were limited. She was never likely to do outstanding credit to her teacher, such as might serve as an asset when some future post was in question. Of Wyn, on the other hand, something striking might be made, could she but learn to speak intelligibly.

"You've probably pushed her on too fast," said Elsie, "so that you could show her off. No wonder her nerves are all over the place. But that pattern game! A game for two. She'd learned it from somebody, whatever they say."

"If there was, it couldn't have been any kind of trained teacher. If I ask her about Slane Forest she always shrinks into herself, and says she doesn't remember. But for all that . . . you know the difference, don't you, between a child that has always been left quite solitary and one that's been played with and talked to?"

"Indeed I do. Sounds to me like some other child. Some little brother or sister? Small children often do a lot, in that way, without knowing it."

"Well! I never thought of that. It might have been some child who died. The surviving children seemed to be quite callous about her. But it was a large family—the sort of family which quickly forgets a child who dies. The mother was fond of her, in a helpless sort of way, and reluctant to part with her. She agreed only because she felt it would be the best plan for

Winsome, as they called her. We shortened it to Wyn. And it was a good thing—for several reasons. The poor woman died soon after they left our neighborhood, and Harper married again, I believe."

"Bet you sixpence it was another child, anyway. Only children play games sitting on inconvenient paths."

"You'll never get that sixpence, even if you're right, for I can't find out now. But if it was a child who died, that would explain an impression I have of some shock, some disaster, that still affects her nerves. And I feel too that she is always in dread of something—not the usual bewildered fear of everything she doesn't understand. It's something definite, which she understands only too well."

"Religion?" asked Elsie, with whom this point was all important.

"None as yet, I think. She pores over the Bible and prayer book, and continually asks for explanations. For a very practical reason: to save herself trouble. In her written work she'll snatch at any text, or passage in the catechism, so as to avoid having to compose a sentence."

"Too clever for her own good, I should say."

"I don't think it could have been only some little brother or sister. She recognized some of our picture books. She'd never seen them in that cottage, I'm sure. And some of the things she seemed to know . . . well, she found an acorn and put it in a dolls' house cradle, and told me that it was a tree's little baby, and she would look after it until it had grown into a great big tree. No child of six could work out for itself the relation between an acorn and an oak tree."

"I agree. Though the things which some people expect our children to have worked out for themselves would make you stare. Did you help her to rear the acorn?"

"Oh, yes. We put it in the mouth of a medicine bottle full of water, so that we could see it split and put down roots. The girls were fascinated, and when it sprouted two oak leaves they were in raptures. We transferred it to a little pot of soil,

and then to a bigger pot, and finally we planted it out in the
park at Trentstoke."

"And you told them," prompted Elsie with a nod of approval, "that Jesus had looked after it? That it's all part of
His plan?"

"No," snapped Christine, who could not pretend to live
with Jesus continually at her elbow.

Elsie taught her children to love their Saviour with all their
hearts. Joy, beauty, wonder, and mystery were continually
associated with Him and His inscrutable "plan." In Heaven
only would they learn why He had permitted them to suffer
so signal an affliction. There they would perceive the reason
to be good, and realize that they had served Him by bearing
it patiently.

Christine had once, in a moment of rebellion, asked why
Elsie should be at such pains to lighten the affliction? Was she
not impeding the "plan"? Elsie replied that she was merely
following the Divine example. We serve Jesus both by endur-
ing pain and by relieving the pain of others. No child would
ask such a silly question.

I shouldn't wonder if Wyn asks it, sometime or other,
thought Christine, and proceeded to describe Wyn's gifts.

"She draws very well. But for a long time she would only
copy pictures that she liked. I couldn't get her to draw from
life. Why should she? Too difficult! Then Lord Seddon let
me get in a first-rate drawing master—Alastair Gordon. Wyn,
for some reason, treated him with extreme awe. She actually
fell on her knees the first time she saw him. And when he put
a jug and a loaf on the table and told her to paint them, to my
surprise, she obeyed him. He comes in twice a week and
teaches the three of us in a row. I've learned a lot from him."

Elsie laughed. She was a devil. This opportunity was, of
course, valuable to Christine, whose art qualifications had been
but mediocre. When undertaking some other little Honorable,
she could now say that she had been taught by Alastair
Gordon.

"Wyn has quite stopped copying Kate Greenaways. Oh,

yes, and I meant to ask you. Do you want any picture books? We have some that the girls have grown out of."

"Thank you. I could do with them. Just as I could do with a few balloons and flowerpots and acorns."

"Oh, dear! Is it very grim up there at Barnesfield?"

A building had apparently been turned over to Elsie, which nobody else wanted because it was next door to a tannery. She had a blackboard and a book or two. Her pupils ranged in age from eight to fifteen. Some could hear a little, others not at all. Some had been deafened by illness, but could remember sound. Others had no notion of it.

"A wonderfully advanced place," she stormed. "Think of the poor taxpayers if it was compulsory, like Scotland! Goodbye. I must go. I wish I wasn't always so nasty to you, Christine, for you're a nice woman at bottom."

It was a blessing, in some ways, that Elsie took so little interest in Christine's problems, since questions about the Seddon household might have been embarrassing.

Myra's mother loathed her only child. That fact was apparent to everybody, despite occasional gushing parades of affection. For eleven years Christine had tried to protect Myra from the truth. Lady Seddon would not probably have cared much for a daughter in any case, and her failure to bear a son must have been a bitter blow. Nor could she tolerate Wyn, who disliked scent, and held her nose when submitting to her share of fondling, grimaces, and "poor darlings."

"What a pity she's so ugly!" Lady Seddon would complain.

This word, often repeated, at length caught Myra's attention.

"Hooeel . . . lot . . . hucklee," she hooted in protest.

"Is she trying to say something?" asked Lady Seddon.

"She says that Wyn is not ugly."

"Oh, dear! She understood me?"

"I think they both did."

"You're wonderful, getting them on so well. . . . No, darling! Wyn is not uglee. Wyn is veree prettee."

This was too much for Myra, who could not think Wyn

pretty, but rejected ugly as a term of abuse. She burst into tears, and her mother fled. After some soothing and comforting, she summed it up in her own way.

"Wyn not ugly because Wyn dear."

In all save matters of the heart Myra was slow-witted. Wyn sometimes suggested a charge of dynamite, but seemed to have no heart at all.

Life in the Belgraves was not as easy as Elsie supposed.

THREE

The carriage stood at the door, and Lady Seddon sailed out as Christine came up to the house. The two paused for a moment to make civil faces at each other. Wyn was quite right; the woman wore too much scent. Her smell epitomized her insincerity.

"Venice! So wonderful that Myra wants to go. All your doing, I'm sure. Please get everything you want for her."

"I will," promised Christine a little grimly.

"Bertrand will get you a gondola. He'll see to everything like that. He's most reliable. I won't burden you with any introductions. I don't know if any of my friends will be in Venice just now, and I'm sure you'd all rather amuse yourselves in your own way."

With an amiable nod, the bonnet, the gleaming hair, the brilliant complexion, the evasive eyes, the petulant mouth, the gloves, the card case, the flounces, and the smell vanished into the carriage.

Her friends! Valerie Seddon had friends in all the places where the wealthy congregate. She knew of every skeleton in their cupboards. She had avidly discussed their misfortunes behind their backs. Did she imagine that there were no shrugs or nods over *that child*, hidden away somewhere. A cripple? A cretin? Nobody knew for certain, but the mystery was enough to qualify her as "poor Valerie" from Venice to Boston, Massachusetts.

On the top floor, Myra and Nellie were lying in wait. They

fell upon Christine, Myra exhausted with weeping, Nellie spluttering with indignation.

"Which I wish to give in my notice, Miss Maxwell, if their word is to be believed against mine . . ."

"Hush, Nellie. I'll listen to you afterward."

After some soothing and kissing in Christine's room, Myra managed to tell the story. Wyn had been bad in the park. Nellie had talked to a lady. Myra had not seen what they said. She had been feeding the ducks. They made Wyn angry. When the party reached home she hit Nellie, and called her a bad name. Nellie said Wyn would be sent away, and put into a cutter.

Christine disentangled a gutter from a cutter, and assured Myra that Wyn would be consigned to neither. When the sobbing and shivering had quite stopped, she went in search of Nellie who had, she suspected, been listening at the keyhole.

"Now, Nellie! Tell me exactly what happened."

"I wish to give in my notice. If you like to listen to their rubbish, Miss, you can suit yourself. I'm not staying here, not for any wages. It's not what I expected."

"What happened?"

"I've nothing against Miss Myra. I knew I was to wait on a young lady that wasn't quite right. It's that Wyn. I don't look to wait on a child that's come out of the gutter. She should be in an asylum or something. And she's artful. Hears more than what she lets on to do, and then makes mischief. Anybody can't say a thing when she's there."

"You haven't told me what happened."

"Why, soon as we got back up here she turned on me like a mad thing. Pulled my hair right out. Yes, she did! Look!"

Nellie held out a wisp of hair.

"Did you talk to somebody in the park?"

"I might say good afternoon to a girl I was in service with, before I came here. Why not?"

"Could it be anything that you said that made Wyn behave like this?"

"What's it matter what I said? She's supposed to be deaf, stone-deaf, isn't she?"

"You know perfectly well that she understands a great deal of what people say."

"That's just it. She's artful. Shams deaf when she's not, and then tells stories, and I'm to suffer for her spite. But it's well known, Miss, that you favor her more than what you do Miss Myra. Remarks are passed on that downstairs, believe me. I wish to give in my notice. I don't like favoritism."

"Then you must give it to Mrs. Hurst."

"I don't know but what I won't give it to his lordship. He ought to know what goes on up here."

Nellie flounced off, and Christine turned in to the schoolroom. Wyn was waiting for her with a white face and blazing eyes. A statement of the case was proffered, written in an exercise book. Agitation had made it less coherent than her normal written work, but it was as scriptural as ever.

Park verily verily I say unto you evil speaking lying slandering. She say we give her the Willys. What the Willys? Nobody wants we no use. Kittens down at Berse. Where Berse? What do kittens down there? Ladyship wishes Myra dead. True. EVIL. Commandment in this house. THOU SHALT NOT THINK. Myra comprehended it not safe beholding ducks. I see her mouth. She say you give her the stick. LYING. You beat not. She say money nobody stay us unless. You Sam. Money you Sam loving kindness at us. More money you run off Sam loving kindness other girls. Park godly sober righteous. House I chastise the harlot. Not penitent. Em Em Em forsake us not money. We die. Verily verily I say unto you we die. It was once long ago. My friend foresaked me. I was dead. You rose me again. Em Em Em not two times?

This then was the mysterious disaster, this the abiding fear, of which Christine had always been aware. Some kind of betrayal or desertion had created tortured mistrust. A reply must be given with no pause, no hesitation. Wyn was waiting, rigid with anxiety. Christine heard herself say: "Of course Myra's father pays me money. I must earn my living, you know. But I will never leave you or Myra as long as you want me. I promise."

Wyn's response was startling. The child normally disliked caresses, and shied away from them like a frightened horse. She would treat with no one save on an intellectual basis; she ignored all those messages of reassurance and goodwill which can only be conveyed by touch. Now she came up and put one finger for a moment upon Christine's wrist, as though acknowledging the pledge and signifying her own confidence in it. They both smiled.

"I think," said Christine, "that Nellie said 'sick,' not 'stick.' "

"Where Berse?"

The phrase had probably been *drowned at birth*, and Christine was reluctant to elucidate it. She said: "I don't know. But, Wyn . . . who was that friend?"

Wyn stiffened, and drew back. Presently she said: "Ca."

"Did Ca show you picture books once?"

"Don't remember."

"A lady who was kind to you?"

"No. Little girl."

A child! Elsie was right, as usual, and Christine owed her sixpence.

They were interrupted by Mrs. Hurst, the housekeeper, upon which Wyn rushed out of the room. Christine's domain was seldom invaded by this stately potentate. She came to say that Nellie had given notice, and, if Miss Maxwell agreed, it might be as well to send the girl packing on the spot. One of the housemaids could wait on the schoolroom for a while. Miss Maxwell agreed with relief. Nothing was said as to the cause of Nellie's departure, but much was understood.

There remained the problem of securing another attendant before the party set out for Venice. Mrs. Hurst had a suggestion to make. Annette, Lady Seddon's maid, was on the point of leaving, since she had repeatedly failed to do her ladyship's hair becomingly. Although not really qualified as a first-class lady's maid, she was a very good-natured creature and fond of the girls. Nellie's place might suit her, if rather better wages were offered. Since she was an experienced traveler, and bilingual, she would be worth the extra money.

Christine could ask for nothing better. Annette's visits to the schoolroom had always been welcome, and a friendship had already sprung up between them. She disliked Nellie, but had hitherto found no grounds for getting rid of her. The transfer was arranged on the spot, and she went to bed with a lighter heart, to lie awake marveling at that rash promise given to Wyn.

It might bind her for an indefinite period, ruling out any more distinguished post. Not that she regretted it: she would say the same again, but she was astonished that there should have been no struggle or debate between her heart and her prudence. She really must be, as Elsie had put it, a nice woman at bottom. In their profession it was all or nothing. One could set no cautious limit for obligations taken toward creatures so helpless.

Reassurance must be of first importance to Wyn. It might soothe tense nerves, and assist that gargled speech. Christine was conscious of growing remorse concerning the child. She had been too eager to make an immediate spectacular success of promising material. She had pushed Wyn continually, forcing on her, perhaps too soon, the intellectual effort of reading and writing. She should have been content with less, and Wyn might pay dearly, all her life, for her teacher's ill-judged ambition. Amends must in future be made, even at the expense of other little Honorables.

Investigation of the mysterious Ca had better be deferred. She asked no more questions and was rewarded, two days later, by a further statement in the exercise book:

Long time ago I could hear. I played happy all the time with my friend a little girl. She was in a big house with children and ladies. A lordly house. Not so big as Trentstoke. Peradventure a very little lord. We bowed the knee to them. In the road all people ordered lowly and reverently to their betters. She foresaked me in a black dress. People in black dresses stood to behold it. I cried unto her hear my prayer hold not thy peace at my tears oh spare me a little. She shut her eyes. I became dumb and opened not my mouth. I saw her no more. That all I remember.

The claim to have heard once could be discounted. Ever since Wyn had grasped some notion of this mysterious faculty, she had at intervals laid claim to it upon no grounds whatever. In time she might submit to the truth; she had by no means done so yet.

It looked as though Ca's father might have been the local Squire. Christine's records showed that Harper had come from Slane St. Mary's. *Burk's Landed Gentry* supplied a Manor House and a baronet with four sons and eight daughters. Caroline, born in 1875, might very well fill the bill. As for that dreadful occasion when everyone wore black dresses, some death, some infectious epidemic, might have caused an interruption of the children's intimacy.

All this Christine explained to Wyn, suggesting that poor little Ca might have been equally miserable but quite unable to explain. She must now be a big girl of sixteen. Perhaps she might like to get news of Wyn.

"She never wrote to me," objected Wyn.

"She may not know where you live now."

"Everybody knows."

"No. Everybody in the world does not know where you live. Shall I write to her?"

"No. I write."

This was dangerous. Ca might have been a dear little girl eight years ago, but a whole village had meanwhile been bowing the knee to her. Nor was Wyn likely to compose the humble, grateful letter expected from a cottager to a young lady who had once been kind to her. She might invite a snub rather than reassurance.

"Show me your letter before you send it."

"Why?"

"I could tell you if I think she would like it."

"My friend. Not your friend."

"She is older. You are older."

"Still my friend, like my letter. I must know."

"Very well. But don't put in anything from the Bible."

Although Wyn stuck out her lip, she did, in the end, show her letter, over which she had clearly taken immense pains.

Dear Ca,

Your friend Winsome writing. Remember? Wyn now. I live at London with Myra. New sister. I adopted this family. Miss Maxwell teaching. We can hear. We can speak. We do everything like other people. Have you been at London? Why did you shut your eyes in a black dress? Miss Maxwell says not unkind. Some good reason. I know french. Ouvre moi ta porte pour l'amour de dieu. Do you know french? Write french. I shall understand. Soon we go to Venice. Have you been at Venice? Beautiful. No streets. Sea. No cabs. Gondola. A pretty little boat. Write answer to this letter if you like this letter. I send 3 pictures. 1 Myra. 2 Miss Maxwell. 3 Gondola.

Love from Wyn Harper.

After a long battle Wyn agreed to delete the statement that she could now hear. The claim to know French was equally unfounded, but did not merit further dispute. Christine had written English words under French words in a nursery rhyme book with pictures that had taken Wyn's fancy.

You mustn't boast," she warned.

Wyn frowned, struggling with a word only seen in print. "She will think . . . ssseeeldiss?"

At Christine's puzzled look she put on her Bible face and added: "When I became a man I put away . . ."

"Oh, childish! It's *child*ish, like a child . . . not *chill*-dish, like children."

What a language! reflected Christine. No consistency. The

wonder is that anybody masters it. She roused herself from this
marvel to hear and mentally translate Wyn's urgent question:

"Ngoogeelik sseek? Ngoogeelik sseek?"

"*Will she?* Will she think you childish? No. Only if she is
very childish herself. But. . . ."

Should they have another wrestle with those intrusive noises,
of which *ng* was the most formidable?

No! Wyn had labored enough for one day.

FOUR

On the morning of their departure for Venice two letters
arrived for Wyn. She read them, announced that they came
from Ca, and from an unexpected cousin, and stuffed them
inside her stays. Since they seemed to give satisfaction, Christine, busy with the task of getting the party off, inquired no
further. The world that morning consisted of trunks, bags,
umbrellas, rugs, cushions, tickets, letters of credit, and smelling
salts for Myra.

The journey proceeded smoothly. Annette turned out to be
a treasure—an expert at jumping out of the train and securing
basins of soup whenever their spirits were low. The courier
vanished when he was not wanted, and reappeared at the right
moment. Venice, pearly in the twilight, received them. A
gondola took them to their hotel.

Only wealth could have got them there with so little fatigue.
Who, thought Christine, could look at Bertrand, and suppose
them to be nobodies? Yet only one of the party was rich; four
of them traveled because Myra's parents had money.

They spent most of their time dawdling about on the
lagoons. Occasionally they visited churches, but Myra was
frightened of the beggars, and Wyn picked up Italian oaths
with astonishing celerity, often rolling them out with no intrusive *ng*. One old woman, a squalid bundle of rags sitting
every day and all day on the steps of the Salute, engaged her
particular attention. She frequently asked to go and look again
at that old woman.

Her sketchbook lay idle. At last Christine reproached her

for this, and suggested a picture of Francesco nel Deserto, floating lovely and lonely amid its cypress trees.

"Sometime I paint that old woman," conceded Wyn.

"Why? She's not beautiful!"

"For Ca. She wants."

"She's still your friend?" ventured Christine.

With a nod Wyn fished down her neck, produced two crumpled letters, one of which she handed to Christine.

Dear Wyn,

I cannot tell you how happy I was to get your letter. I would have written to you long ago if I had known where to find you.

I wore a black dress that day because my sister was dead. It had nothing to do with you and me. I shut my eyes because my eldest sister said our games were foolish and forbade them. I thought I had to obey her. I was miserable because I could not explain that to you.

She is married and lives in London in the Victoria Road, and I stayed there once. I wish I had known you were there, but I do not think it is very near Belgrave Square.

I have never been abroad. Everyone says Venice is very beautiful. I have seen pictures and read a book about it by John Ruskin. I cannot imagine it. All the pictures look the same. How do the people get about if there are no streets? Do they swim? Please write and tell me what it is really like for the people who live there.

Nous n'irons plus aux bois. Les lauriers sont coupés. They have cut down the laurel hedge where we used to play. I am not very good at French. My sister Lallie is further on than I am.

Thank you for the pictures. Please send me one of Venice that is not exactly like all the other pictures.

Your cousin Ida is still our schoolroom maid and she was so pleased to hear about you, since she did not know where you were either. She is writing to you.

With very much love from Caroline.

This struck Christine as the letter of a genuine friend. There was no hint of patronage, no parade of kindness, no tactless surprise over Wyn's progress. The French quotation, moreover, was inspired, since it figured in the same nursery rhyme book, and Wyn would recognize it.

"You'll write again?" asked Christine.

"Yes. Tell her Venice smells."

"Only the little canals."

"Where Venice people live. They walk. Pictures are stupid. I paint that old woman for Ca. Tell her . . . that Venice."

These two, thought Christine, might really have a good deal in common. Ca wished to know about "Venice people" who could not afford gondolas. Wyn would tell her. That old woman would correct the monotony of all the Guardis and the Canalettos.

"Was your cousin's letter nice?"

Wyn made a face, and handed it over.

Dear Winsome,

Miss Carrie have showd me your letter and I am very pleased and proud of your letter. Fancy you talking. I always thought you might if somebody learnt you. What good people they must be. Are they foringers?

Mother, your aunty, was vexed when she heard you was adopted into a family. She thought people ought to keep there own child. We never rightly knew where youd gone. We did not tell anybody in the villidge or the House or anybody. It seems it as all been for the best but I have ask Miss Carrie to keep it to Herself. I am shore it is alright her writing to you. Only not tell Miss Lallie for instants. She would make a tail of it and it would be all over the Place in no time and mother would be vexed. I said not put it in the post bag they are such Paul Prize in the Hall. I will post them next time I go to Slane Bredy.

There has been a lot of changes her Ladyship passed away last year. Miss Sue and Miss Barbie and Miss Flo all married and Miss Kitty away half the time stopping with them.

Miss Flo got a title and a House In Darbishire bigger than this. She wanted me to go there it was more wages but I am better off here it is an easy place with no Lady. Mrs Peters her rehumatism so bad she does not get after us girls much.

What nice pictures. A sweet pretty girl and the Governess a real lady has anyone can see. You must of worked hard to learn so much. You are a good girl dear to work so hard. Well Winsome if ever I get to London town to see the Queen I will go to see you to. Miss Carrie was so pleased to get your letter you cannot think. No more now dear from your loving cousin I Brent.

"She sounds very nice," commented Christine.

"Not Winsome now. I forget all those people. Bad spelling!"

"She probably left school and went to work when she was twelve. Some wonderful people never learned to read or write at all, remember? Think of Alfred the Great. Wouldn't you like to send something to Ida? Some Venetian beads?"

Wyn brightened. Ida's letter had offended her, but a gift of beads might set matters right.

"Picture for Ca. Beads for Ida," she agreed.

Myra, rousing up from a placid reverie, asked, "Who Ida?"

Upon learning that Ida was Wyn's cousin, her face clouded. The word had no pleasant association for her. Some little cousins, invited to tea, had laughed at her and teased her.

"I take Ida the Great to see the Queen," said Wyn, who was still revolving plans for putting Ida in her place. "At London."

"London," repeated Myra, catching the word. "I like here better. No streets. No horses. No running. No cousins. All day safe in our little boat."

The life suited her, and she had never looked so robust. In London she was often frightened. At Trentstoke she seemed to be conscious of exile, peeping wistfully into the great empty rooms as if in search of somebody who was never there. Secure in this tiny world of the gondola, she could glide through the tranquil days, disturbed by no demand beyond her powers, conscious of no life going on about her in which she could not join.

"Here always," she decided. "Never go back. I ask Dada."

"Oh, no," said Christine, with a twinge of panic. "He would not be here. You would not like that?"

"He come in the train. Often. I ask. He say yes."

He would. What Myra demanded, Myra got. Nothing would suit Lady Seddon better. Myra's money had brought them to Venice. Myra's money might keep them there for the rest of their lives.

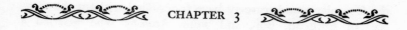

CHAPTER 3

The Greco Lark

1896

ONE

MARK NORRIS fell in love with Kitty Knevett when he was painting the portrait of her sister Flo, who promptly made up the match. It was Flo Dacre who persuaded stupid old Sir Richard that artists are not invariably long-haired, penniless, and immoral. Mark could offer his bride a handsome red brick mansion a stone's throw from Leighton House, his lineage was respectable, he was received everywhere, and he made a great deal of money.

For a time he regarded Lady Dacre as the most amiable of women. He might have gone on doing so had she remained in Derbyshire. When she pushed her poor baronet into politics, and took a house in Queen's Gate, he liked her less. She was forever invading his household, criticizing his wallpapers, snubbing his friends, and commanding him to dine at short notice when other guests had failed her.

All this he could have endured better had Kitty resented it on his behalf. She regarded such licence as natural in a sister. Flo, she said, had always upset everybody, but was nevertheless the loveliest and cleverest of a family renowned for beauty and wit. All Knevetts were perfect, although the flower of the flock had been her exquisite sister Clemmie, now long dead. Her brother Dick was heir to the stateliest home in Great Britain. The Home Office, the Indian Civil Service, and

the Consular could scarcely have functioned without the services of Edmund, Bob, and Tom. Anyone who married a
Knevett automatically acquired consequence. Barbie's Mycroft
was a formidable scholar, Sue's Preston a brilliant barrister,
and Flo's Dacre a dynamic politician. Mark himself was fore-
most among British painters; any demur on his part was an
insult to the family.

After four years Mark had grown heartily sick of the
Knevetts, but until his father-in-law died it never occurred
to him that his irritation might be shared by other victims.
He and Kitty, summoned from Paris, did not reach Slane
St. Mary's in time for the funeral; they could not escape
the subsequent baked meats—a tribal luncheon party which
lasted, as it seemed to him, for about three weeks. He sat next
to the new Lady Knevett, Dick's Dora, a pale, sharp-featured
woman, heartily loathed by all her sisters-in-law. Since most
of her attention was given to the Bishop of Severnton, on her
other side, he had plenty of time to look about him. His eye
fell upon three possible sufferers from Knevett megalomania:
Mycroft, an obscure don at a shabby little college; Preston,
a careworn Junior who could never, probably, afford to take
silk; and Dacre, whose existence might be occasionally remembered by the Whips but by nobody else. So far as he knew,
they were all content with their wives, but must they not
often have wished every other Knevett at the bottom of the
sea? John Preston, looking up suddenly, caught his eye. The
two men gave one another a hard, surprised stare as if to say:
You too?

But they, at least, were not midgets, he thought morosely.
His own lack of inches oppressed him at the Manor House.
Kitty stood on a level with him, but the rest positively stooped
when they talked to him. He had thought, at one time, to
counter this by growing a beard. It sprouted so sparsely that
nobody observed it or perceived any difference when, in
despair, he shaved it off.

He had not sat at this table since his own wedding. By
one excuse or another he had managed to avoid visits to Slane
Forest. On that single occasion he had been overwhelmed by

the number and height of his sisters-in-law. Six giantesses. Now, scanning the company, he could identify only four: Sue, Barbie, Flo . . . Grace . . . where were . . . where were. . . .

Dora at this moment turned to him, and he demanded: "Where are . . . er . . . Lallie and Carrie?"

"Upstairs. All this would be too much for Lallie, and Carrie is staying with her."

Lallie's heart! How could he have forgotten it? Anything was liable to kill Lallie at any moment. Some years ago an attack of rheumatic fever had saddled her with health so precarious that it could never be mentioned save in oblique references.

She never left home, and he had not seen her since his wedding. She had then been a pink, pert schoolgirl, determined to figure as bridesmaid, although all feared that this might be too much for her. The doubt somewhat eclipsed Kitty's consequence as a bride. Lallie was the heroine of the day. A hymn was omitted in order to shorten the time during which Lallie would have to stand. The news that Lallie had survived syncopated all the congratulations offered to the wedded pair.

Dora was waiting for him to say something else. He inquired politely after her child.

"We've sent her to my mother," snapped Dora. "So as to make more room. So many people staying. . . ."

Too many, her dry voice implied. Too many Knevetts. On that point, at least, he could agree with her.

"And such an inconvenient house," she added. "No bathroom."

She turned again to the Bishop.

A neighboring landowner, on Mark's other side, murmured in his ear, "And a ghost."

"What?" exclaimed Mark, to whom this was news.

"Oh, yes. Most inconvenient. When it walks, they sack the butler."

Mark guffawed just as ten seconds' silence fell on the table. All the Knevetts glared at him.

Nothing lasts forever, he told himself, refusing cheese. Nor

did this. Dora at last rose and took all the women away. The
men then made for a privy at the end of a long stone passage,
one of two installed by the late Sir Richard as a concession
to modernity. It was not, after all, the middle of the night.
The Bishop and the neighboring squires were dispatched on
their several drives home across the forest. The brothers and
brothers-in-law betook themselves to their selamlik, the smoking room. No woman had crossed its threshold since the days
of wicked Sir Harry. Any urgent message from the harem
was delivered by a manservant. Here all fell into a profound
slumber save Dick, who bewailed the dilapidation of his inher-
itance. His father had accumulated capital instead of putting
money back into the estate, and with this capital he had made
provision for his unmarried daughters.

"Four hundred a year apiece those girls have got," he cried
to his comatose companions. "Twelve hundred among them!
My father was an only child . . . born late in life!"

He paused to consider this statement and amended it, although nobody had blenched. It was easy to imagine the
deceased as an elderly infant.

"I mean his parents were married for fifteen years before
he turned up. If *he'd* had a dozen brothers and sisters he'd
have looked at it differently. One property can't provide for
a family that size, even with the Madeira fortune thrown in.
The girls must marry. The younger sons must work. I do
believe the property is in a worse state now than when my
grandfather took it over. Dry rot! Riddled with dry rot!"

Edmund, the only younger son present, rose and flung a
wasteful scuttle of coals upon the fire. Dick scowled at him.
He grinned.

"Can't think why they call it *dry* rot," boomed the rival
baronet, suddenly waking up. "Comes from damp. Flo and I
had a lot of trouble with it at Connington. In the billiard room,
of all places. Had it quite a while before we spotted it. I was
in there. Happened to look up, I don't know why. What's
that? I said. Up there by the cornice, just to the left of the
door? Looks like some kind of fungus, I said. We sent for a

stepladder. There was this huge fungus, must have been nine
inches long, sticking out of the wall. Well, to cut a long story
short, I sent for a builder. Local man. Knows his job. He said
it was dry rot. Nothing for it but to pull the wall down.
Awful mess. . . ."

The oppressive occasion, the reek of cigar smoke, the prospect of long stories cut short until nightfall were too much
for Mark. Murmuring something about fresh air, he fled.
Country walks were not to his taste, least of all in midwinter,
but he must get away from this beastly house.

He took a path uphill into the forest. The ground was damp,
and the going was heavy. There was nothing to see save tree
trunks, nothing to hear save the forlorn lowing of a cow away
down in the valley. At the top of the ridge the path plunged
downward again. He paused, frustrated, wondering if it was
possible to get a glimpse of open country.

"If you go a little way along to the right," said a voice at
his elbow, "you can see as far as the Welsh hills."

A tall young creature stood beside him. Four years ago
her dark hair had tumbled in a mane down her back. Carrie?
His tongue rejected such a stupid name.

"Caroline! Where on earth have you come from?"

"Didn't you hear me coming? I was just behind you. Come
this way. You were looking for some place where you could
see out?"

"Yes! Yes, I was!"

She led him along a faint track. He remembered to ask after
Lallie.

"Oh, she's quite happy now they've all gone up to her.
She hated missing everything. We heard you down in the
dining room talking and talking. And once we heard somebody laugh!"

"I'm afraid that was me. An awful brick!"

Remembering why he had laughed, he asked about the
Manor House ghost, at which she said uncertainly:

"Oh, it's not a ghost. It's something . . . scientific. It's . . .
it's a coach driving somewhere in France."

This sounded unlikely, but he inquired no further. Carrie, according to Kitty, was the only stupid Knevett; the simplest matters defeated her understanding. His information about her was scanty, since Kitty seldom talked of her. If mentioned at all, she figured as a useful nonenity: "Carrie was carrying the baskets and. . . ." or "We sent Carrie to the vicarage to ask if. . . ."

The trees thinned suddenly. To the west lay a gap in the ridges through which they could see a wide prospect. Under a ragged winter sunset, fields and copses stretched away to distant hills. Mark drew a breath of relief, and exclaimed, "That's better!"

She sat down on a fallen log. Presently she laughed—tranquil laughter indicating pleasure rather than amusement. She would, he felt, have sat there and laughed even if alone.

Since she was quite absorbed in the view, he was able to stare at her. Why had Kitty never mentioned her beauty? It was, to be sure, not in the Knevett style. She was darker than her sisters. She lacked their fine complexions and regular features. But . . . he smiled to himself as a comparison occurred to him. Some Spaniard he had met described a Greco "in my church at home. It is unique because in this picture the features of the Madonna are drawn perfect correct." And that, thought Mark, also sitting down on the log, is Caroline. A Greco, but not in any sort of holy fit. A matter-of-fact Greco. Face only a shade too long. Exquisite nose and mouth. And what eyes, when she likes what she sees!

"Ah!" she murmured. "Now!"

The sun looked out for a moment from among the thin drifting clouds, and the whole scene changed color. Bare woods warmed to a friendly brown. Caroline's white scarf blushed pink. The plain below emerged in greater clarity so that he could see smoke rising from a farmhouse chimney, and a distant church steeple among trees. Then the light was gone again.

As all sank back into a winter monotone, a chill breeze sprang up. Their log was damp. Mark rose, remarking:

"Into my heart an air that kills
From yon far country blows:
What are those blue, remembered hills,
What spires, what farms, are those?"

"The Welsh hills," she told him. "The church is Stretton Courtney. That farm is Millthorne."

"I meant to say that we shall catch cold if we sit on this log any longer. There's quite a wind."

"Oh, I see. I thought you said an air that kills just to make it rhyme. We needn't go back the way we came. There's a shortcut."

As they plunged down again into the valley she asked if that poetry was Tennyson.

"No. This year's new poet. Do you like poetry?"

"No. But I thought there weren't any poets, now that Tennyson and Browning are dead. We don't hear of them down in the forest."

He could believe it. The wonder was that they had heard of anybody since Chaucer.

"Is he very young, this poet?" she asked.

"No. Must be nearly forty. He was up at Oxford with my eldest brother. Rather fancied himself as a classicist but only got a pass. Went into the Civil Service. Now he's come up with these poems."

"How odd! I mean a civil servant writing poetry."

"They all do," declared Mark, "on the sly."

"*Do* they?"

She looked quite stunned, as though she believed him. Kitty was literal-minded enough, but for Caroline fantasy of the mildest kind was evidently unintelligible.

"I'm sure Edmund doesn't," she exclaimed.

"Perhaps not. They do it because they are bored. I daresay Edmund likes being a civil servant."

"Oh, no. He'd much rather be a farmer."

"Then why isn't he? Surely he can do as he likes?"

This also seemed to puzzle her. Presently she said:

"Does anybody do what they like? Even men? I used to think men could. But all the men I know keep saying they wish they could do something else. Dick doesn't want to live here. Tom says it is a dreadful bore being a Consul; it stops him from writing his book. Perhaps artists are different?"

Were they? he wondered. What was he doing save paint portraits, year in, year out, of stupid women, dressed up to the nines? Did he like it? Why was he doing it? Everything had been, perhaps, too easy. He had mastered technical problems too soon. Success had come before he knew what he really wanted. *Early struggles* . . . some unconscious process might go on which he had missed.

"People don't wait long enough," he said. "They tie themselves before they know what they really want."

"Nobody waits unless they have to."

"Sometimes it's a good thing to have to. Something goes on while one waits, though one doesn't know it."

"Oh? I didn't know. I'm glad. Thank you!"

Her grateful glance suggested that he had solved a problem. The house now sprawled below them, an unprosperous-looking expanse of moss-grown roofs and smokeless chimneys.

"Oh, dear!" she sighed. "I do hope they've finished. I came out because I didn't want to hear any more of it."

"Finished? What?"

"Settling about Lallie. Where she's to go? Who's to have her?"

"Why, is she going away?"

"We're all going. Didn't you know? Dora doesn't want us here. And we don't want to stay. But Lallie . . . weren't the men settling about it in the smoking room?"

"No. We talked of nothing but dry rot."

"Dear me, how nice!"

"But where are you all going then?"

"Flo wants Grace at Connington, and Barbie wants me at Boar's Hill. But nobody wants Lallie."

"What? Surely they're all so devoted to her?"

She gave him a sad look.

"Nobody is fond of Lallie. Everybody is very sorry for her, but that's not the same thing. Still . . . I think Sue would take her, only there's no room at all in Victoria Road."

A ghastly idea occurred to him. In his house there were empty nurseries, prepared for a stillborn child who had never claimed them. Kitty had always professed profound affection for Lallie.

"And you can't," continued Caroline. "Kitty was explaining that when I came away. You have to go abroad so much. For your art. To get inspiration for your art."

Thank God for that, he thought, and broke into a near run in his anxiety to reach Kitty and support her.

They rushed into the house. Grace, pale and anxious, met them at the top of the stairs.

"It's awful," she said. "Kitty won't, and Flo has already told Lallie that she *is* going to Kitty, and Lallie is simply delighted. She'll be terribly upset. Flo says if it kills her, Kitty must take the blame."

"Where are they?" asked Mark.

"Fighting in Barbie's room."

Grace indicated a door. Voices raised in dispute could be heard within. He recognized the tones of Barbie, Sue, and Flo, but failed to detect Kitty's plaintive treble. Sue and Barbie both seemed to be talking at once:

("Moo-ma-moo-ma-moo-moo-moo-ma-mooo!")

("Yak! Akka-yakka-yak-yak-kakka-yakka-YAK!")

Then came Flo's deceptively pleasant contralto:

"Ruther? Uruther-uther-ruther-ruther-ruther?"

A moment's pause, and then a dual protest:

("Yak!")

("Mooo!")

"Kitty doesn't sound to be there," observed Caroline. "I'll ask Dick and John. They're Lallie's guardians."

"They're in the smoking room," said Grace.

Caroline turned and went downstairs.

"You can't go *there*, Carrie!"

"Where's Kitty?" asked Mark. "Where is our room?"

"She can't go into the smoking room," protested Grace. "Whatever will the men think?"

She led him up steps and down steps and round corners, adding: "Sue and Barbie are angry with Flo. She tried to force Kitty's hand by telling Lallie it was all settled this morning, before you'd even arrived. It wasn't very fair, but just like Flo."

Kitty, as he had expected, was in floods of tears.

"Oh, Mark! Have you heard? Dora . . . turning those poor girls out . . . how Dick could . . . his own sisters . . . their home . . . poor little Lallie even . . . utterly determined, thinks of nobody but herself . . . there ought to be a law, Lallie's not of age, John is a lawyer . . . but even if . . . Flo could easily take her and Grace at Connington. Heaven knows we hear enough about the size of that house. And *then* . . . to say that *we* have room, as if nobody ever expected us to have another . . . poor little Lallie can't do her own hair. She mustn't lift her arms. She mustn't stoop to lace her shoes. Everything has to be . . . and one can never leave her for a moment. She's so reckless. She doesn't understand the risks, and naturally she can't be told. It's not that I don't love her. I do, quite as much as they do. More, probably. And now, *now*, they say *we've* got to tell her we don't want her! Oh, what shall we do?"

"Find out what Dick and John think."

"Oh, they'll think whatever their wives tell them to. And anyway they've shut themselves up in the smoking room, where nobody can get at them."

"Caroline, I believe, has gone to tackle them."

"Carrie? You don't mean it. She can't do a thing like that!"

"The matter seems to be urgent, if Lallie is unlikely to survive the news that she is not coming to us."

"But nobody ever . . . even Barbie wouldn't . . . that's the worst of Carrie. For months she seems sensible, and does what she's told, but she can't manage to be like the rest of us. Suddenly she does something insane . . . worse! Unladylike."

"If the house was on fire, would you women let us be

burned to a cinder rather than run in and warn us in the smoking room?"

"Phelps would tell you," said Kitty fretfully. "And you could get out through the window. It's on the ground floor."

Then she began to giggle and added: "Flo once . . . when she was about fifteen . . . really, Flo . . . hid in a cupboard. She wanted to find out what they talk about when we aren't there. She hoped they'd say something . . . well . . . improper."

"My dear Kitty. Nothing even faintly improper has been said in that room since wicked Sir Harry died."

"No. Poor Flo. She had a horrible time, shut up for hours. She said they don't talk like us, all at once. One talked, and the others went to sleep, in turns. First one went on and on about a horse drench. Then another said what a nuisance it is having no good dentist in Severnton. Where are you going?"

"Down there to see if Caroline needs support."

"You don't have to call her Caroline. We never do. And they'll have sent her packing by now."

The smoking room, when he reached it, contained no Caroline, but traces of shock were discernible. Everyone was sitting bolt upright and wide awake.

"Those girls!" said Dick to Mark. "None of us can very well take all three of them. But it won't do to part Lallie from the other two, and they are too young to set up on their own. Lallie is only eighteen."

"Can't see why they shouldn't," said Edmund, "if you hire a dragon to look after them. They've got all that cash, and dragons don't cost much. Might get old Fitzy back. She's only been gone a year."

Dacre and Mycroft made sounds of approval, but John Preston objected that Fitzy was half-witted. She could not spell Wednesday.

"Nobody wants her to spell Wednesday," argued Edmund. "She's had charge of those girls ever since my mother died. And she's of royal blood."

"What?" cried everybody.

"Claims to be descended from William IV on the wrong

side of the blanket. It's her great qualification as a dragon
for nice young ladies."

This led to a digression until Dick called them to order.

"Let's get this settled. If Fitzy comes back they could all
go on as they have in the past. In a house of their own. And
I think I know of the very house!"

He explained, with some enthusiasm, that he possessed a little
house near Millthorne which would just suit them. It had been
standing empty for a long time and needed substantial repair,
but that need not trouble young women with twelve hundred
a year among them. At the thought that this money, so
inequitably left, might find its way back into his pocket he
grew almost cheerful.

Nothing at all was said about Caroline. Mark's curiosity was
unappeased until he could get Edmund alone.

"My dear fellow! You should have seen us! We all leaped to
our feet, and stood in a bunch like a flock of frightened sheep.
Poor simple Carrie thinks we are the stronger sex. Oh, no . . .
she didn't say much. Just outlined the problem, and expected
us to provide wisdom and counsel. When Dick got his breath
back he told her to hop it. Said that this was neither the time
nor the place. After she'd gone he apologized for her. Said we
must make allowances. She wasn't herself. Shock of her
father's death and so on. But if she hadn't tipped us the wink,
I daresay the women might have killed Lallie among them
before we'd ever tumbled to the facts. We can thank Carrie
that Lallie is still alive and kicking."

TWO

The four husbands confided Edmund's suggestion to their
wives while dressing for dinner. The women discussed and
approved of it over the coffee. At bedtime they put the men
in their places. This obvious solution had, of course, occurred
to the harem before it was ever mooted in the selamlik.

Sue, Barbie, Kitty, and Flo addressed themselves next day
to the agreeable task of purloining furniture. The girls would

need chairs, tables, beds, china, plate, and linen; all this gear must be snatched from Dora.

Flo, being the most unscrupulous, fought for the more expensive items. Barbie secured a domestic staff. Kitty ran about collecting important trifles: books, clocks, knickknacks, and cushions. Sue invaded the attics, which had once been full of treasures won by wicked Sir Harry at play; when short of money he and his friends had often staked anything they had about them, from mistresses to shoe buckles.

Little of value was left, since servants, throughout the century, had been helping themselves. The most conspicuous relics were a wig stand, a Bible, and a portfolio of watercolors. The wig stand and the Bible she ignored. Having never heard of a "Wicked Bible,"* it did not occur to her to search for a missing *not* in the seventh commandment. The pictures she brought downstairs. The girls would need some to hang upon their walls, and the portfolio contained some large blue ones, signed J. R. Cozens, which would look nice in a drawing room.

"I wish Mark hadn't gone back to London," said Kitty. "He could have told us if they are good pictures."

"I should hope we know good pictures when we see them," replied Barbie huffily.

Mark never saw the pictures until they hung in their new home. Since he had not been consulted, he said nothing, but he thought that he could identify a Girtin, a Cox, a couple of Munros, a Hills, a Towne, an Edridge, a Nicholson, and a small Constable. This last was allotted to Carrie's room, as the least impressive item in the collection, and he was pleased to think that she had got it. Knevett stupidity had its compensations.

Her invasion of the smoking room had freed him from a dire menace, for which he was grateful. Renewed acquaintance with Lallie brought home to him the magnitude of his escape. To pity the poor girl was obligatory; her health had deprived her of all the amusements and interests natural to her age. She might, he told himself, have been much worse. She

* A "Wicked Bible" was a rare edition with a misprint. M. K.

did not whine, nor was her fixed grin the sweet patient smile of the pathetic invalid. In normal circumstances she might have been reproved for some of her jokes. Immune from reproof, praised for her courage, she liked to be daring, although her audacity, for want of solid material, seldom took her further than mildly indecent limericks. He once asked Kitty if it would kill Lallie outright to be occasionally sat on. Kitty feared that it might.

His sense of escape diminished when he learned that his sisters-in-law were to be established in a block of flats overlooking his own house in London. John Preston had refused to spend their money on repairs to Dick's property. Dora, anxious to get them out of the neighborhood, had suggested London, where they might live under the supervision of Sue and Kitty. The girls themselves were enchanted by the idea. Within a couple of months the whole bevy—Lallie, Grace, Carrie, Fitzy, and two maids, with all the plunder from the Manor House, were whisked into their new quarters.

These comprised two reception rooms, five bedrooms, a bathroom, and a lift, worked by a porter who pulled a wire cable. Such luxury threw them all into raptures. The flat rang with laughter and music. Fitzy and Lallie played duets on the Broadwood snatched from Slane St. Mary's. Grace sang in the bathroom. Ida's Bissel squeaked hilariously down the long corridor. Even Jane in the kitchen burst, now and again, into a lugubrious contralto:

> "When the dewy light was fading,
> And the stars in beauty smiled,
> Came a whisper like an echo
> From a pale and dying child. . . ."

Caroline did not sing. She was not fond of music. She enjoyed herself as much as anyone, in her own way, because she could *see out*. She told Mark that from her bedroom window she could see his chimney pots, just below, Richmond Hill, the Crystal Palace, the Albert Hall, the House of Lords—all

London in fact, including an inch-wide glimpse of the Thames.

"Isn't that a lark?" she cried. "We'd never seen the flat before we came. Sue found it. 'Here's your room,' she said, and I went in not knowing what to expect. To be able to see out like this!"

Fitzy and Grace, he discovered, had smaller, darker rooms at the other end of the corridor. That Caroline should be so much better lodged was unusual, but the explanation, when it emerged, was characteristic. Lallie, established in the best bedroom next door, was given to thumping on the wall in the middle of the night if she wanted a cup of tea, or a fresh hot-water bottle, or sympathy for insomnia. Repose counted for more with Fitzy and Grace than a view of Richmond Hill.

Ought not Grace to take her turn in these nocturnal labors? Kitty's reply to this epitomized the Knevett ethic as he had observed it in the course of four years. If Carrie did less, then Grace would be obliged to do more. Carrie never observed the chief end of man: that of standing up for himself. Had she done battle with Grace, her sisters might have sympathized and sided with her. Lack of pugnacity amounted, in their eyes, to a moral lapse for which she must pay the penalty.

To his great relief he saw but little of Fitzy and the younger pair. Caroline was always welcome in his house, and was sitting to him for a portrait which he privately christened "The Greco Lark—or Caroline Seeing Out." He wanted to catch that particular glow which happiness awakened in her, although he could never locate its source. She suggested some strange musical instrument upon which nobody could play but which, brushed at haphazard, gave forth a haunting note or two. What pleased her? Why, having got the Constable, had she particularly asked for the Nicholson, among those watercolors? Was it the highlights?

When asked, she gave him a startled look, and then laughed.

"Light! Yes . . . *light*. That's what makes anything real. But what are highlights?"

He explained highlights, and added, "In a watercolor you get them by stopping out. Nicholson . . ."

"Mark! There's one on your nose like a comma. Are high-lights on noses always the same?"

"No. You have a thin line on the ridge of your nose. Many people have just a blob at the end. But Nicholson . . ."

"When you look . . . everything is sparkling with high-lights."

"Nicholson was a pioneer in stopping out. He . . ."

"What? I didn't know my pictures were *by* anybody!"

"You wouldn't have got them if anybody had thought so. Hold your tongue and hang onto them. And stop wriggling about looking for highlights. Sit quite still, please."

She obeyed, and he did some intensive work on "The Greco Lark" which was beginning to take hold of him. He wished that he had more time to give to it. His livelihood, at the moment, involved labor with a lady in a diamond tiara. When he audibly regretted this, Caroline exclaimed that diamonds must be all highlights.

"Quite. So what do I do with her nose?"

"You make it smaller," said Caroline.

"You've noticed that, have you? It's what I'm paid for—to pare down the boko if there's too much of it, or supply one if it's missing. Oooagh! I ache when I think of Lady Bostock's nose. It's like an onion. I think I'll knock off and have some beer. What would you like? Lemonade?"

To his surprise she asked for beer too. She had acquired a taste for it, so she said, in the schoolroom. All the servants at the Manor House had beer, and an ignorant maid, deputizing for Ida, had once brought up a mug of it for Fitzy, thus rating her as a servant. The children had whisked the mug away before Fitzy could observe the insult, and later they sampled it themselves. Grace and Lallie disliked it, but Caroline liked it so well that she had continued to sneak Fitzy's beer until the maid, better instructed, ceased to provide it.

"I'm learning more about you all the time," said Mark as he opened the bottles. "Tell me, what do you want to do with your life?"

"Me? I don't know. I'm waiting."

"What for?"

"You said yourself that people don't know what for. The day of Papa's funeral. You said people must wait till they find out what they really want to do."

"Profound of me! But waiting can be an awful bore."

"I used to think so. In the forest. But here one can have larks while one waits."

"You'll get married, and that'll be the end of it."

"The end of larks. Oh, dear, yes! Only I can't imagine it somehow. And we haven't met people. Flo says when she comes to London she will take us about so that we can meet people."

He tried to picture Caroline married, and failed. Flo can take her about, he thought, but she won't marry unless some fellow turns up who knows what tune to play.

"What I want, more than anything," she told him as she sipped her beer, "is to get to Venice."

"Venice! Swarming with romantic tourists? How banal!"

"Some people live there all the time. Not only Italians, I mean. Some English people live there."

"Only funnies live there all the time, though plenty of people buy a *palazzo* and clean it up and never go there. The permanents have all got a screw loose. Had to run away, like Byron."

"Browning lived there."

"And who can have been funnier? No—they're packed off to Venice by families who don't want them. They're kleptomaniacs, or they have cleft palates. Where's dotty Aunt Delia who used to turn cartwheels in Piccadilly Circus? Living in Venice with a paid companion."

He shivered suddenly. The room was very cold, although the fire flickered away, and the door was shut. Then he perceived that Caroline was angry. Her wrath, which he had not previously encountered, took the form of a frightening withdrawal. She sat in the model's chair, her beer mug in her hand, but she was not there any more. A source of warmth and light had been quenched. A lifeless deputy thanked him, and departed at the end of the sitting.

Crouched beside the fire he puzzled over the episode. He

had teased her often enough; she had never resented this before. That warmth, so suddenly extinguished, had become
valuable to him. He liked her company because he liked himself when in her company.

How could he apologize? What had he done? He had but
spoken the truth. There were doubtless funnies in all Conti-
nental resorts, but those in Venice stood out more sharply
against the gorgeous unreality of their background. One knew
them by sight, yet never met them. He should not, perhaps,
have called them funnies, since it was not to be supposed that
they enjoyed their lot. Callousness? Inhumanity? Had that
been his offense? Would Caroline forgive him if he undertook,
in future, to call them *les misérables?*

Apology proved to be needless. When next they met she
was her warm self again. The incident was closed, and he took
good care never to offend in that way again.

They were now seeing a good deal of each other. Kitty was
off on a round of spring visits. Bullied by Barbie at Boar's
Hill, mortified by Flo at Connington, she was recapturing a
cherished childhood. Larks with Caroline occupied most of
his leisure.

He could not share her taste for vigorous exertion. Some
mild tennis was all that he needed to keep his liver in order,
and this he played with her in the garden of a friendy neigh-
bor until the neighbour's son took to joining them. Since the
fellow was a crack player, the attraction of their pat ball was
obscure, unless he was after Caroline.

Mark dropped tennis, and took her to Richmond where they
hired a boat. He rowed with moderation, she with ardor. At
Richmond also they went riding. He knew that he cut a poor
figure on a horse, but was unlikely, out there, to be seen doing
so by any of his friends.

They went, once or twice, to the theater, of which she was
critical. The people, she complained, did not talk like real
people, and that curtain coming down all of a sudden was in-
furiating. Why should it descend just when the hero had said:
"There was . . . no other woman!" The heroine must surely

have been very much surprised, on learning this, and should have been allowed to say so. The scene should continue until one or both quitted the room for some sensible reason.

He feared that she had no aesthetic sense whatever. The rearrangements of the actual, necessitated by art, offended her. She was, however, strongly responsive to visual beauty, and their visits to picture galleries were more successful.

"I wonder what you'd make of the French Impressionists," he said one day.

"Are they in France?"

"Most of them. Very few here. But there's to be a sale next week. Some eccentric bought a lot of them, and his collection is to be sold, and it's on view first. I'll take you."

Their larks in future were likely to be restricted, for Kitty had come back, but he was nursing a scheme that should make up for this. Kitty was in a fretful mood. The Dacres, she said, were on their way to London, and Flo would be sure to criticize everything she did.

"Let her," he said. "We shan't be here. I'm taking you to Venice as soon as I've finished Lady Bumblebee and her fender. And Kitty . . . why shouldn't we take Caroline along?"

This proposal had a mixed reception. Kitty was pleased that he should wish to invite one of her sisters; he had never done so before. But why Carrie? It could not matter to him which of the girls they took, and she would prefer Grace.

Next day she had changed her mind. She would have to take Grace about, and chaperon her. A girl is a bore when one's friends are mostly young married women; she hampers conversation. Carrie could go dozing about in gondolas with Mark, and was, moreover, obliging and helpful. She would pack and unpack and sit backward in the train, whereas Grace suffered from travel sickness.

"Then you'll invite her?"

"Oh, yes. I'll speak to Sue first, and get her to back me up if Barbie and Flo disapprove."

He refrained from telling her what to do with Barbie and Flo. He must not antagonize her. Very soon she would believe

the whole plan to have been her own. He would let her give
the invitation, and he would play the part of a tame Knevett
husband, escorting his sister-in-law in gondolas because instructed to do so.

This discretion survived until the afternoon when he took
Caroline to see the French Impressionists. Then it suddenly
deserted him. He must tell her himself. Kitty might give the
invitation when he was not there, and he would miss the first
flash of ecstasy.

"Oh, these poor girls!" she cried, pausing before a couple
of Renoir bathers. "How they're going to peel!"

"Caroline! I've something to tell you. I . . . we. . . ."

He broke off to glance round the room. It was not very full.
The sale had aroused no great interest. Everyone seemed to
be intent upon the walls, yet, a moment earlier, he had felt
that he was being watched.

"Kitty and I are going to Venice shortly. And we very
much hope that you will come with us. Will you?"

She grew quite pale, and for once suggested a Greco holy
fit.

"Oh Mark! Oh . . . not really? Oh, Mark!"

"Will you?"

"Will I? Oh, I can't believe it. Oh, Mark! How kind! How
very, very kind."

"Not kind a bit. We want you. Kitty is going to invite you
all in due form. But I had to drop a hint. Don't expect too
much. It won't be as wonderful as you think. But we'll have
larks."

Again his shoulder blades pricked as though sharp eyes
were stinging them. He swung round. An elegant woman,
near the door, was discussing a Sisley vivaciously with her
companion. He felt sure that she had been watching him a
second ago.

"Flo!" cried Caroline, following his gaze.

"Yes. Don't say anything about Venice! Not till Kitty. . . ."

Flo now turned and rustled gracefully toward them. She
had in attendance a quidnunc called Beddington whom Mark

knew slightly. The fellow posed as an art critic, and had a most malicious tongue.

"Well, you two!" said Flo. "What do you think you're doing?"

"Looking at pictures," stated Caroline, who was still pale with excitement.

"And that's the long and short of it," chuckled Beddington.

A reproving smile from Flo emphasized the contrast between tall Caroline and dapper little Mark, standing at bay in front of their Renoir.

"And what brings *you* here?" demanded Mark. "Wasting your time on a show like this?"

"Oh . . . I'm making discoveries. Mr. Beddington has been telling me the difference between a Manet and a Monet."

She threw a proprietory glance at Beddington, which was not acknowledged. He was looking at Caroline. The white transport was passing, and Caroline had never been better worth scrutiny. She glowed at them all. When Flo had introduced her, he asked what she thought of the Renoir.

"I'm so sorry for them! Getting so badly sunburned. They'll be in agonies tomorrow."

"They will! They will!" he agreed, enchanted. "Poor, poor things! They little know! But then, you see, there won't be any tomorrow for them. They've just got today, and the glorious warm sun, and the cool water, for ever and ever."

"Oh, yes . . . I see," said Caroline thoughtfully.

"They're too plump," objected Flo.

"We like 'em plump, don't we, Miss Knevett?"

If he's going to make eyes at Caroline and snub Flo, thought Mark, we're in for trouble. Damn! Damn! Damn! Why did I let the cat out of the bag. Nobody can look at Caroline, and not guess that something is up, or suppose that Renoir is at the bottom of it.

"Have you seen the flat yet?" he asked Flo.

"Oh, yes. I've come on from there."

In pursuit of Caroline? They knew at the flat where she had gone. She and Mark made no secret of their larks.

The other two moved on to a Degas, and Beddington burst out laughing at Caroline's comment. Mark hoped that Flo thought well of Lallie's looks. She did. *Fitzy* and *Grace* were obviously taking great care of Lallie. But how did Mark come to have so much time on his hands nowadays? Had clients fallen off? Last year he had been so busy that one could never get hold of him for dinner.

"I think I'd better get a hansom, and take Caroline away," he retorted. "She's monopolizing your cavalier."

"*I'll* drive her home."

"Oh, no. That would be quite out of your way. Caroline and I live next door to each other now, you know."

"I'm quite aware of that. I'll see you *both* home. Carrie! Come along! We're going now, and I'm driving you home."

They were all herded toward the door at which Flo paused to glance at Caroline's hands.

"Gloves?" she murmured.

"Gloves," cried Caroline. "Oh, dear, yes. Gloves . . ."

"You have them?"

"I started with them. I took them off here. One can't look at pictures in gloves."

Beddington guffawed again as Mark rescued the gloves from the settee in the middle of the gallery.

"Put them on," commanded Flo.

It was clear that they must all stand waiting while this awkward rustic creature made herself fit to be seen. To Mark's delight she took her time about it, showing no flurry or discomposure. It was a pleasure to watch her as she fitted the gloves onto her shapely hands, and smoothed down the fingers.

"*Les gants,*" said Beddington. "Who would have painted it? Manet?"

"Now we can all get away," sighed Flo, as the last button was fastened.

Beddington was to go with them, and to be dropped in Belgrave Square. He had evidently decided that Caroline was a wit, and her indiscretions intentional. She had told him in the gallery that she disliked pictures of saints in haloes, but supposed this convention to be necessary in order to distinguish saints from good people. As they drove he rallied her for this.

"So saints aren't good people? How true! They don't know right from wrong. They're foreigners. They come from somewhere else, and they don't know the rules. They try, poor things. They try like anything. But they never get the hang of it. Never manage to be like the rest of us, so they're always in hot water."

"But there aren't any nowadays," objected Caroline.

"Oh, yes there are. Not in the Calendar, of course, but you can spot them if you know the signs. For instance: they do what they like. Nobody else does."

"He doesn't mean a word of it," said Flo kindly.

"Oh, yes. I know what he means."

"Thank you, Miss Knevett."

"I have a birthday book with quotations from saints. On my birthday there's one from St. Augustine: Love God, and do what you like."

Beddington's laughter became a trifle strained. There might be limits to the wit which he thought acceptable in an ingenue. The inference that good people cannot do as they like, because they do not love God, might be diverting, but God in Flo's brougham was out of place. There was a short pause. For the rest of the drive he and Flo discussed the lady whom he was to visit in Belgrave Square. They laughed over her a good deal, and called her "poor Valerie." Caroline in her corner glowed away. Venice! Mark cursed himself again and again for his indiscretion. Flo was on the warpath.

No immediate storm burst, however, when they had dropped Beddington. Flo became frighteningly pleasant, and demanded news of Tom, who never wrote to anybody except Caroline.

"He's had a holiday," said Caroline, rousing herself from her private transport. "So he went to the desert with Donald."

"Donald?"

"Donald Fraser. Tom's friend at school. He used to stay at

the Manor House. After you were married, but I'm sure
you've seen him."

"A sort of mute scarecrow? I vaguely remember. Is he in
the Consular too?"

"No, but he's in White's Bank at Tabriz. So he and Tom
take holidays together in the desert."

"What desert?"

"The Takla Makan."

"Heaven help us! Where's that? Why do they go?"

"They think there was a town there once. The town the
Magi came from. It's buried. But the people there were
Christians even in B.C. And someday . . ."

"Someday they'll take their little spades and buckets and
dig it up, I suppose. Here we are. Hop out, you two."

They hopped out, and watched her drive off.

"She's in a wax," said Mark.

"Oh, no. I think she's rather pleased about something."

"She's up to tricks of some sort."

"That! Yes. It's when she can't get up to tricks that she's
in a wax."

"Have you," ventured Mark, "any idea . . . ?"

"No. I never do. If one started to wonder about Flo, one
would have no peace. And never, *never* listen to anything she
says!"

"How can one not listen?"

"I say some poetry to myself, that Fitzy made me learn. I
don't like poetry, but this is useful because it's so long. It lasts
longer than Flo does, generally. When I feel she wants to be
upsetting, I start off, inside my head: *Lars Porsena of Clusium.*
. . . And after a bit, she knows I'm not hearing a word. She
generally stops by the time I get to a bit that says: *And e'en
the ranks of Tuscany could scarce forbear to cheer.*"

THREE

On the following day he learned what Flo was up to. Kitty
returned, greatly excited, from a tribal tea party in Victoria

Road. Flo had come forward with a wonderfully generous offer—a London Season for Grace! She would do the thing properly, present the girl, take her about—Ascot, Henley, everywhere—and give a ball for her. Grace was in the seventh heaven at the news. She was to stay with the Dacres in Palace Gate, since they could not be continually calling for her at the flat and returning her in the small hours. The scheme to take Carrie to Venice must, of course, be abandoned; somebody must look after Lallie. One could not entirely rely upon Fitzy, and Lallie would pine, bereft of both sisters. Luckily nothing had as yet been said to Carrie, so that she would not be disappointed. They could take her abroad another year.

Fury kept him silent for some time. When able to speak, he asked why Grace should thus be singled out, rather than her elder sister.

"Why . . . Carrie is a dear . . . we are all very fond of her. But one can see why Flo . . . she's rather awkward to take about. She never seems to know quite how to behave. Think of that business in the smoking room! You never know when she'll . . . and she says such disconcerting things. Flo complains that she treated you all to a lecture on St. Augustine driving home yesterday. Hugh Beddington was there, and you know what a tale he's likely to make of it. Flo didn't know where to look."

"Flo has her knife into Caroline, and I'll tell you why. She regards Beddington as her property, and he was very much taken with Caroline. Talked to her instead of to my lady."

"Oh, nonsense. And do call her Carrie, like everybody else. Flo says it was really painful; he was obviously laughing at her."

"You seem to have enjoyed yourselves, pulling her to pieces."

"Well, Sue was a bit inclined to think that she should have the first chance of a Season, not Grace. Not that Sue would have backed us up over Venice. I spoke to her about that before Flo arrived. She said no. Not *Venice*. Carrie, it seems, has a very undesirable friend in Venice."

A friend! So that was at the bottom of it—the mystery and the glow. He felt quite dizzy with rage.

"Who is he?"

Kitty laughed.

"How like a man. A friend must be a *he*. No, poor Carrie! Her swains are likely to be few and far between. The friend is a girl, but not the sort of girl . . . if you'll believe me, she's Ida's cousin!"

Ida? That maid they have at the flat?"

"Umhm! Just a cottage child. Carrie used to play with her when they were children, and we all thought her quite imbecile, but it turns out she's only deaf and dumb. Still! Isn't that just like Carrie? It seems that some people who live in Venice adopted this child, and Carrie has been writing to her for years, even in the schoolroom, behind our backs. Really, you know, Flo is quite right. She's just a little bit underhand. She pretends to be sensible and tractable, but underneath it all she's quietly going her own way, and doing exactly what she likes."

"Underhand? She's the most simple, open, straightforward . . ."

The protest died on his lips. He could not believe Caroline to be dishonest, but she was a baffling creature. Why had she never mentioned this friend in Venice? She was, in her own way, devious. Undetected, she had for years secured herself against Flo's venom by inwardly reciting *Horatius*.

"So you may think till you get to know her. Well . . . it seems that a couple of years ago, when she was only nineteen, these people wrote, coolly inviting her to stay with them in Venice, and offering to pay her fare! Sue forgets the name—Maxton or something. And she went to Papa, and asked if she could go, and then it all came out. Papa was quite bewildered, but luckily Sue was staying there at the time. She dealt with Carrie, and told her it was quite out of the question. We know nothing about these people, and it's most unlikely they're in our class."

"Why have I never heard of this before? I thought I know every smallest detail about every Knevett."

"I was surprised myself, and reproached Sue rather. One expects to be told things. But she says she promised Carrie to hold her tongue about it if all this nonsense about going to Venice was given up. Ida doesn't like it to be known that her cousin was adopted out of charity. Her people are very respectable; these cousins, the Harpers, not so very. He was only a kennelman. But Sue felt she was free to tell me about it now, since Carrie still threatens to get to Venice. Look, Mark, we must dress. We're dining with the Talbots."

Kitty ran off, averting an explosion which would have been, as he later perceived, unwise. He could not but guess Flo's motive in this maneuver, since he knew her only too well. Impeccably virtuous herself, she had a keen nose for intrigue in others. He had been seeing too much of Caroline. The thing must go no further. Venice, and larks in a gondola while Kitty visited her friends, might break up the marriage. He could almost foretell, word for word, the account of the episode which Flo would later circulate.

"I think I acted just in time. Kitty, of course, suspected nothing, and I said nothing. But they were always together. He was obviously losing his head, neglecting his work. Carrie? Well . . . I caught a glimpse of them once when they didn't know they were being watched, and nobody who saw her then could have felt any doubt about it. Quite ecstatic! So I saw to it that she did *not* go to Venice, and I think I did it very neatly. Grace, I said, must have a Season. . . ."

Larks with Caroline must stop. Angry protest from him would merely support Flo's case. He could only curse himself for having so rashly proposed the plan, and trust that Caroline would not give him away.

She did not. Venice was never again mentioned between them, and some second thoughts arose to soothe his regret. This queer friend might have turned out to be a nuisance; he had not bargained for larks with the deaf and dumb, although Caroline's silence on the point might be explicable. She might have told him more, given the chance. She had confided her strong desire to visit Venice, and he had discouraged her by laughing at funnies. If his invitation in the gallery had not been interrupted by Flo, he might have learned more then.

He soon became reconciled to the family decision. The thought of Caroline's inevitable disappointment made him feel uncomfortable and disinclined for further larks. Nor did he finish that portrait. The glow that had inspired it was now extinguished. He threw it into a cupboard full of half-finished pictures.

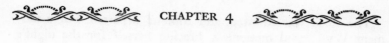

CHAPTER 4

Arrpairr

ONE

ANNETTE need not have taken so much trouble to settle Wyn's frills and puff out her hair, as though this toil would make any difference to the final effect. Wyn knew that well enough. She grinned at herself in the glass, while Annette hooked up her bodice. A square suety face, grinning back, told her that she was not invited to parties for her looks.

Beautiful Myra would have been better worth the trouble, and it was bad luck for Annette that Myra never went to parties. Myra had cupboards full of exquisite clothes. On their spring journeys to Venice, on their autumn migrations back here to Paris, Myra's jewel case was closely guarded upon Annette's knee during the long railway journeys. The diamonds, emeralds, sapphires, rubies, and pearls were kept in a wall safe in Myra's room, since she was fond of wearing them, although the world never saw them.

When the bodice was hooked, Wyn pinned to her waist belt a little slate in a gold frame, hanging by a chain. This pretty toy, a present from Myra, accompanied her everywhere, since nobody in the world, except Em and Annette, could understand what she said. Those rattles, gugs, and clicks had never been conquered. To be completely mute among strangers, to write down anything that she wished to say, was the least embarrassing course. None of the students in her class at Atelier Cruchot had ever heard her voice.

The cloak was adjusted, and Annette departed. For a moment Wyn stood motionless, bracing herself for the night's ordeal.

To venture out alone into the great world was a tax upon her strength. She would have no Em to protect her in situations that might prove difficult. She must fend for herself among people who cared little for her predicament, and scarcely understood it. She must be on her guard lest she make a fool of herself, or appear to be claiming their compassion. This she must do as a step toward independence. Should she fail in her resolution, she must remain a passive creature accepting whatever was given to her.

Not go! Stay warm and cozy with Em and Myra.

Go! Dive into a sea of trackless tossing waves, people moving, mouths speaking, a hundred things going on at once—incomprehensible, important, trivial, dangerous things. Plunge in, and swim for dear life. Harper enjoys parties. We invite her because she can amuse us and is never a bore. Go! Go!

She ran into Myra's room next door to say goodbye. Em was there fixing emeralds into Myra's pretty, useless little ears. The dressing table was heaped with sparkling stones.

"Daisy is coming to supper with Myra," explained Em, "and she wants to see the jewels."

Daisy Hopper was a useful young woman, recommended by one of Lady Seddon's friends. She ran errands and did odd jobs for Britons and Americans in Paris, and would, so her sponsor said, "do anything for anybody." She had been hired to take Myra out during a crisis when Em and Annette had both been laid up with influenza. An intimacy ensued, which Em encouraged, since she was always anxious to widen Myra's circle of acquaintance. The walks continued, and Daisy was invited to supper when Wyn went to parties. Em, on these occasions, left Myra and Daisy to their own devices, partly because Daisy bored her and partly because Myra should be gently pushed toward some degree of independence.

"I shall go to bed," she said. "Bastien will stay up and let you in when you get back from your party."

"Take!" suggested Myra, pointing to her treasures.

Wyn shook her head. She would never borrow Myra's jewels. Turning her back on Myra she said, "Daisy will take."

Both she and Em took Daisy's professions of attachment to Myra with a grain of salt. She was out for what she could get, despite her plausible, affectionate manners. Em also moved out of Myra's vision to say: "Nothing very valuable. She has too much sense. Myra likes to give presents. If it makes her happy to give some little. . . ."

Annette appeared to say that three gentlemen had called for Wyn. This was a surprise, for she had expected only two. Bill Taylor and Hal Gouge were both in her class *chez* Cruchot, and they always undertook to fetch her, and to see her home on these occasions, although she insisted on paying the cab fares since neither of them had much money. Nor did she see a third when she ran down to the foyer. Bill and Hal were standing there at attention side by side. She thought that she must have misread Annette's message until Bill, looking round him, exclaimed, "Where's Whiskers?"

"Vanished!" discovered Hal, and he added to Wyn: "Chenet. He came with us, I don't quite know why."

Wyn frowned. She disliked Jules Chenet. He was often to be seen at student parties; since he was good company, he was accepted, although he was no student and no artist. Nor was he as young as he would have the world to suppose. His smooth face, pink cheeks, and bright eyes were not tokens of youth but of a life so tortuous that it could leave no outward record. Nobody knew whence he came or what he did.

To herself he had been, at one time, assiduously agreeable. He gave her unmistakable looks. He sent her flowers. He was forever contriving to touch her. She gave him no encouragement, since she knew a dirty type when she saw one. Of late he had completely dropped her.

On a sudden impulse she went down the foyer and looked into a salon seldom used at this time of year because it was cold. Now it was icy, since the long window, leading to a small courtyard, stood open. This yard was bounded on three

sides by houses, but had a short fourth wall looking upon a
narrow alley. When she had grown accustomed to the darkness of the room she could see, out in the yard, two people
faintly outlined against a whitewashed wall. Then one of them
rushed forward into the room. Her arm was seized, she was
marched back into the foyer, and the door slammed behind
them.

"*Veen!*" cried Chenet. "*Enfin! Nous vous attendons tous!*"

She shook his arm off angrily. She had never given him leave
to call her Wyn. Only Bill and Hall did so. Most of the students *chez* Cruchot called her "Arrpairr."

They all went out to a cab. There, in the dark, he talked to
the others, probably explaining his disappearance. She could
not see what they said, but doubted if they believed him. The
three of them lodged, at the moment, in the same hotel, somewhere off the Boule Miche.

She was almost sure that he had been talking to a woman in
that courtyard. He was a rogue. Once she had observed him in
a crowded room while he pretended to watch some dancers.
Step by step he had moved backward toward a table upon
which somebody had left a gold cigarette case. His hand stole
out of sight while his eyes never left the dancers. Later there
was a cry and a hunt for that case.

Rumor had it that he haunted student gatherings for the
sake of Nella Kloster, a rich, spoiled brat who had come from
Chicago to Paris to study art. She had worked with Cruchot
for a month. He objected to female pupils, and accepted Wyn
only on a very warm recommendation from her Italian teacher;
upon discovering that Nella had boundless conceit but no
talent whatever, he threw her out. Bets were laid as to whether
Chenet would have to marry her in order to lay hands upon her
dollars. Men thought this needless. Women were disinclined to
underrate Miss Kloster, who was laying a determined claim to
him.

The cab was drawing up. Wyn must forsake its seclusion,
and plunge into that alarming sea. Slipping the fare into Hal's
hand, she allowed them to help her out. Upstairs they went,

toward the jarring and shaking caused by a lot of people making a great deal of noise. There was a moment's respite while
she took off her cloak, and glanced at herself in a mirror. Was
it, she wondered, an advantage or a disadvantage to look so
much like a Toulouse Lautrec?

She took her plunge, and received a warm welcome. *Chez*
Crouchot she was popular, although her sex was against her,
and her deafness would have secured no tolerance had she been
a bore. Women, in that community, were not accepted as
artists, despite the achievements of Morisot and Cassatt; Wyn
was now the only girl in the class. Her vogue sprang from her
gift for brilliant pantomime imitations, coupled with her un-
broken silence. Inspired mimers should never talk. If they do
they break a spell.

Gravely she acknowledged their salutations, accepted re-
freshments, and was led to a chair. Here she sat and surveyed
the scene. Her host would later approach her with hands
joined in supplication, begging for some of her turns.

This gift for pantomime had never struck her as amusing
until she went to the class. She had used it as a help in conversation, a quick way of telling a story, or indicating her view
of a character. One day, when they were all waiting for their
master, somebody had given a crude sketch of his manner
when going round their easels. She thought it so inadequate
that she proffered a better one herself. They were enchanted.
Thenceforth she was asked to parties, and begged to repeat the
performance. Her renown grew as she added other items to
her repertoire. This evening her meditations in the cab had
suggested a new one, never attempted before. It would be daring, but very good fun.

They were all singing, crowded in a bunch round the piano.
There was a sudden stir. Chenet had been standing close behind
red-haired Nella Kloster, and she had spun round and slapped
his face. A lightning spasm of fury crossed it before he doubled
up with mirth. Everybody laughed. Wyn nodded to herself.
That little caper would adorn her new turn admirably.

They had embarked upon an endless ditty which was in vogue that year. The last verse ran:

> *"Et si cette histoire vous embête*
> *Nous allons la, la, la recommencer, cer, cer!*
> *Nous allons la, la, la recommencer!"*

Upon which somebody would recommence and they would go all through it a dozen times before they grew tired of it.

Nella was talking in a corner to a model called Lulu. Amid that caterwauling, nobody would have heard what they said. Wyn could see a good deal of it. Nella was explaining that Chenet needed, at times, to be brought to order. Lulu was trying to keep a straight face. She was a cat with sharp claws as everybody knew save that fool of an American. Now she was talking, "... *Une petite sourde ... non, non ... une autre ... bien jolie même, et tellement riche. ...*"

Nella moved her carroty head between Wyn's eyes and Lulu's mouth.

Who was this pretty little rich deaf ... *Myra?* No! Myra had never met the man. Yes! Walking in the Bois ... Wyn, Em, and Myra ... Chenet there suddenly, forcing an introduction ... but only once. Myra never went out alone without Em or Annette or ... or ... Daisy Hopper?

Many little facts fell into place. Both Wyn and Em had lately noticed a change in Myra. Sometimes she was restless and anxious, at others rapt away in a blissful dream. There was obviously some emotional disturbance. When questioned, she only laughed and kissed them, explaining that she had a lovely secret which would be revealed when her father came at Easter. To win her affection must have been easy, for she was ready to love everybody, but Chenet must have gone about the business very cleverly, since she was not naturally secretive.

Nor had she any notion of a truth long apparent to Wyn. They were unlikely to marry. Men would not want them. This had become plain during their later teens. Myra's beauty attracted attention. In Venice male mouths exclaimed, *Bella!*

Bella! as she passed by. Should her voice be heard, the mouths closed, disconcerted. One handsome youth, radiating admiration, picked up a scarf that she had dropped. Smiling happily, she thanked him. The admiration was eclipsed by furious dismay. He gave her the reverent bow which he might have given to a nun, and fled.

Em, realizing that Wyn disdained shelter and protection, had been quite frank about it. They must accept the fact that, for most decent men, they were nuns. Their affliction placed a gulf between them and other people in which desire was likely to founder. Wyn pointed out that a notable Venetian funny, a woman so badly disfigured by burns that she always wore a thick veil, possessed a young and comely lover who escorted her everywhere. Em replied that the poor woman paid him for his services and got, presumably, value for her money. But, insisted Em, no woman can hope to get full satisfaction from a man whom she despises, since contempt is liable to breed frigidity. Nor might Wyn confuse such pathetic transactions with "love."

Nothing of all this had been made plain to Myra, since she seemed to be content with a completely sheltered life. Wyn, observing a larger world, came to accept Em's view. She was never likely to get a man worth having, and she preferred to be a nun. She might, at one time, have slept with Chenet. He had indicated as much, and she had often wondered what his motive could have been. It was not, she felt sure, a perverted impulse for intimacy with an ugly little freak. He must have reckoned upon some solid advantage to himself.

Had he hoped to enlist her aid in getting hold of Myra? His attentions had suddenly ceased about the time that Daisy Hopper came upon the scene. *It had been Daisy with him this evening out in the courtyard.*

A gold cigarette case. Myra's dressing table sparkling with red, blue, and green. Myra crying, "Take!" to anybody she loved.

Somebody nudged Wyn gently. Her host stood before her, his hands joined in supplication.

TWO

"I say," said Bill to Hal as Wyn was escorted out of the room, "do you think Whiskers was really only looking for the bogs at Wyn's house?"

"No. I expect he was after the teaspoons. What possessed you to bring him along? Wyn can't bear him."

"I didn't. I thought you'd brought him along. Oh . . . we've all got to move back. She's going to do Cruchot."

A space was cleared. A roar greeted the Master as he crept in reluctantly to inspect his pupils' work. After a bleared and bilious scowl at the room in general, he did the round. There could be no doubt as to which victims were in question. At a curt nod, dismissing adequate but mediocre work, several spectators laughed uneasily. A cocked eyebrow, indicating interest, long meditation, a sudden single stroke of correction—all heads turned toward a young Italian thought to be the most promising pupil in the class. Nor did Wyn spare herself. Cruchot, at her easel, always betrayed embarrassment. He used signs and gestures which were unnecessary and ludicrous. He smiled a rusty, disused smile, pointed at himself, pointed at Wyn's picture, took a brush and pointed at that, pointed and nodded like a mandarin at each stroke of correction.

The callous had never concealed their mirth over this, but the compassionate found it distressing. Wyn's attitude toward it raised her in their opinion. Amid the laughter there were some mutters of *brave gosse!* Applause shook the room at the finale, which owed much to a prevailing contempt for Nella Kloster. An easel, obviously hers, was kicked over and Cruchot, struggling with nausea, rushed out.

"Really, one almost forgets it's Wyn," said Bill.

"Yes. If she can't sell her pictures, she can always make her living on the halls."

There was another roar as M. Muller, doyen guest at the hotel off the Boule Miche, trundled in to his dinner. Course after course vanished down his throat at lightning speed, the nature of each being clearly indicated. Finally, taking out his toothpick, he discovered that his dentures were missing.

"Really happened," said Hal, who had been longer in Paris than Bill. "They found his teeth in the bouillebaisse. Somebody thought he'd be good copy for Wyn, and took her there to watch him!"

"It wouldn't come off in England, all this," said Bill. "Everyone would be too embarrassed for words. Awful beasts, the French, in some ways."

"I expect she likes to be accepted entirely on her merits. She must get damn tired of kindness. Hullo! This looks like something new."

Their host had come in. He borrowed a little gold mesh bag from Lulu and put it on a table. Then he signaled through the door to Wyn that all was prepared.

The door was thrown open. After a second's pause Chenet, flashing his brilliant smile, made an entrance. There was a concerted gasp. The laughter diminished a little, since everyone was intent upon capturing the inferences of this new turn. Through the room he went, greeting this friend and that, always with a certain air of complicity. Every woman, so his eyes said, had been indiscreet. He would not tell. Not he! Every man, if all were known, might be glad to count on his good friend Jules Chenet. He moved toward the piano, and recoiled suddenly. His face had been slapped. For a moment he looked murderous. Then he doubled up with laughter.

All heads turned to see how the real Chenet and Nella were taking this. Nella was scarlet. Chenet? A polyglot whisper proclaimed that he had vanished:

"Où est il donc? . . . Dóve? . . . Nicht hier! Disparu . . . When did he go? . . . Chut! . . . Ssh . . . Regardez. . . ."

Chenet was beating time to some imaginary music as he moved back, step by step, toward the table upon which lay Lulu's bag. His right hand continued dreamily to beat time. His left stole behind his back. When he moved away the bag was no longer there.

To a gasp and a roar Wyn curtsied low. She gave the bag to Lulu, and returned to her seat.

Somebody immediately struck up a waltz. Prolonged applause after Wyn's performance was not encouraged. People began to dance. Hal seized Nella and whirled her round. He was a good-natured young man, and he thought that Wyn had been rather hard on her. He soon regretted the impulse.

"Harper just has to be spiteful, I guess," she said. "Deaf people always are. And she can't paint. Cruchot only lets her stay in the class because he's sorry for her."

He said nothing to this. He liked Wyn, but it went against the grain with him to admit that she, or any woman, could paint.

"It's a pity Jules missed seeing himself. He must have slipped out before she started. I never saw him go, did you? But I know why she's got her knife into him, and I can guess where he's gone, too. He used to make eyes at her for a joke. Maybe she took it seriously. And now it's that other deaf girl she lives with. Lulu says she saw them spooning in the Luxembourg Gardens. So I guess it's the green-eyed monster. Lulu says that girl is supposed to be very rich. Some lord's daughter. She calculates Jules means to have a shotgun wedding."

This he could scarcely believe, even of Chenet. He and Bill had met Myra, and thought her infinitely touching. As they danced past Wyn, he caught her eye earnestly fixed on Nella, who giggled and added: "Maybe he'll get one. But not the one he thinks."

The music stopped, and he broke away without ceremony. Nella was a bitch. So was Lulu. He hurried over to Wyn, who wrote a message on her slate. She was tired. She wanted to go home at once. He and Bill must not trouble to come with her, but could he get her a cab?

"We've had quite enough of this," he assured her, and went to collect Bill.

As they drove home, it seemed to him that she was tense and anxious. He feared that she might have seen what Nella said. It was difficult to believe that a cad like Chenet had been allowed to come within a hundred miles of Myra, so tenderly cherished and protected, but he would have liked reassurance. Wyn was in a frantic hurry to get home. Could she possibly suppose that Chenet was there already?

On alighting from the cab she ran off immediately down the street, away from the house. They pursued her, as soon as they had paid the fare, and caught her up in a narrow side alley.

"What on earth . . ." panted Bill.

"Tell you later. I think she's frightfully worried."

Suddenly she pulled up, pointing to a short space of wall between two houses. Dangling over it, discernible in the faint wintry moonlight, was a rope.

A strange jangle of noises broke out. She was trying to speak. She was struggling desperately to say something of which they could not make out a word. Hal at last lit a match, and held it to his mouth while he told her to write on her slate. He then lit several in succession while she wrote, and he read her message: *Our wall. Wait here. I go. If Chenet comes kill him.*

"Whiskers?" cried Bill in amazement, as she sped off.

Hal explained his fears and added: "Why did he come with us tonight? What was he doing in the house? I think she's sure he left the party to come here. If she hadn't done that turn nobody would have spotted he'd gone, perhaps. He couldn't have foreseen that she would."

"Good God! And we wait till he comes down that rope?"

"No, you ass. He can't have gone up it yet. If he had, he'd have pulled it up after him—not leave it dangling for anybody to see. We must stay here till it's removed, or till he comes."

Bill shinned up the rope and reported that it was, at the top, fastened to a ladder propped against the inner wall.

"Let's not stand in the moonlight," said Hal.

They moved into the shadow. A cat howled somewhere. Bill said: "I never heard her speak before. Did you?"

"No. Ghastly. No wonder she never does when you think what brutes. . . . I doubt if she really enjoys these parties. I'd always thought before that we were giving her a good time."

"Why should she come if she doesn't?"

"And rot at home all her life? I was thinking about it in the cab. I daresay they aren't fun for her at all; just a job she feels she's got to tackle."

"But why?"

"If she wants to be a painter, she's got to go through it, along with all of us—all her own generation. It wouldn't be the same thing working alone. Cruchot . . . the classes . . . we know what they do for us. We know why we scraped the cash together to come here. She wants to get what we get out of it."

"Pity she's a girl," sighed Bill.

"Umhm. But she's not bad, you know."

"A man's brain weighs more than a woman's brain. I forget how much. Half an ounce, I think."

"Which man and which woman?"

"On average, I mean. I wish Whiskers would come. I'm getting cold. Do we kill him, by the way?"

"I think not. I'd like to oblige Wyn, but I don't fancy the gallows. We'll just see to it that he doesn't climb ropes in comfort for a long, long time."

"Right. It'll warm us up."

They waited and listened. Hal murmured: "All her life. All her life. Year after year. No letup till she dies. Always struggling against these odds."

"Ssh!"

A figure had appeared at the end of the alley. They shrank back against the wall. As Chenet grasped the rope, they stepped forward and seized him.

THREE

Bastien had gone to bed at the top of the house, with a slight stomachache. Mélanie, his wife, who cooked for them all, was waiting up for Wyn. Not expecting so early a summons, she fell into a doze until awakened by frantic peals upon the bell. At length she shuffled off to open the door. Wyn pushed past her, and rushed upstairs.

She found Myra, tranquil and content, stowing the jewels away in the wall safe. Where was Daisy? Gone downstairs to look for a book, reported Myra.

Christine was hard to rouse, for she had taken a headache powder, and she followed Wyn's speech with unwonted slowness. Still very much mystified, she agreed to go down to the courtyard, where they found Daisy in the act of removing the ladder and the rope. Wyn flew at her, and held her while Christine returned to the house. Myra was told that Daisy had gone home. Bastien was hauled out of bed and goaded into action. When, after much delay, Christine returned with him to the courtyard, Wyn was sitting on Daisy's head. Both young women were the worse for their tussle; they were bruised, scratched, and bleeding. Daisy, faced with a possible police charge, had fought like a demon.

The ladder was identified as one which lay on its side under the wall, and was used when the courtyard was freshly whitewashed. Before removing it, Bastien climbed up. Nobody, he reported, was to be seen in the alley below. It was, by then, nearly forty minutes since Wyn had got into the house.

Both he and Mélanie wished to summon the police. Christine flinched from such a step. If Wyn's surmises were correct, the publicity of a police case must be avoided; she was sure that Lord Seddon would think so. Daisy Hopper was given her choice. She could tell the truth, and go free. She could hold her tongue, and be handed over to the police.

She chose to talk, although she volunteered nothing. Information had to be squeezed out of her, drop by drop, in answer to questions. Yes, she had carried letters and messages between Myra and Chenet. She had arranged meetings. Yes, he had paid her for it. Myra believed herself engaged to him, but that the engagement could be revealed to nobody until her father came at Easter. Chenet would then ask for her hand in due form. Lord Seddon would assuredly consent, and the delightful secret could be told to everybody. Daisy herself expected to be out of Paris before Easter; she was going with some patron to Tangier.

No, Chenet and Myra had never been alone together. This was the first time that he had tried to get into the house. It was to be a surprise visit. Daisy had agreed to put the ladder and the rope for him, and to let him in by the salon window when the coast was clear. She had gone down to wait for him, at the appointed hour, but he had not appeared. Eventually, hearing some racket inside the house, she had tried to remove the ladder.

How should she know his intentions? To do anything for anybody, on cash terms, was her vocation. Yes, she might have told him about the jewels. Yes, he had asked her to arrange for a display of them tonight, but she would have seen to it that he pocketed none on this occasion. If he wanted them he must get them by some other means. No, she could not be sure that they were his sole object. He might really have intended to marry Myra, who was of age, and had inherited a large fortune from her maternal grandfather. Plenty of men might regard her as a profitable match. Since she seemed to be very susceptible, she would certainly marry some fortune hunter sooner or later.

This seemed to be all that Daisy knew or would tell. Christine, dismissing her, felt that it had been her own fault for accepting a testimonial from any friend of Valerie Seddon. Chenet had probably meant to entrench himself so firmly in Myra's affections that Lord Seddon would be obliged to buy him off; at Easter, heavily bribed, he would vanish.

Wyn disagreed. She did not believe that Chenet could afford to wait until Easter, since he was obviously anxious to escape from Nella Kloster. The jewels had been his object. Having seen them, and assessed their value, he might hope to get them from Myra on some pretext or other. She was always only too ready to give. He would then vanish well before the arrival of her father.

A telegram summoning Lord Seddon was dispatched next morning. Some immediate consultation seemed to be necessary. It had never occurred to any of them that Myra might fall into trouble of this sort, and a stricter guard must in future be kept on her. As yet she knew nothing of the night's turmoil; she had better remain tranquil until her father came. She loved him dearly. He, rather than anyone else, must tell her that she had given her heart to a scoundrel.

The shattered household got through the day as best it could. Toward evening, Hal called. Christine saw him, since Wyn was upstairs, nursing a black eye. Hal also had a black eye. Many people, according to him, had got black eyes; he wanted Wyn to know that her pal Chenet had been attacked and beaten by thugs on the preceding night. Nobody knew for certain when and where this outrage had occurred. It could not have been immediately after his disappearance from the party, for some cronies had met him coming out of the house, and had detained him for a long while, being much amused by his obvious anxiety to shake them off. Nella Kloster, on hearing the news, had turned up at his hotel. She had removed him to her own apartment where she was now tending his bruises. There was no serious injury. Wyn need feel no alarm.

All this Hal retailed with a straight face. Chenet's delay in keeping the tryst was now explained. Christine longed to know how he had been smuggled out of the alley before Bastien inspected it, but thought it wiser to know nothing. She thanked Hal, and promised to deliver his message to Wyn.

Lord Seddon arrived next day—a prosperous, heavy-jowled, brokenhearted man. He listened to the dreadful story, and checked Christine when she accused herself of negligence.

"No. I should have foreseen it. I know the world. But Myra. . . ."

He broke off with something like a groan. Myra was still for him the charming baby who had captured his heart before anything amiss had been suspected.

"No great harm has been done," he said.

"I'm afraid Myra is in love with him," sighed Christine.

"She'll forget."

"Oh . . . I hope so . . . but . . . we've always thought of her as a child. She has all the natural feelings of a woman, and I'm afraid he has roused them. He's quite an expert with women. We may, in future, have difficulties over other men. And, in any case, if she never sees or hears from him again, without a word of explanation, she will suffer. How can we tell her that he is a very bad man, and did not love her at all?"

"Oh, my God. . . ."

They sat in miserable silence, scanning the disaster.

They had been friends and allies for so many years, planning together every step that might secure some measure of happiness for Myra. She knew the depth of his bitterness toward his wife. His case was not, as she had once ventured to hint to him, unusual. Elsie Spender had often spoken of it. Parents who face the tragedy of a handicapped child with equal candor, fortitude, and common sense are rare. One frequently cares too much, the other too little. One will sacrifice a whole family for that single claim. The other grows impatient and jealous.

Reluctantly he had agreed to the establishment in Venice, although he hated to lose Myra, and spent as much time with them as he could. A winter house in Paris had given him more opportunity for this. With each sign of improvement his hopes soared high. At each proof of incurable limitation he was wretched. He was continually seeking new methods of instruction. Christine strove to make up for the deficiencies in her own training; she read everything published on the subject both in Europe and America. Some of her labors had been of service to Wyn, but it seemed impossible to push Myra beyond a certain point. Happy and secure among people who loved her, she had no ambition to make a place for herself in the world, and lacked Wyn's incentive for continual effort.

That perhaps had been his hardest cross. He had been able to do so much more for the alien child than for his own, though he had no affection for Wyn, and had adopted her only for Myra's sake. Year by year he had been forced to see Wyn improving and Myra dropping behind in everything save actual speech. He now said, with some impatience, "Myra would never have come across the brute if it hadn't been for that girl and her bohemian friends."

"Not this particular brute. But she might have met another,

later on, when we were even less on our guard. And Wyn was very quick to stop it."

"Oh, yes. She seems to have behaved well. But I wonder if she is now the best companion for Myra. This painting . . . it takes up too much of her time. Some girl, more of our own class, might do better. We could make other arrangements for Wyn."

"This is no time to part them. Myra will need everyone she loves just now. Could you stay with us for a while, till she has got over the shock a little? Whatever we decide to tell her, you will be her best comforter."

"Yes, I'll stay. We must get her out of Paris. I'll take you all off . . . somewhere warm. As soon as possible. I'll tell my wife we've had another scare over Myra's lungs. She need know nothing of this."

"Wyn will have to break off her classes," murmured Christine.

"She will," agreed the father. "But where is she? Where's Myra? Does she know I'm here?"

"No. We didn't tell her you were coming."

She took him upstairs to Myra's room where the two girls were playing chess. They were better matched than might have been expected, since Myra kept what mind she had on the game, and Wyn did not. At the sight of her father, Myra gave a gasp of ecstasy, and flung herself into his arms. The other two retired to Wyn's room where they sat down and wept.

Presently Wyn produced a written statement of her views. She still did this, even with Christine, when she had anything very important or complicated to say:

Take Myra away and tell her that he is dead. No use to tell her that he is wicked. She will never understand. Never believe it. She loves him. If she thinks he is dead she will always love him. Never forget him. Never any other man. She will be safe from other wicked men. Her own heart will keep her safe. She will be true to him because he is waiting for her in heaven. If you will not tell her a lie, I will tell it for you. Almost the truth. The man she loves is not alive. Stay away from Paris till he is gone. I think he will go soon. Nella will take him away to America.

"I'll suggest that to Lord Seddon," said Christine, folding the paper. "I expect you are right. In any case, we are leaving Paris at once. I'm sorry about your classes, my poor Wyn. And all our plans for asking Ca to stay."

Wyn shook her head, tenderly fingering her black eye.

"Ca will never come now that Grace is married. She can never leave Lallie."

"Poor Ca!"

After a pause Wyn again shook her head.

"No. Not poor Ca. Not poor Wyn. We are in the world. Sad. A sad world. But we choose what we do. It's poor Myra . . . poor Myra . . . she can never choose. . . ."

Her voice was lost in sobs.

She had spoken the truth. Somehow or other she was scrambling her way into the world. Inclement it was likely to be for her. She knew that, and preferred to live in it. She accepted her affliction, was resigned to its discipline, but she would recognize no stigma of inferiority. She would not be "poor Wyn."

Christine had hesitated over those classes, fearing that the rough-and-tumble of student life might prove too great an ordeal. She saw now that from this test the girl had emerged as "Arrpairr," a very rum little customer, standing valiantly and precariously upon her own two feet.

CHAPTER 5

The Aunt Heap

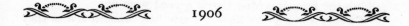

1906

ONE

IT WAS Sue Preston's self-appointed task to circulate tribal news. She saw to it that none of the Knevetts could complain that they had "not been told." This activity she described as keeping the family together.

Anything connected with Slane St. Mary's was regarded as important, and the fact that Ida's cousin had two pictures in the Salon went, at the turn of the century, to every Knevett in Great Britain, also to Grace in Madrid, Bob in India, and Tom in Persia. They must surely remember Winsome, who snorted so dreadfully? She was now, it seemed, living in Paris with a kind lady who had taken an interest in her. One could not help wondering if this sort of thing was right for that sort of girl; it would have been kinder to train Winsome to some more practical trade. These rich eccentrics often do more harm than good; they waste money in an attempt to turn geese into swans, and they give their victims swelled heads. Not that the Salon could be compared with the Royal Academy. It probably exhibited a great deal of rubbish.

Thereafter it became a feudal duty to inquire after Winsome when calling at the flat. Ida's meager and abrupt replies discouraged the civility. She was affronted by persistent references to *Winsome* when she had made it clear that her cousin was now called Wyn. They had tittered enough, as she well knew, over that awful name in the old days. Now they clung to it as though the change was affected and pretentious.

Amusement and disapproval were so obvious in these inquiries that she took to being very short with them. They had died away when, in 1906, Myra Seddon died, and Wyn announced her own return to London. Ida felt no inclination to publish the fact, and Miss Carrie agreed with her.

"Twenty-three years since we saw her," mused Ida as they read Wyn's letters. "Time flies. Ten years since we came here."

And changes! Such a pack of wild girls, and old Fitzy as bad as any of them, laughing and singing like mad things, getting this lovely place all to themselves. Oh, they had had a high old time, ten years ago, as if something wonderful was starting.

Where had they gone to, those girls? Miss Grace married. Poor Fitzy carted off to a Home by Miss Barbie, after she had that stroke. Miss Kitty and her little baby. . . . Oh, that was a dreadful thing, her going like that, one still couldn't hardly believe it, and Mr. Norris gone off nobody knew where as soon as they were buried. Ida herself close on forty. No chicken! Jane weighed fifteen stone if she weighed an ounce. Miss Carrie didn't look much different, but you couldn't remember she had ever been a girl—so quiet and watchful, seeing Miss Lallie didn't tire herself. Miss Sue's children, they called the flat the Aunt Heap, and so it was these days. The least changed was Miss Lallie. Didn't look twenty-eight, so dressy always with her frilled blouses and her hair done just right. Well, she'd had nothing to age her. She could go on just the same, laughing and joking when anybody came, but a terror to live with, all right.

Blount's Hotel. That was where Wyn would be stopping, along with Miss Maxwell, who was coming too. Why not the Ritz? Wyn was rich now. Poor Miss Myra had left her money. Have you heard anything lately of *Winsome*, Ida? Can she earn her living by painting these pictures? Oh, yes, Mrs. Mycroft, she's in London and stopping at the Ritz. And she don't have to earn her living, not Wyn, she has private means, and I'm just off to have tea with her. I've bought a hat.

Miss Carrie said that Blount's was a very good hotel; more style about it really than the Ritz. Quieter. She and Ida were to take tea there on Wednesday, because on Wednesdays Miss Lallie always went to Victoria Road, supposed to, so as to give Miss Carrie a few hours to herself. And if it really happened once a month they were lucky. Miss Sue might talk as if she never put anything in front of her promise to take Miss Lallie on Wednesday. Talk was all that Miss Sue had ever been good for.

Wednesday came, and with it the usual disappointment. A niece, Daphne Dacre, had been sent from Derbyshire to have her teeth straightened. She must be taken to the dentist, and Miss Lallie must be put off.

"You go," said Miss Carrie, when Ida's indignation had subsided a little. "You are Wyn's cousin. I'll go another time."

"All very well to say that, Miss Carrie. I know these other times! Poor Wyn! She'll be so disappointed. All these years you've both waited. And such friends. Close as if you'd been living next door to each other."

"So we can wait a day or two longer. You've got that new hat especially for today. You must wear it."

Ida was longing to wear the hat, but she would have argued further had it ever been possible to argue with Miss Carrie. Wednesdays were often the worst day in the week. Miss Lallie, if balked of her outing, was enough to make anybody say their prayers backward.

Half the glory of the treat was gone. She did not relish marching into a grand hotel all by herself, hat or no hat. She had looked to Miss Carrie to do all the talking and to inquire for Miss Harper in a ladylike way. A good thing it was not the Ritz after all! Blount's, when she got to it, looked less alarming. A gentleman was talking to the young chap at the desk. When they had finished, she would go up and say that Miss Harper was expecting her.

She waited nervously. A lady got up and came forward. Miss Maxwell! Just like in Wyn's sketches.

"Oh, yes, ma'am, I'm Ida. Miss Carrie couldn't come. She's ever so sorry, but she couldn't leave Miss Lallie. She said to tell you she'd arrange something as soon as ever she can. She's dreadfully disappointed. I'm sure Wyn would rather she came than me, but it couldn't be helped."

"Never mind. We've got you! And I've an apology to make. Wyn may be a little late. She had to go to the lawyers with Lord Seddon. Come upstairs."

Over as easy as anything, thought Ida, as they sailed up in the lift. Now she could begin to enjoy herself. A private sitting room! Something like! They sat down, and they both laughed.

"So much to say. So much to ask," said Miss Maxwell. "We don't know where to begin."

"Oh, yes, ma'am, but there's one thing I must say first. How sorry I am! Poor Miss Myra! Quite sudden was it?"

"Yes. Pneumonia. She was never very strong."

"And her poor . . . his poor lordship? Did he get there in time?"

"Yes. She said her last words to him. Italian. Just before she died. *Grazie per tutte*. Thank you for everything."

"Oh, dear, it does seem sad! It must have meant a lot to Wyn. I mean somebody she could study. I've a notion Wyn is all for Number One generally, isn't she?"

Miss Maxwell gave Ida a sharp look, and laughed.

"You're quite right. She is. But she often put Myra first."

"Excuse me, ma'am, but does Wyn sell her pictures? I'm often asked, and she never says in her letters."

"Yes. She has sold quite a number. And people who are good judges think well of her work. I'm no judge myself, but I can see that there is something very real and solid about it. I think she's doing very well. She has attracted attention, though she's not thirty yet."

"That's good. But . . . I don't want to seem inquisitive . . . does she have to earn her living now?"

"No. Myra left her enough to live on. But of course she'll go on painting. Did she tell you that we are going to America?"

"No. She never said about that."

"She has some friends there, who have bought a couple of

her pictures. They live in Massachussets, and have often asked her to stay with them. We thought it a good opportunity as I'm going too. You see, besides providing for Wyn and me, Myra left a great deal of money, the bulk of her fortune, in trust to be used for educating deaf children. I'm one of the trustees, and before we settle how to spend this money I thought I'd better go over to the United States and see what they are doing there. They are a good deal ahead of us Europeans."

"They've got more money?" hazarded Ida.

"They've got more sense. Here we've been held up for a hundred years by the wars and jealousy between France and Germany. The French teach by signs, and the Germans by lip reading, and they won't even attend the same conferences."

"Foreigners are all alike."

"Well, even here, if you follow the one method, you sniff at the other. The Americans aren't so silly. They have studied and combined the best of both methods. They have set an example to all of us."

"Fancy!" said Ida, who did not really believe that anyone could set an example to the British. "And Wyn? Is she going to study it up in America too, so she can help you?"

"I fear not. Wyn hasn't much sympathy with the enterprise."

"What? Trying to help deaf children. Why, she was one herself."

"The whole subject bores her. It makes her impatient. She doesn't like to be classed with 'the deaf': a lot of people with whom she feels she has nothing in common, except one disability. She has been successful, in spite of it. That's her attitude."

"She wouldn't have got anywhere, only if people had helped her."

"I know. She rather overlooks that. But, Ida . . . I'm rather glad to have got you to myself, for I want to ask about Ca. Your Miss Carrie, I mean. I've been calling her Ca for so long that I don't think I'll ever be able to call her anything else. . . ."

Tea was brought in, and Miss Maxwell broke off to pour it out. Then she resumed: "Why can she never leave her sister? We've asked her to stay with us again and again, you know. Does she get no holidays?"

"It's Miss Lallie's heart. Somebody has to be with her always."

"But why always Ca? It's a very large family, I gather."

"Why, yes. There's some abroad. But there's two brothers and three sisters got homes in England. Only. . . ."

Only . . . there was no one answer to Miss Maxwell's question. There were a dozen. It had not always been so. Ten years ago there had been Miss Grace and Miss Fitzroy. Really it had been a sort of accident, and all very well to say that Miss Lallie could stay by herself with some of them while Miss Carrie got off on a holiday. Mr. Tom had said that, last time he come home. Very angry he had been. Called them all selfish brutes till Miss Barbie fired up and said she'd no objection, not any, to looking after Miss Lallie while he took Miss Carrie to the Highlands. And after a week she had to send a telegraph, and Miss Carrie had to come rushing back. Miss Lallie as ill as could be, not putting it on, properly at death's door. Well Miss Barbie was enough to make anybody ill, even if they were as strong as a horse. They might be selfish, but that wasn't the whole story. If they'd been ever so unselfish, not one of them could have kept Miss Lallie alive for long. There'd have been ructions, and she'd have made herself ill and died.

Miss Carrie, she could manage anything without seeming to. Without raising her voice. Even Miss Barbie . . . that time they carted poor old Miss Fitzroy off, she said no need to store all the rubbish in her room, throw it out, she'll never want it again . . . and pulled open the drawers and laughed at all the photos and keepsakes . . . oh, Miss Carrie, she just stood there and *looked*. Never said anything, but the way she looked was enough to turn a person into a frozen statue. Had Miss Barbie crawling out of the room in no time. *Oh, all right! Do what you like!* About the only time in her life, most likely, Miss Barbie had ever told anybody to do what they liked. Oh, no,

Miss Carrie wasn't one to be pushed about, but it wasn't easy to explain.

"Is she," asked Miss Maxwell, "so very devoted to her sister?"

"Not specially," admitted Ida. "But whatever she does, there's a reason for it, you may depend."

"Does she think it's her duty?"

"It isn't quite that, ma'am. She isn't that sort—always going round doing their duty. She's very patient. But she only once, *once* in her life, did something because she was told to; that was when she shut her eyes to Winsome, twenty-three years ago. It went against her so much that I think it put her against duty, and all that, ever since. And she doesn't care two pins what anybody thinks. But it doesn't show because she's so quiet and gentle and ready to oblige."

"Not all for Number One?" suggested Miss Maxwell. "I'd got that impression. I suppose it's because most of us are, more or less, that we have to worry about duty."

A bluff, odd little creature burst into the room gargling angrily.

"She couldn't come," said Miss Maxwell. "But here's Ida."

The newcomer ignored Ida, and said something at which Miss Maxwell winced. It sounded like Mairdalawk. Ida protested: "Language! Language!"

They both stared at her.

"You know French?" exclaimed Miss Maxwell.

"No. But I know what's vulgar even if it's double Dutch."

Wyn cackled with laughter, slapped her on the back, and produced a present from Paris—a blouse in *broderie anglaise*. After an interval of gargling Miss Maxwell interpreted: "She thinks she remembers you. Did you go to their house once and walk all round the room with a red jug on your head?"

"I might do," said Ida unhappily.

She was overwhelmed with disappointment. Impressed by Wyn's achievements, she had come to imagine her cousin as completely cured, as looking and talking like other people. These noises were not talking. After years with the elegant

Miss Maxwell, Wyn did not look worthy of Blount's Hotel. She was no lady. Now she gave Ida an accusing stare, and gargled again. Miss Maxwell obviously refused to translate, upon which a slate was snatched up. A scribbled message was handed to Ida.

"*You are disappointed in me.*"

"The idea! Of course not."

"*Yes you are. Don't tell lies.*"

Losing patience, Ida said: "Well, perhaps I am, a bit. I thought you'd be more considerate of other people's feelings. You may have learnt a lot, but you don't seem to have much notion of the things that matter most, all said and done."

Miss Maxwell sighed. Wyn stumped off into the bedroom next door, and stayed there. I'll never look forward to anything again, not anything, thought Ida, straightening her expensive hat.

"She'll be sorry soon, and say so," suggested Miss Maxwell. "She's upset and disappointed over Ca. She still has a great deal to learn about those things which you rightly say matter most. Only . . . we can go on learning those things all our lives. She may never manage to speak better. We can't push our minds or our bodies beyond a certain point, and then they fail us in old age. But the heart can go on growing."

"I was silly," said Ida. "I expected too much. Her speaking . . . that was a shock. Somehow I'd thought. . . ."

She wiped her eyes.

"And what does Ca expect?" asked Miss Maxwell, a little nervously. "I . . . to tell you the truth, I've been dreading this meeting. She is so sure that Ca will understand what she says. She may get a fearful shock. I've told her it's most unlikely. One has to be used to her. She seems to think that Ca is unlike anybody else."

"So she is," said Ida. "I can't say how, but she is. I wouldn't worry, ma'am, if I were you. Miss Carrie understood Wyn before Wyn could talk at all."

Wyn suddenly bounced in again with a fresh message on her slate.

"*Sorry. I'm a camel You are Ida the Great.*"

"Don't be so farfetched," said Ida, kissing her. "Sit down, do, and have your tea."

She did not stay very long after that, lest she begin to cry. She had taken such a pride in Wyn. A good thing they were going to America. The sooner the better. If The Family knew the truth about "Winsome," some very sarcastic remarks might be passed.

TWO

"For goodness' sake, Daphne, stop fidgeting. We've got homework. I daresay your wire does hurt. *Il faut souffrir pour être belle.*"

"Is that supposed to be French?"

"You must suffer to be beautiful. You don't want to wear your teeth outside when you grow up. I thought you *knew* French."

"I didn't understand your accent. It's like Aunt Lallie's. *Eel fo sooffreer por aitrer bell.* Mother says that's just one of the things against a high school."

Stella and Rosemary Preston exchange glances. Cousins were a chronic nuisance. They suffered enough from Cecily, the youngest of the Mycroft girls, who went to Oxford High School, and insisted that it was immeasurably superior to Kensington High School. Daphne Dacre, an inveterate exhibitionist, yet impervious to snubs, came at the bottom of their list.

"Aunt Barbie," said Stella severely, "thinks you ought to be packed off to boarding school to find your own level."

"And what is my level?" mused Daphne.

"Jolly low," muttered Rosemary.

"Who says so?"

"I do."

"My dear Rosemary!" For a ten-year-old, Daphne achieved a very fair imitation of her mother's arrogance. "Is what you say so very important? Does one have to take it seriously?"

"I happen to be two years older than you are. At school you wouldn't speak to me unless you were spoken to."

"Oh, shut up, both of you. I've got algebra to do."

"I think," sighed Daphne, "I'll go and sit with Aunt Sue."

"She won't want you. She's got Aunt Lallie on her hands, though it's not Wednesday. Aunt Carrie insisted that she wanted to go out somewhere. You get a book. You say you adore reading, but we never see you do it."

"None of your books appeal to me particularly. I like poetry."

Stella went to the schoolroom bookcase, pulled out a large battered volume, and slapped it down in front of Daphne.

"There you are."

"Shakespeare? I've read Shakespeare."

"All of him?"

"Of course."

"Have you read *Venus and Adonis* or *The Rape of Lucrece?* Ha! I thought not. You never heard of them. Read them now."

Silence fell. Stella labored with her algebra. Rosemary wrote an essay on Christopher Columbus. Daphne thumbed her way through *The Rape of Lucrece* in search of a quotation that might impress grown-up people. Warned by experience, she did not start at the beginning. Too early, a quotation might give the impression that she had not read the thing all through.

Where is Daphne Dacre? Sitting on the library steps with her nose in a book. That child lives in the library. And the books she's read! Why! The other day she came out with something from *The Rape of Lucrece!* You wouldn't have thought she'd understand it! A very unusual child. . . .

Who is that beautiful girl with a tragic face? (Nobody can have a tragic face if their teeth stick out. It hurts, but I'm bearing it very bravely) . . . Oh, that is Daphne Dacre. She grew up all alone in a wonderful old house . . . she had three brothers but they were away at school . . . a very lonely child. And then came the great tragedy. I must decide sometime what it was. Now she is quite, quite selfless and devoted. Living for others. Not like Aunt Carrie, though. Aunt Lallie laughs too

much. The blind? I would play and sing to them and lead
them about and read poetry. Or if there was a war I would
nurse the wounded with my gentle hand. Her lover was killed
in the war. Was that the tragedy? I wish there was a war.
Here's something about a war:

> "And from the walls of strong-besieged Troy
>   When their brave hope, bold Hector, marched to field,
>   Stood many Trojan mothers, sharing joy
>   To see their youthful sons bright weapons wield;
>   And to their hope they such odd action yield
>   That through their light joy seemed to appear,
>   Like bright things stained, a kind of heavy fear."

Do you know what that strange child Daphne said, when
she saw all the soldiers marching away? *And from the walls* . . .
but there isn't a war. Father says there won't be, ever, because
they know we always win. . . .

The door flew open. In rushed Aunt Lallie with her odd
little gasping shuffle.

"Well, old chaps! Did you think I was never coming? What
shall we play at?"

Stella welcomed her glumly, and explained that they could
not play because they were doing homework.

"Oh, that! I'll do it for you in two twos."

"You can't," said tactless Rosemary. "Stella has algebra, and
you don't know algebra."

The corners of Aunt Lallie's mouth went down. Stella, with
a frown at Rosemary, said that they might have time for a
very short game, and suggested Old Maid.

"No. That's a dead bore. Scramble Patience."

"Aunt Lallie! That's much too . . ."

"Get the cards, Rosemary. They're *downstairs*."

"Are they? I thought . . . oh . . . I see. . . ."

Rosemary vanished with a conspiratorial air. Aunt Lallie
sat on the table, swinging her legs.

"Hullo, Daph! How's your Pa? Got over the elections yet?"

"Yes, thank you, Aunt Lallie. I mean no. It's very tragic, isn't it? For the whole country."

"Must be. I don't know what I'd do if I lost my *seat*. He must be in agonies! And everyone saw, with a feeling of awe, that he couldn't sit down for he hadn't *de quaw*."

"Ha! Ha!" tittered Stella mirthlessly. "Uncle Dick says he may as well emigrate. They've even got a Liberal at Severnton. He went on and on about it, when he was here. How the country is going to be ruined."

"What? When was he here? He never came to see *me!*"

"Last week. Only for the night. He hadn't time, Aunt Lallie. You know there's only one good down train to Millthorne."

"Oh, yes. We all know that he goes by the town drain and takes two rags and a bug."

"Ha! Ha!"

"Daph, old man! What's that hidjus contraption in your mouth?"

"My wire. I have to wear it always. It hurts."

"Throw it out of the window then."

"They'd only get me another."

"Throw that out, till they get tired of it. That's the way to treat 'em. What say I throw it out now for you? They can't stand me in the corner."

Grinning at Daphne's dismay, Aunt Lallie jumped off the table, and advanced.

"No!" cried Daphne retreating. "No . . . no. . . ."

"Yes! Yes! Yes! I'm not frightened of your ma, though everybody else is."

"Oh, Aunt Lallie! Don't tease her."

"Why not? A little teasing would do her all the good in the world. The whole family says so."

Rosemary returned with the cards, and held up five fingers behind Aunt Lallie's back. The table was cleared. They embarked upon a gruesome game of scramble patience. The children played doggedly. Aunt Lallie screamed and gasped and snatched until their mother came to remove her.

"Now, Lallie. Rules are rules. This is their time for homework."

"Poor little blighters! Is this a prison or what?"

"You mustn't spoil them. Come along."

"Boo! Goodbye, old chaps."

"Goodbye, Aunt Lallie. Thank you for coming."

As soon as their elders had departed, Stella scolded Rosemary for failure to repeat this formula.

"I'm not going to, in future," said Rosemary. "We hate it when she comes. Why must we pretend we like it?"

"Because of her heart. What ages Mother took to come!"

"She said five minutes wouldn't matter and she'd come up after that. But it felt like five hours!"

Daphne felt obliged to protest against this callous heresy.

"Aunt Lallie is wonderful, isn't she? So brave and cheerful."

"We have too many aunts," said Rosemary, getting back to her essay. "I like Aunt Muriel best."

"What? Uncle Bob's wife? In India? But we never see her!"

"That's why."

THREE

Boys were flying kites. They soared in the bright wind blowing from the west over Kensington Palace. Little boats scudded across the Round Pond. The air sparkled. The day danced. *The day!*

At the top of the little hill in the middle of the broad walk, Wyn paused and said: "Wait here. We shall see her coming."

She had insisted that Ca should meet them in Kensington Gardens, not shut up in a room, but out in the space and air where they had formerly met.

"When she comes," said Em, "I shall go on to see Elsie Spender, in Bayswater. And you'll both come on to join me there when you've had your tea."

An old man went past wheeling a beautiful great ship in a dilapidated perambulator. Wyn's eyes followed him with interest. Then they turned again to the path leading past the Palace to Palace Green.

"There! Coming now!"

"Which is she?"

"Guess."

"That tall lady in dark blue?"

"Of course."

"You're quite sure? After twenty-three years?"

"So are you."

Em laughed.

"She is very like my idea of her."

The lady came up the hill, paused, saw them, and approached.

"How clever we are!" she said, shaking hands with Em.

Ca! Ca! Why do you waste time talking to Em? Saying things you both know already! Courtesy! You are pleased to meet. You have heard so much about each other. Em turning her back. I know what she is saying. Horses and motors on the left in London. Poor Wyn run over. Take me to that house and the smelly-little-deaf-children-woman, I stay outside. Not a smelly little deaf child. Finished? Go away, Em! Go away! Then we can look at the boats.

Em was walking away. Ca and Wyn, without any preliminary discussion, set off to look at the boats, drawn to the Round Pond by an identical impulse.

The old man had got his great ship off the perambulator and was squatting over it, trimming its sails. They watched him, so eager, so old, curved dark in front of the bright water.

"It's the best ship," said Ca.

"He looks quite poor," said Wyn. "Ask where he got it."

Ca went nearer and pointed to the sails on which he was working. She asked what they were called. Wyn could not see his answer, but Ca passed it on: "Main sail. Main topsail. Main topgallant. Main royal."

Wyn repeated the incantation and he looked round curiously.

"No, lady. Topgallant not topcallant."

"Where did you get it?" demanded Wyn.

"Arr!"

He looked pleased, but would not tell them. Some rough boys pushed in to look at it.

"He made it himself," said Ca.

Of course he had; Wyn saw that when she thought it over. They retreated to a seat nearby. Quite a crowd gathered round the old man, blocking their view of him.

"Do they sail boats like that in the Bois?" asked Ca.

"Not on the big water. On a little stream. Poor children sail stick boats."

"Can you see what I say quite comfortably?"

"Ca!" Wyn laughed with pleasure. "I can almost hear what you say. Little girls choose best sticks. Not so impatient. Put them in carefully. Girl boats sail away. Boy boats sink. That makes boys angry. They throw stones. Sink girl boats. Say not real boats. Only girl boats. Men say that, when we do any-thing."

"Poor men," said Ca. "They don't like to be laughed at. We don't mind, as long as we get what we want. Tell me more about the Bois."

"You see when you come."

"I see when you tell me."

Wyn made a face. It was understood between them that Ca would some day pay that long-promised visit.

"Old men play chess. Little tables under trees. I painted that. My friends in America bought that picture."

"Nobody plays chess out-of-doors here."

"Here they put on hats and gloves and faces. There you see them living lives. Two lovers rowing. He rows ten rows. Stop. Kiss. Ten more rows. Stop. Kiss. No lovers here."

"Oh, yes. Lying about on the grass all over the place."

"All look the same. *Pas de cachet.* Ah. . . ."

The crowd parted. The ship had been launched. Her little sails filled, and she set off across the pond. The old man took his perambulator and boathook round to the far side, followed by a train of enraptured boys. Wyn and Ca watched the voyage across the glittering water amid fleets of smaller craft and ducks. Neither spoke till it was completed. Then Ca said: "Yes. I don't like it when people all look the same. What makes them look different is more important."

They rose and sauntered across the grass, stopping every few minutes to look at things that caught their fancy. Twenty-three years were nothing. They were still of one mind, as they had been on their path between a laurel hedge and a ruined hothouse. Into the total silence of Wyn's world there crept again a faint awareness, a vestigial whisper from Ca's mind and Ca's world, where dogs barked and birds sang and the wind whispered in the trees.

Everyone shut up in a thick shell. Making faces. LOOK AT ME. SEE WHAT I SAY. Ca no shell. No fighting through two walls. Only one wall. Only mine.

"Who is Miss Spender?" asked Ca.

"Em's friend. Like that thing on the road. Crushing all into flat. *Cylindre*. Tells dull things with hands. To stupid little children. Nice for them, *hein?*"

"Yes. If she tells them what they want to know."

"She tells them about soap. And Jesus."

They found a table on the sheltered side of the teahouse. When their tray was brought to them Wyn asked after Lallie.

"She is still so unhappy?"

"Dreadful!" said Ca, with a face of despair. "She's so lonely. I was thinking how ghastly her life is, when I was coming here to see you. Nobody tells her anything she wants to know. Not even about Jesus and soap. They only tell her what isn't true. They say they love her. They don't. They say she is very witty and clever. She's not."

"Where is she now?"

"Gone to Susan. She will try to play with the children, and they won't want her. She is a child still. A rather dreadful little girl, but of course they don't understand that. She's been kept from growing up in case those hard things, that make people grow up, might upset her. She's had no real sorrow in her life, like your Myra."

"Yes," agreed Wyn. "Myra was a woman. She jumped from a child to a woman. In a week. When she knew how sad her father was to see her so unhappy. But . . . Ca . . . you can't

make Lallie happy. Why stay? Not worse for her with some-
one else."

"Something might turn up for her. I can't think what. But
she is so anxious to live. I feel sure she is waiting for something.
If it turns up, I shall see that she gets it. *They* might not approve. They might think it was. . . ." Ca wrinkled her delicate
nose in disgust ". . . *wrong*. They think the life she has now
is *right*. If I wasn't there she would be quite in their power.
Kept alive. But never allowed to live."

"Poor Lallie. All same . . . when I come back from America
I take a studio in Paris. With Annette. Good life. Friends there.
And a room for you, when you come."

"I'll come. Someday. Your friends . . . you know a lot of
artists. Did you ever meet one called Mark Norris?"

"Norreese?" cried Wyn, with a hoot of laughter. "*Le maître
sans œuvre?* Everyone has met him."

Some years earlier he had been a standing joke. He knew
everybody, was to be seen everywhere, and had an impressive
studio, but never apparently put brush to canvas. Hence his
nickname. Some wits had once amused themselves by supply-
ing him with the missing commodity. Each had dashed off his
his own idea of a typical "Norreese." All styles and schools
were represented, but the most popular exhibit had been a
study of three very fat women leaning over a balcony and
seen from the rear. *L'Exposition Norreese* had been housed
for a week in an empty studio, and its fame spread through
the Quarter. Wind of it might have come to his ears, for he
vanished from Paris as suddenly as he had come.

"*Mais tu le connais, toi?*" asked Wyn when she had told all
this, partly in English, partly in French, partly in pantomime.

"He's my brother-in-law. He was married to my sister
Kitty, who died. We heard he had gone to Paris, but we've
quite lost touch with him. I'd often meant to ask you."

"He painted pictures once?"

"Lots. He was a great success. He painted a portrait of me
once. He called it 'The Greco Lark.' "

Wyn stared at her friend.

"*Comment! Outrée? Dévote? Religieuse?*"

"Oh, no. I was laughing. Or just going to laugh."

After some reflection Wyn shook her head.

"Those Greco people . . . all gone away somewhere else. Not here, with us, like you."

FOUR

Elsie Spender was now teaching in London. Her labors overflowed into her leisure hours and into the Bayswater house which she shared with some friends. When Christine arrived, her sitting room was occupied by a handicraft class for older girls. She herself was wrestling in the dining room with a very dirty and apathetic little boy.

"Four o'clock already?" she said, by way of welcome. "Really, Saturday is my worst day. Sit down, and I'll get tea."

The room was littered with raffia mats, papier-mâché bowls, and variously shaped bricks. The top of a cardboard box had been cut into holes matching these bricks. Elsie had evidently been teaching her pupils to post squares, circles, oblongs, and triangles into the right apertures. Presently she bustled back with a Spartan meal of bread, margarine, and damson jam.

"Montessori methods, I see!" said Christine, holding up the box.

"That? I made that. Gives them an idea of shapes. What's Montythingummy?"

"This Italian. Maria Montessori. She's doing some wonderful work with backward children."

"You're daft about Italians. Always were. Plain English kindergarten is good enough for me."

"Good old English word . . . *Kindergarten*," agreed Christine.

For once Elsie was winded. Christine followed it up:

"Froebel and Pestalozzi! I suppose when people have been dead long enough they cease to be foreigners."

"You cut yourself a slice of bread," said Elsie, "while I take some tea to Miss Lecky."

Off she went, slopping the tea into its saucer. In her own

time, as ungraciously as possible, she would give the advice that Christine sought. When it came it would be valuable.

"Voluntary helper," she explained as she came back. "Teaches papier-mâché work. There's quite a demand for it, and they can do it at home. So I put up with her manners, though they're filthy. What is it, Arthur? Oh, come along!"

Arthur was dragged from the room. Christine, taking a fresh grip on her patience, wondered how Ca and Wyn were getting on. Although she had felt strangely reassured on meeting Ca, she still feared disaster. It would be a miracle if anyone unused to Wyn's gugs could, on a first encounter, make anything of them.

"He didn't really want to," complained Elsie, returning with Arthur. "Merely likes to attract attention. No wonder. Spends his life tied to a kitchen table leg. What have you done with your prodigy this afternoon? These freak successes! Personally I think they do more harm than good."

"So you've said. Often," snapped Christine.

She was, however, doomed to hear it all again. She munched bread and jam and watched Arthur crawl furtively out of the room. Lucky Arthur! Elsie inveighed against the exceptionally brilliant deaf mute who had, down the centuries, queered the pitch for his fellow sufferers, served as a focus for exaggerated claims and advertised quacks. Over the lost talent of mute inglorious Miltons, Elsie wasted no sleep. It was for poor little Hodge that she did battle, especially since these prodigies frequently turned up their noses at their comrades in misfortune. Christine's Wyn was typical.

"No thanks to people like her that we've at last got compulsory education for our children and a lordly grant of five pounds apiece. Little she cares if the Royal Commission classed her as an imbecile. Does she even belong to the Association?"

"I'm afraid not," admitted Christine. "Myra did. She signed that petition to the King they sent in. But tell me, Elsie, is there any chance that the Board will ever recognize our diplomas?"

"I don't know, and I don't care. Half you college-trained

teachers never come near *our* children. You float off to little Honorables. I suppose you want to earn more than two pounds a week! But about this Seddon money, Christine . . . you say you want to lay it out in the best possible way. I think it's the very little children who now need it most. State education begins at seven. Till then the child is left to rot, though those seven years are the most important in any child's life. Look at my poor Arthur! What good will five pounds a year be to him when he's seven? By then he'll be so far behind that five hundred pounds couldn't do much for him. What we want most of all is prompt diagnosis, of course. But no money will secure that; you can't force people to take their child to the doctor, even if they can afford it. What we *can* do is make up to Arthur all he's losing in these years when he's tied to the table leg. Nursery schools. People trained to go and play with them in their homes. Arouse all their faculties. Get them ready for school. If we could start some center. . . . Oh! There's the doorbell. No rest for the wicked!"

"I expect it's Wyn."

"It would be."

Elsie went off with her grimmest face. She came back, looking almost sunny, with Ca who explained that Wyn was waiting out in the street.

"If she likes to do that, nobody is stopping her," said Elsie. "Miss Maxwell is in the middle of her tea. Yes, they are nice bowls, aren't they, Miss Knevett? Some of my girls made them."

The history of the papier-mâché class was related. Ca was disposed to buy a bowl on the spot in the hope that it might interest Lallie, for whom occupations were hard to find. A craze for shellwork was waning; papier-mâché might take its place.

Elsie dived into a cupboard for more bowls, and Christine took the opportunity to ask how the afternoon had prospered.

"Did you . . . could you understand Wyn at all?"

"Oh, yes. Ida said she was impossible to understand, but I didn't find her so. I think she speaks very well."

"Who speaks well?" asked Elsie emerging from the cupboard.

"Wyn."

"Wyn Harper? Speaks well? Why, she can't speak at all. Hideous gibberish, after all poor Miss Maxwell's labors. She's the very worst example of oral methods I ever met."

"But I found her quite easy. Really! Her voice sounds terribly tired and strained, as if she'd been shouting for hours on end, and she mispronounces some things. But I can't see why you call it gibberish."

"In that case she doesn't talk to you as she does to everybody else."

"Ooh!" cried Christine. "Oh . . . perhaps. . . ."

A perfectly new possibility dawned upon her, and was driven from her mind by a raucous clamor in the passage. The door flew open. A little woman with a yellow face and a cockney accent rushed in and thrust a bleeding hand under Elsie's nose. Behind her clustered a group of frightened girls.

"He bit me. That filthy brat bit me."

"Who? Arthur? Isn't he . . . where. . . ."

"He came into my class. I don't bargain for brats of that age, but I was fool enough to let him stay. I even gave him something to do. Two of our bowls had dried crooked, so I let him paint them. He did one quite nicely. When I gave him the second, and showed him the pattern, he bit me. Look!"

Elsie hurried off to get lint and a bandage. The others went into the next room, which was littered with bowls and painting materials. Miss Lecky, wrapping her hand in a dirty pocket handkerchief, pointed to a crooked object, daubed in red and green, which stood on the table and to another, partially striped in black and yellow, which lay on the floor.

"Who put on the stripes?" asked Ca, picking it up.

"I did. To show him. But when I tried to give it to him. . . ."

A chorus of hoots from the class drew their attention to Arthur's ashen face poked out from under a sofa. At the sight of the bowl in Ca's hand he yelled, and vanished again.

"It frightens him," she said.

"Nonsense. Why should it?"

While the bleeding hand was being dressed, Christine conversed with some of the girls, admiring their work. Ca stood very still in a kind of trance, gazing at the bowl. Her absorption began to be felt in the room. At last everybody turned and looked at her.

"A wasp," she said.

"There was no wasp," snapped Miss Lecky.

"Not today. But these stripes are just like a wasp. He might have thought it was the black and yellow that hurt him so much. When the wasp stung him."

"But he was!" exclaimed Elsie. "Last year. Stung by a wasp. Quite badly. Miss Knevett, how clever of you!"

Arthur again poked out a cautious face.

"Oh, tell him!" cried Ca. "Somebody tell him that we won't let it hurt him."

She threw the offending bowl on the floor and stamped on it. The pupils, who had begun to enjoy the drama, all took a stamp too. Some signs from Elsie seemed to reassure Arthur, for he crawled out, ran to her, and butted his head into her skirts.

"Did you say something about your house?" asked Ca, making a pointed gable with her hands.

"Yes. I told him that children don't get hurt in my house. Why? You know these signs? You've had experience?"

"No. No . . . only once, a long time ago, you know, I used to play with Wyn Harper. When we were very little. And we had a sort of language that we made up for ourselves. At least . . . we must have, I suppose. And our word for house was the same, I remember. We had an empty bird's nest, where we kept our treasures, and we called it the 'little bird house.' "

She put her thumb and finger very close together, flapped her arms, and made a gable.

"The sign for a bird is this," said Elsie, putting her clenched fist to her lips and extending her first finger.

"But you got *little* right, and *house* right," said Christine.

"Well! That's a life-long puzzle solved. I always thought that you and Wyn managed to converse, but I couldn't make out how."

"Didn't she remember any of our signs?"

"No. She always insisted that she could hear you. That you talked."

"You must have a knack for it, Miss Knevett," put in Elsie. "You'd learn very quickly."

"Could I? Could I?"

"I'm sure you could." Elsie seized Ca's arm, as if to press her into service on the spot. "And it was so quick of you to guess about the wasp. So few people, so very few people, seem to have any imagination."

"We really ought to be getting after Wyn," said Christine.

"Oh, hang Wyn."

Ca however agreed, and they took their departure. As soon as they were in the street she turned a glowing face to Christine.

"Oh, Miss Maxwell! Where is the best place to learn? Where did you learn?"

"In Fitzroy Square. And there's a very good college now at Ealing. But are you really interested? Would you think of taking it up?"

"I'm very much tied at present, as you know. But . . . if . . . when I'm free, that's what I shall do."

"I hadn't realized."

"I've only just realized it myself. When I was looking at that bowl, and trying to think myself into his mind. I've been very stupid. I always knew there was something. But I thought of it as going back. To that time. That place. When I played with Wyn. I've never been so happy as I was then. But one can't go back. And I thought of it as a kind of game only. Trying to see how much we could say when we couldn't talk. I never thought of going on. I knew people did, but I imagined it must be something quite different. I see now. One could go on, and learn it seriously."

They found Wyn sitting on some church steps. She was

plunged in a reverie so deep that she had not observed a policeman who stood in front of her, and exhorted her to move on.
Nor did she look up when Christine, having explained her
case, undertook to remove her. With one hand she made a
curve, and with the other a second curve crossing the first.
These mysterious gestures always signified the incubation of
a picture. At a touch from Christine she looked up, smiled at
them, and rose.

"That old man," she said to Ca. "With the boat. Curved
over. No sky. All water. Sky in the water. Only trees behind
and grass. He must go this way, boat that way. Tomorrow I
go there. Take my paints."

"He might go again on a Sunday," agreed Ca. "Tell him
you want to paint his boat, and he might let you."

"Main sail. Main topsail. Main topcallant. . . ."

"Topgallant. . . ."

"Topgallant. Main royal."

Christine gradually got her breath back, but she could still
scarcely believe her ears. Wyn had never talked like this.
There were no intrusive rattles, gugs, or clicks. It was a hideous voice, nasal and metallic, bearing witness to the dire over-
strain to which it had, for years, been subjected, but it was
perfectly intelligible. At last, at last, Wyn was relaxed.

Ca caught a bus to Shepherd's Bush. Having seen her off,
they turned into the Gardens to walk back to Blount's Hotel.

"How very beautiful she is!" said Christine.

"Ngeegass," agreed Wyn.

They walked on in silence. It was a great temptation to say:
"Can't you pretend I'm Ca?" It might, however, be dangerous
to do so. The improvement was apparently quite unconscious.
With Ca, Wyn was perfectly at ease and confident, free from
all sense of effort, quite sure of being understood. To call her
attention to this miracle might ruin everything. It would be
wiser to wait.

"Is there any chance," Christine asked, "that Ca will ever
get away from Lallie?"

"Oh, yes. Soon, I think. Then she will come to me in Paris."

This was almost too good to be true. It solved all problems. Christine had felt some misgivings over Wyn's future and her ability to live alone in Paris with no companion save Annette. Now Ca would join her, and, in Ca's company, she would talk freely, as she had never talked before, could face the world almost as a normally equipped human being. Nor would Wyn be the sole gainer from this delightful plan. Every letter from Ca had breathed a longing to travel, and to see the world.

"She'll live with you for good?"

"Yes. Till she finds . . ."

"Finds what?"

"Something. I know she is always waiting. Something for her . . . like my painting for me."

"Oh."

A shadow fell on the bright vision. Ca, that very afternoon, had hinted as much, and had spoken as though the long waiting were over. I'm glad I got her away from Elsie promptly, thought Christine. She will enjoy Paris so much; nothing must stop it. Only a saint would hesitate. I wish I could be sure she isn't one.

Saints are tiresome and inconvenient, she decided. They hear *calls*, and after that there is no holding them. They are, in a heavenly sort of way, abominably selfish. It would be just like a saint to sacrifice Wyn to Arthur.

CHAPTER 6

Postbag to Washington

 1907

ONE

MRS. PRESTON to Lady William Davenport.

Victoria Road.
April 10th.

Dearest Grace,

It is good news that you are keeping so well. But I do wish you would come home to have the baby as you did the other times. I don't like to think of you with only American doctors. I suppose they are quite good but it is not the same. *Family News.*

(1) Dora wants to go and live at Cheltenham. She has always hated the Manor House and wants to be near a good school for all those girls. Dick wants Edmund to come and run the property for him, taking an agent's fee and living in the Manor House. Edmund won't. We all think that he ought to. He has given up the Civil Service and taken to farming so it would be just the thing. Down there in Devonshire he is far too much involved with his in-laws who are, frankly, just ordinary farmers. And he will eventually come into the property, since Dora can't seem to produce a son. And Molly, at the Manor House, wouldn't be able to hob-nob with the local farmers' wives, as she does at present. She'd have to take her place in our class, not drag Edmund down to hers. Not that she could ever take Mama's place.

Flo says we ought to thank heaven Bob wasn't the second son. Muriel, with her bangles and her face powder, would have been much worse. Edmund talks now of letting the Manor House. It breaks one's heart, when one thinks of that glorious old place.

(2) Tom is now sharing a house with that friend of his, Donald Fraser, who has been transferred from Tabriz to Kermanshah.

(3) Charlie Mycroft has mumps, and Barbie is going on as if he had bubonic plague. Of course it is more serious for a man than a child. Men sometimes get it in the wrong place. And he will be taking Schools next term, so it is a worry for her. It might interfere with his getting a First! Nobody save Barbie expects him to get a First. He has never done any work.

(4) Things have not been going too well at the flat. Lallie has made a most undesirable friend, a Miss Lecky, imported by Carrie to teach papier-mâché work. Really it is what the children call a "rave." The woman is getting on for forty, I should think, very plain and dowdy, not a lady, and extremely rude to us all. She is continually at the flat. Carrie is quite pushed out and is being very spineless about it, won't stand up for herself. After all these years of devotion to Lallie she should not be treated like this. It is *wrong*. She has taken to going off and getting some training for teaching invalid children, which is all very well, but she ought not to leave the field to this Miss Lecky. We have all told her so, and pointed out that we entrusted Lallie to her.

However, Flo is doing something. Carrie and Lallie, as you know, usually go up to stay at Connington in September. Flo says that this year she wants them *now*. That will break up this Lecky nonsense.

(5) Poor old Fitzy is dead. We all sent flowers and Carrie went to the funeral.

Take good care of yourself, my dear.

Your loving Sue.

Lady Dacre to Lady William Davenport.

Connington.
April 17th.

Dearest Grace,

How are you? I hope that No. 3 does not interfere with your *menus plaisirs?* Is it true that in America one is expected to go into Purdah for six months on these occasions? Helen Palgrave told me that she had to when she was in Washington. Other embassy ladies used to ask her to tea and promise that the parlor maid, not the butler, would open the door. Whereas, with an earlier baby in Paris, she had to attend public functions till the very last minute and a table full of gallant Frenchmen used to leap to their feet with the toast of: *Au petit voyageur, Madame!*

I'm interested that you met the Pawletts in New York. But it's not really so very surprising, is it, that Wyn Harper is staying with them? They are great art patrons and are said to have a remarkable collection. It's time, I think, that the family should grasp the fact that she is thought to be a good painter. And stupid, by the way, to go on calling her Winsome. Hugh Beddington was talking about her not long ago and seemed to take it for granted that one had never heard of her. He opened his eyes rather when I told him that we knew her as a child, that she comes from our part of the world, and she still writes to one of my sisters.

Carrie, by the way, is letting us down, as I expect you've heard. I've not met this Miss Lecky but I gather she is a terrible person and a positive *schwärmerie* on Lallie's part. Barbie says it is too embarrassing to see two women in their thirties behaving like schoolgirls and giggling over silly private jokes. When she was there they were giggling over somebody called Jemima. When she asked who Jemima might be, Lallie said: My rascally ticker. Her heart! Which we have been so careful never to mention in Lallie's presence. She is reckless enough as it is. If she is allowed to regard her health as a joke, Heaven knows what she may do. Miss Lecky is in every way a bad influence and she goes out of her way to be rude to the family. Barbie says she laughed at Lallie's French accent and called it *Fitzy atte Slane*. Lallie is so besotted that she seems to like it.

However, the girls are coming to me shortly and when I've got them here I shall get to work. I think they'd better leave London for good. Buxton might suit them very well. It is only a short run from here, now that we have the motor, and I should keep a sharper eye on them than Sue does. If I can only plant an enthusiasm for Buxton in Lallie's tiny mind, I don't see what Carrie can do. Mind you support me over this.

I'm having a time with Daphne who has suddenly become extremely religious. She crosses herself on the least provocation and genuflects till she makes one giddy. In consequence she nearly crippled poor George who fell over her in the aisle in Church when she unexpectedly paused to duck at the altar. The sight of them both sprawling was too much for Eddie and me. We had *fous rires* all through the Service. That boy is an oasis in a desert of Dacres. He takes after us, which none of the others do. I suppose Gee, being the eldest, had better be a thorough paced Dacre, but I wish Frank wasn't so solemn and I cannot imagine how I ever came to have a daughter like Daphne.

I understand that Barbie is rather huffed because Gee does not go up to Boar's Hill oftener, now he is at Oxford. But really he has nothing in common with the Mycrofts. He and Charlie were never congenial. You've heard about Charlie's mumps, by the way? And the threat to Charlie's *First?*

I caught sight of your mother-in-law once or twice when I was last in town. Who makes her hats? A bower bird? Or are they survivals from the time when she was a Lady in Waiting?

Fondest love.

Flo.

Mrs. Mycroft to Lady William Davenport.

Boar's Hill.
April 26th.

My dear Grace,

You will be glad to hear that Charlie is getting over his mumps very well. No complications. It is a great relief.

I have ordered and sent off to you four dozen diapers of good quality, as you may not be able to get them in America. The baby clothes that you had for Pamela and Peter ought to be still serviceable if you have taken proper care of them, but let me know if you want anything sent. Take plenty of exercise and avoid constipation. If I remember rightly you have a tendency to it when pregnant.

You will have heard all the family news from Sue. Lallie has now gone up to Connington but Carrie has refused to go! She says she doesn't want to break off some kind of training she has taken up. I rather sympathize. An invitation to Connington is too much like a royal command. One is expected to drop everything and go.

I shall be interested to see just how long Flo and Lallie will hit it off without Carrie. Flo has never taken her on single-handed. She may now have a taste of what I went through that time I took Lallie when Carrie went to Scotland with Tom.

Oh, about Tom. I met a Professor Lowrie who really knows all about Chinese Turkestan. He assured me that there is no such place as Tom's "lost city." Tom apparently still means to write a book some day, proving that it is there. He won't. When did he ever do anything he meant to do? Do you remember his stamp album? A handsome album but —no stamps in it.

Yours affectionately,
Barbara.

Alice Knevett to Lady William Davenport.

Owl Wood Cottage.
Nr Devizes.
May 8th.

Dear Grace,

This is my address for the rest of the summer. I am staying here with my friend Martha Lecky. As a matter of fact
we elloped!! I was shipped off to Connington and Martha
came and rescued me. The Dacres all went to a Conservative
Fate. While they were there Martha came and packed my
bags and whisked me off. She hired a motor. When Flo
found me gone she drove straight to the junction but our
train was moving out as she rushed on the platform. I waved
to her.

This is the jolliest little cottage. Martha bought it some
years ago but never lived in it. Now she means to spend a
lot of time here. We have a piano and she says I must learn
music! I thought I knew, but she says not. She plays beautifully herself. The Rector called when she was playing and
asked her to play at the next village concert. He is a nice old
cove and we go piously to Church.

We are reading Esther Waters by George Moore. We
have also collected a puppy, an irresistable creature, we call
him Pompey. Carrie did once get me a puppy in London,
you remember? Bonny. But since it was Carrie who took
him for walks he got devoted to her instead of me. I have
never had so much fun in my life.

Martha's father was a solliciter, but she never knew how
rich he was till he died and left her all the money. He was
very strict and never gave her a latchkey and made her do
all the housework. She says there is no tyrranny like familly
tyrranny and I agree with her. When he died she was rich
but very lonely. She made friends with a girl in a hotel who
was very ill. Martha nursed her and bought this cottage.
They meant to live here but then the girl went and got
married.

I must stop and feed Pompey. Looking after him is *my* job.

                    Best love from Lallie.

Caroline Knevett to Lady William Davenport.

                    180 Selwick Court.
                    May 14th.

My dear Grace,

The others will have kept you abreast of the news. This is to say don't let them worry you with gloomy forebodings. I think that Miss Lecky is very fond of Lallie, fonder than any of us are, and will take great care of her. She is not an attractive person, but very sensible. I talked to her, some time ago, about Lallie's heart. She quite understands the dangers, and what to look out for, and what Lallie ought not to do. I'm sure she will take no risks. But, with Lallie, she treats it in a lighthearted way, as a sort of joke. I daresay this is better than the solemn attitude we had got into.

I have been down to Owl Wood to see them. They are very snug there and have got a good maid. Miss Lecky has taken great pains to make it comfortable for Lallie. She does Lallie's hair for her but will not put up with demands for fifty strokes with the brush twice a day. She just bundles it up and Lallie is quite content. They are as happy as possible. Anyone can see that.

Since they seem to be settled there for some months I am off to Persia to pay a visit to Tom. He has often begged me to go and this seems a good opportunity. When I come back in the autumn we can make more definite plans for the future. It must depend upon how the Owl Wood household goes on. We are lending the flat for the summer to Bob and Muriel; it fits in nicely that he gets his leave this year.

                    A great deal of love,
                    Caroline.

Part II

For a crowd is not company; and faces are but
a gallery of pictures; and talk is but a
tinkling cymbal, where there is no love.

FRANCIS BACON, "Of Friendship."

CHAPTER 7

A Journey into Silence

ONE

TRANSLATED FROM the Manor House to Connington, Flo Dacre was a little inclined to mock at both. The Knevetts might claim to have figured in Domesday Book; they had figured but little elsewhere in the course of a thousand years. To be chatelaine of so great a house as Connington was fine, in its way, but everything in it was so splendidly respectable as to be boring. She was enchanted one day when she discovered, hidden away, an illuminated address of condolence presented by the tenantry to the regnant Dacre on the Abolition of the Slave Trade; this iniquitous measure had, it seemed, injured family interests in Jamaica. His descendants had learned to regard it as disconcerting. Flo, encouraged by Hugh Beddington, hung it on the wall at the top of the great staircase. She insisted that it was a period piece and a terrific joke, although poor Sir George winced whenever he caught sight of it.

Eddie, her second son, was the only member of the family who thought it funny. He was fond of his mother. He never took her very seriously, but with him she could be herself insofar as she had discovered any self to engage her constancy. Everyone else was afraid of her; she would have been uneasy if they were not. Eddie laughed at her, and teased her unrebuked. He frequently guessed what she was up to.

It was he who first perceived the importance of Donald

Fraser, Tom's friend, in the great Lallie-Lecky drama. This name recurred, with increasing emphasis, whenever Flo discussed the affair.

Why had Carrie so suddenly absconded to Persia? Tom, to be sure, was her favorite brother, or so she said. If she wished to pay him a visit, why had she waited for ten years before astutely engineering her own escape from the Aunt Heap? She could, had she been so minded, have gone at any time.

Donald Fraser had recently left Tabriz. He was now sharing a house with Tom in Kermanshah.

"When one thinks it all over," declared Flo, "one realizes. She was always talking about that man, letting slip little things . . . things about this book he is going to write. How could she know, unless they corresponded?"

To correspond, thought Eddie, sounded much more sinister, for some reason, than merely to write letters.

He suggested: "But even if they did . . . er . . . you know . . ." he managed to blush and mumble the shameful word . . . ". . . *correspond* . . . wouldn't Aunt L. have found out and told everybody?"

"I'm not sure. Carrie is very secretive. She was writing to Wyn Harper for years, and we none of us suspected."

"A clandestine correspondence with a deaf female artist!" cried Eddie in horror. "Only a Knevett would think of doing such a thing!"

Flo was obliged to laugh, but she returned to her conjectures.

"They saw a good deal of each other at one time. Tom used to bring him to the Manor House before they both left England."

"What was he like?"

"Exactly like a stork. Immensely long thin legs, and the rest of him hunched on top, with a great beak of a nose. A complete oaf. Nobody ever heard him speak."

"He mayn't have been very good at getting in a word edgewise. But if there had been a . . . a partiality . . . you'd have spotted it. You're so sharp about things like that."

"I only saw him once, when I was staying there after I was married. I daresay I should have noticed more if I hadn't been very busy at the time, getting Kitty married to Mark Norris. But now! I shan't be in the least surprised. Bear me witness, Eddie. I've been expecting it."

"You need a witness? Surely you've prophesied to Aunt S. and Aunt B.?"

"No. I've said nothing to them."

Very little had indeed passed between Flo and her elder sisters that summer. She knew that they were amused by her discomfiture on the junction platform. Her reputation for successful diplomacy had been considerably damaged, and she was biding her time for an opportunity to reestablish it.

In September an enormous letter arrived from Sue. Carrie had returned from Kermanshah, but was off shortly to Paris with Ida's cousin, who could not talk at all, and who had come back from America to Blount's Hotel. Lallie was remaining for good in Wiltshire. The Aunt Heap, and Ida with it, was to be sublet as soon as Bob and Muriel went back to India. Two strange women called Maxwell and Spender were taking it; they meant to open a nursery school in South London. It had been Miss Maxwell who, years ago, had invited Carrie to stay in Venice, and she also was staying at Blount's Hotel. Carrie was as obstinate as a mule, although Barbie had told her that, in the case of a sublet, all the furniture ought to be returned to the Manor House.

This letter Flo gave to Eddie as they sat in the rose garden on the morning of his return to school. Her spirits were low. For thirteen dreary weeks she would have to live without him. The house would be full. There would be continual shooting parties. She would be very busy, and very bored. It was a piece of luck that this entertaining letter should have arrived before he went. They could chuckle together in a final tête-à-tête.

Frank was also going back to school, but he knew when he was not wanted, and had gone to say goodbye to his horse. Gee was in Scotland, and Daphne shut up with mademoiselle.

"What fun!" said Eddie, giving back the letter.

"I think I must go up to town," said his mother.

"Why? What for?"

"I'll see when I get there."

"You will do such things! What they are yet you know not, but you will do them."

"I've asked you before not to quote *Hamlet* at me."

"I know. I don't. Honestly I don't. But why must you go to town? To find out what Aunt C. has done with Donald Fraser?"

"One likes to know things."

"One certainly does. But how will you find out? Shall you ask her?"

"Don't be silly. I shan't bother to see Carrie at all. It's never any use talking to her. She seems to manage not to hear what one says. I don't know how. One can talk, and talk, without making the slightest impression."

"I know how. She recites *Horatius* to herself."

"What? Eddie! You made that up."

"No, I didn't. Cross my heart."

"How do you know?"

"Well, years ago she found me being sick in the shrubbery. Gee had told me how to kill a pig so as to bleed it white, because he knew it would make me sick. Just a bit of brotherly fun. I said to Aunt C., I wished I knew of some way of not hearing things I didn't want to hear. And she instructed me in the *Horatius* technique. Said she'd found it very useful for years."

"Why did you never tell me this before?"

"Very unselfish of me to tell you now, but I thought you needed a stimulant. I've enjoyed myself so much, watching you both, when you were saying things intended to disconcert her. I know, by her rapt expression, just when she takes refuge with Lars Porsena."

"I still don't believe it."

"Oh, yes you do, or it wouldn't annoy you so much. You and Aunt C. are like the hare and the tortoise. She's always ahead, and you can never think why, because the explanation is so simple."

"Next time I shall challenge her. Tax her with it."

"Tax away, my dear mother. You can't stop her doing it."

At the moment Flo could not deny this. She returned to Donald Fraser.

"What happened out there in Persia? What made him sheer off?"

"Perhaps she sheered off when she saw him again."

"Unlikely. After all, she's getting on. It's most mysterious. A thing which has lasted all these years!"

"Ever since the Manor House days," agreed Eddie, who perceived that this boy and girl romance was now an established fact, so far as his mother was concerned.

"And then . . . this Miss Maxwell . . . that's all rather mysterious too. Putting two and two together, I think she must have been governess to Valerie Seddon's daughter."

"Oh, yes, and now you'll be able to find out what was really the matter with poor Lady Seddon's daughter."

"One knows that now. But a lot seems to have been going on. . . . I shan't, by the way, oppose the subletting of the flat. She'll find me a pleasant change from Barbie and Sue."

"Who? The governess? Mother, are you going to tackle the poor governess? Isn't that potting at a sitting rabbit?"

"I hear the motor coming round for you. We must go."

They went round to the front of the house where the servants were bringing out the luggage. George, Frank, and Daphne were standing on the terrace. Before they joined the family group Eddie pulled up, exclaiming: "No! Not the governess. Ida's cousin. Carrie's great friend. Knows all about her. But she can't talk. How can you hope to get anything out of her?"

"There are ways and means," said Flo laughing.

She kissed both her sons, and watched them drive away.

If I did not love him so much, she thought, I should be better off. Then I should love nobody at all, and would miss nobody. Oh . . . my life . . . my life . . . going past so quickly.

What do I want that I haven't got? I have everything. Everything!

A whimper at her elbow reminded of one unwanted possession. Daphne was decorously squeezing out a few tears for her departed brothers.

"Must you?" demanded Flo savagely.

"You looked terribly sad yourself," retorted Daphne. "You looked like a Trojan mother watching her sons go away."

"Did I really? I'm sorry to hear it. People who go about looking sad are bores. Do try to get that into your head. And run back to mademoiselle."

Daphne, suitably crushed, crept back into the house.

She could scarcely have hit upon a more damaging accusation. Sad! People who look sad, save upon licensed occasions, lay themselves open to a derisive "poor thing" from their neighbors. Triumphantly at terms with the world, that was how one should look, especially when one had everything— beauty, wit, wealth, consequence, a husband, children, and a host of important friends.

It was true, on the other hand, that she had never perhaps been completely happy. Looking back on her life, she could recall only one transport of flawless satisfaction, and that had been a moment of anticipation rather than fulfillment. She was newly engaged to George. She had escaped from the prison of Slane Forest to all the glories of Connington where she would do such things! For the first time in her life, she sat in a box at the opera displaying her beauty and her success to all the world. For the rest of her life she would do exactly as she pleased. On the stage a young bride, arrayed for her wedding, echoed that certainty. A voice leaped up, like a lovely fountain, and its echo still rang faintly in Flo's inward ear twenty years later:

"I mean to rule the earth
    As he the sky
We really know our worth,
    The sun and I!"

The Mikado, she remembered. It was new then. Everything was new then, and she had been certain, perfectly certain, that she could, if she chose, rule the earth.

So she did, more or less. Whenever she chose to do so, she ruled. She was forty-one. She had kept her complexion and her figure. George had failed as a politician, but he never thwarted her. Although three of her children bored her, she had them well under her thumb. She did as she liked, and never paused to ask herself whether she liked what she did. Nobody could have any excuse for calling her "poor Flo." She would miss Eddie, but he would come back at Christmas. He would always come back.

TWO

At a first glimpse of Miss Maxwell, sailing across the public lounge at Blount's Hotel, all condescension and patronage vanished from Flo's smile. Here was no sitting rabbit. Here was a woman accustomed to hold her own in any company. A governess? No governess ever dressed so well or carried herself with such calm assurance. Governesses might, upon occasion, bridle and flounce, but they were more easily put in their places than most housemaids. They had their gentility to preserve, poor creatures. One must alter the approach.

"Miss Maxwell? How very kind of you to come down! I'm Caroline Knevett's sister, you know. I expect you may have heard of me, though there are so many of us, I'm sure it must be impossible to remember us apart."

Miss Maxwell had, so she believed, now met them all except Lallie, and she countered with Lady William Davenport, of whom she had caught a glimpse when she was in Washington seeking information at the Volta Bureau. They had met at a garden party, at the White House. Round one to Miss Maxwell.

Since Flo managed to know a very little about everything, she seized upon the Volta Bureau, praised its activities, and passed from there to her old acquaintance, Lady Seddon, for

whose daughter the Bureau must have done so much. Miss
Maxwell's smile informed her that poor Valerie rated as low
in this quarter as she did among her dearest friends. It would
be wiser perhaps to stick to the daughter and the Bureau. All
these new experiments must be very fascinating to an expert
like Miss Maxwell. For thirty seconds Flo chattered glibly on
the conquest of deafness, and then found that she had been
pushed back onto her opening square—Wyn Harper, who was
also deaf, and for whom she had inquired at the desk.

"Ah, yes, Wyn! Another very old friend. I wonder if I
could possibly see her?"

There was some demur. Miss Maxwell explained that Wyn
could not talk.

"Oh, I know they are sometimes difficult to understand. But
I find I can generally follow what they say."

"She never talks to strangers. A few, a very few intimate
friends, can understand her. Nobody else."

"But she can lip-read surely? And write things down?"

"Her speech reading is very good. But she doesn't always
feel able to write things down."

"I can understand that. I'm sure I couldn't. But if she will
just listen, it would take a load off my mind. I'm rather
worried about Caroline. I do hope Wyn will see me."

"I'm afraid that she doesn't much want to see any of Miss
Knevett's sisters, just at the moment. I'm sorry if that sounds
discourteous. But, you see, there seems to be a considerable
family controversy over the subletting of the flat, and we
neither of us wish to be drawn into it."

"Oh, yes indeed. But I didn't come to talk about that. I think
it sounds an excellent arrangement, but, of course, it's no affair
of mine. No. I merely want to be sure that Wyn knows something which, for Caroline's happiness, she should know. I
daresay she does, but I want to be certain. It's all rather . . .
confidential."

It was obvious that Miss Maxwell did not trust Flo an inch,
but could not quite decide to send her packing. In the end she
rose, and led the way to the lift.

Fragments of half-remembered gossip recurred to Flo. Poor Valerie! *He*, so one heard, was forever vanishing to Paris on a visit to "that child." Nobody believed it. There was some other attraction in Paris. Looking at this woman, one wondered. She must once have been a beauty; was remarkably handsome still. If one had never included the governess in one's speculations, that was because one had not conjectured a governess like this. Here at least was a discovery which justified the visit to Blount's. It was taking shape as a very good story before Flo stepped out of the lift.

They went into a pleasant sitting room. Money! Seddon must have treated the woman generously.

A stocky little person with frizzed sandy hair stood looking out of the window with her back to them. Miss Maxwell went up to her and gently turned her round so as to reveal the square, suety face of Wyn Harper. This creature, who had once scuffled and snorted in the old kitchen garden, was now several sizes larger. Her suit was well cut. Otherwise she had scarcely changed at all. She stared at Flo for a moment, and then bobbed the uncouth curtsy imposed by the Manor House upon the village.

Flo masked disconcertment by a peal of pretty laughter.

"Oh! Oh! How that takes one back! I'd quite forgotten. But did we? Did we really?"

Turning to Miss Maxwell she added: "Fantastic. One can't believe it."

This open hostility was a tonic. She liked people who stood up to her, and despised sitting rabbits. Since Wyn made no move to welcome her, she sat down, and loosened her furs.

"I remember you quite well, of course," she said. "But you can't possibly remember me. You were only about five years old when you went away, weren't you?"

Six fingers were briefly held up.

"I'll be next door," said Miss Maxwell. "Call me if you need an interpreter."

Her smile told Flo that this was no concession. She was going because she believed them evenly matched.

After her departure there was a lengthy pause. Flo could not immediately turn her mind to Carrie's activities in Persia, since she was now more interested in Paris and Lord Seddon. That woman must be in her fifties. The whole affair was probably over, but it would still be worth discussion. Few men could have lodged a legitimate though handicapped child in an illicit establishment. Nobody would have suspected such ingenuity in poor stodgy Seddon. One would have supposed that even his irregularities must be rigidly conventional. "You don't believe it? I do, because, as it happens, I have *seen* that governess." "Flo! The things you manage to do! When? where?"

The affair must have been going on for many years. There had been, she now remembered, some resounding lamentation, either over the Diamond Jubilee or else over the Coronation. Poor Valerie had been absent from the Abbey, because Seddon was abroad with "that child." Everybody had laughed. Wyn, moreover, as a permanent member of the household, must have known all about it. She was no fool. That insolent little curtsy indicated brains. Could she be induced to tell what she knew? Possibly, if one had come prepared with the right questions. One had not, as luck would have it. This investigation had better be postponed until the more humdrum topic was out of the way.

"I've come," said Flo at last, "to consult you about Caroline. You two are such great friends that your opinion is important."

She paused and then shot her bolt, "I mean about her engagement to Donald Fraser."

That hit a target. Wyn started, and sat down in a chair by the window. Flo, who was an expert in shock tactics, asked if she had known about it, and got a slight shake of the head.

"No? Well, I'm not surprised really. But I think you should know. It's a long story and a sad story. I'm not sure what she would say about it herself, just now. We none of us know exactly what has gone wrong, though we all hope that it may end happily. She may even be feeling hurt and wounded, and inclined to insist that there was never anything between them."

It was an easy story to tell since she now believed a good deal of it herself. Nor need she exercise caution in telling it. She could say what she liked. Nobody could later accuse her of going too far. Since no witness was present, who could say how far she had gone? The poor thing's speech reading might be to blame. Miss Maxwell had been overconfident when she left them alone together.

Donald's visits to the Manor House, long ago, were now described. An attachment had then grown up between the two young creatures. Everyone had perceived it, but a formal engagement was, of course, at that date, impossible. They were too young. They must wait for a reasonable period. The period of waiting had become unreasonable in consequence of Carrie's devotion to Lallie, whom she would not leave. The whole family had regretted this. Repeated attempts were made to set her free, and facts in support of this assertion were offered in profusion. At any time Lallie could have made her home at Connington or at Boar's Hill. She would, however, accept no alternative arrangement. She was difficult, as invalids often are, and Carrie had been too kind.

Then, then at last, an unexpected solution had set Carrie free. What had she done? Without a moment's hesitation she had sped to Kermanshah. Which showed, didn't it, that her feelings had in no way changed, and that she had grounds for supposing him constant? Didn't it?

Wyn made no sign of reply. She was looking out the window at some pigeons strutting and curtsying on the parapet of a balcony across the street. She would surely have protested had she disagreed. Flo warmed to her theme.

What had gone amiss? Why had they settled nothing when, now, there were no obstacles? Had there been some misunderstanding? Tom thought that there had. He was as anxious as the rest of them to see the match made up, and he feared that Carrie's excessive unselfishness had begun to irritate Donald. That was scarcely surprising, was it? The poor man's patience had been severely tried for many years. In Tom's opinion, it had snapped at the news that Carrie was still not perfectly free. Disburdened of Lallie, she had exchanged servitude, and had cut short her visit to Kermanshah because she had promised to join Wyn Harper in Paris. Perfect frankness was best. Might not Wyn herself now be the obstacle? Might she not figure, in Donald's eyes, as another Lallie whom Carrie was too kind to abandon? Would not a true friend send her back to Kermanshah?

Never in her life, save to Carrie, had Flo talked for so long without eliciting any sign of response. For some time she felt this to be an advantage, but in the end it became frustrating. She wanted a gesture of assent, dissent, wrath, regret, or bewilderment.

"I think," she said, "that if you don't answer me, it means that you agree."

Even as she said it the truth smote her. For at least ten minutes she had been talking to nobody at all. Wyn had secured complete immunity from attack by looking out of the window.

A heavy silence fell upon the room.

Flo had always hated silence. It frightened her. All her life she had avoided it. She had never even slept alone. Until her marriage she had shared a room with Kitty. She could not read a book save in company. She liked to break off at intervals for a word or two. Somebody must always be there, making noises.

In this moment of defeat her dread intensified, as though silence, like an incoming tide, was creeping up round the sands of her life. What if, some day, nobody should be there to make noises?

Such an end could, as she well knew, overtake a fellow creature. There was old Miss Kitchin, up at Connington, unable to get out of her invalid chair, abandoned to solitude by neighbors whose dislike had mastered their compassion. It was dangerous, according to the vicar's wife, to call on Miss Kitchin, sorry as one felt for her. One need not believe her scandalous tales, but nothing one said oneself was safe.

"Our apple crop this year has been disappointing," became, within hours, a rumor that the vicar suspected the village of stealing his apples. Flo always looked the other way when she drove past that cottage, lest she see a long white miserable face peering out of the window, waiting in vain for somebody to come and make noises.

She jumped to her feet. It was morbid to dwell on such things. Miss Kitchin was a spinster. She was poor, plain, and stupid. People like that could not afford to quarrel with their acquaintances lest they quench those impulses of sympathy and compassion upon which they might ultimately come to depend. For Flo Dacre there would always be somebody.

Without any attempt at farewell, she fled from that terrifying little room. In the lift she said something to the page in order to hear him answer. Even the noise in the street was a stimulant. She would hail a cab and go to Sue, and they would talk for hours. She would not, as yet, hint at her suspicions about the Maxwell woman. She must collect more evidence, and it would perhaps be a very good joke to see a person like that established in the Aunt Heap. On the other hand, she might venture to say what she really thought about Miss Lecky. In any case they would talk, and talk, and talk.

She stood on the pavement, looking for a cab. A barrel organ was churning out a tune above the roar of the traffic. The leaping notes, tossed high in the air, stabbed at her. It was not the same tune, but it started in her mind another cadence which she had once thought superb, but which now mocked at her. *I mean to rule the earth. . . .* Nor was there a cab to be seen.

A carriage drove past, and a familiar face bowed to her, a woman called Yates. How had she looked, standing there panic-stricken, with that horrible tune in her ears? Had there been a trace of amusement in her friend's smile? Had she given Lucy Yates some grain of justification for describing her as "poor Flo"?

CHAPTER 8

A Journey out of Silence

 1908

ONE

"WHITE WHEELS GOING ROUND. Black behind."

Wyn paused, assembling words. Then she went on: "Round a long green . . . cigar. He saw that, Rembrandt. They said: Paint portraits. Boring. He went to watch anatomy . . . that wrong?"

"Anatomy," said Ca, thumping the table to indicate the accent. "Not anatomy."

"Anatomy. Till he sees something not boring. That doctor said something. Surprised them. All move. Turn. Some look down at the . . . dead thing . . . *cadavre* . . . some look at him . . . some look at the enemy. The Won't-Agree man . . . standing . . . back turned. . . ."

Rapidly she indicated the different poses and expressions in Rembrandt's "Anatomy Lesson."

"And all that white . . . What you hear?"

"Bells," said Ca. "All chiming four o'clock."

"What that white round necks?"

"Roughs."

"White roughs go round. All moving wheels. That picture . . . you see wheels first. Then . . . they stay still. Look at detail. Then highlight going up arm. Satin . . . that . . . not velvet. Eye goes up. Those roughs, they spin. He thought: There a picture! Wheels moving. Not portraits."

[145]

"I wish you'd tell that to those women in our hotel," said Ca. "I said I'd ask you why it's supposed to be a great picture. They thought it most unpleasant."

"Uck! Uck! Uck!"

Wyn gave a parody of herself in the throes of her glottal gargle. She disliked those women; they reminded her a little of Elsie Spender, and they toured Holland briskly giving marks to pictures.

In Ca's company she could occasionally converse with people whom she liked. At any hostility or nervousness her throat tightened, and her hostility was easily roused. Despite the genial confidence distilled by Ca, she still saw life as a battle in which she must fight to secure her place. She resented kindness as a form of patronage. She was always on the lookout for ridicule. Nor would she excuse any faults or shortcomings in people who could hear.

"Poor things," said Ca. "They've only got their guidebook, and that's so dull. What you say about pictures is much more exciting. And quite true. When I first saw that Rembrandt I did think: What are all those white wheels? Oh, Wyn! Turn round. Turn round and look!"

Wyn, who had been sitting with her back to the street, turned, looked, and laughed. Every child in Delft had rushed out of school. The pavements on either side of the canal, so empty five minutes ago, were now thronged with a wild mob.

"Same in Venice," she said after watching them. "Quite safe."

Her train of thought was clear to Ca since their minds ran in unison. Why did no child fall into the water? Because only the bigger ones ran on that side, herding the smaller into safety next to the houses. Who had ordained this drill? It had been in force, probably, for centuries. Children born on canals do not fall in.

"Holland is so sensible," said Ca. "The nicest country we've seen."

Upon which Wyn turned her back to the canal and finished her coffee. They had traveled much, during the past months, and Ca had never said the reassuring thing: I want to stay here forever. She remained a traveler on holiday, even in Paris. And one day. . . .

"You want to climb that tower before we go back?" asked Wyn.

"Yes. But you needn't."

"Don't like staying alone. They speak to me. Think I'm Dutch. I look Dutch? You look Spanish. Nobody spoke to you in Toledo."

"Spaniards don't talk to strange ladies."

Wide prospects with no foreground did not appeal to Wyn. She toiled up the tower behind Ca, grumbling all the time, until they reached the top. Holland lay about them, and, immediately below, the roofs of the Prinsenhof reminded Wyn that one word on the lips can be two words in print. Roughs? *Ruffs!* There were bullet marks on a staircase down there, and a room where a murdered hero had died. Visualizing that death, she had seen more white wheels spinning.

"Poor man!" said Ca, also looking at the Prinsenhof.

This was undoubtedly the assassin, not the victim. She was always sorry for the unexpected person.

"Somebody probably told him it was *right*," she added.

In her view, the evil caused by bad people in this world is negligible compared to that ordained and condoned by good people.

"You will go to hell," chuckled Wyn. "You were never confirmed!"

That incident in Ca's past diverted her greatly. She herself had been confirmed with Myra. They had worn long white veils. Myra, carefully coached, had managed to say, *I do!* very prettily. Wyn, taut with anxiety, had roared GIKADOOKA! so fiercely that the Bishop had nearly jumped out of his skin.

Ca had avoided the rite by dint of considerable double-dealing. She was determined to take no vows that should bind her to obedience. She recognized no spiritual pastors and masters. Civil laws she would keep. That was a matter of common sense. She would oblige other people whenever she could. Moral submission she rejected. Once was enough. She had shut her eyes to Wyn and had, for eight years, suffered tortures of remorse, until Wyn's first letter came to ease her mind.

When commanded by her elders to present herself for confirmation, she resolved on a desperate step. Argue she could not; verbal contention had ever been beyond her. There was nothing for it but to say, *I do not!* when required to take the vow. She hoped, however, that God would spare her this ordeal, since she could never believe that He relished the accounts, so freely given by good people, of His likes and dislikes. Her confidence was justified. The confirmation was held at Slane Bredy at a time when the whole household was in an uproar over Lallie's rheumatic fever. Nobody could be spared to escort Ca save Ida, to whom she confided her predicament. They took refuge in Ida's home, and never went to church at all. On their return, it was assumed by the family that Ca had been duly confirmed.

"Hell?" she said now. "Good people made it up. I know He said *where their fire is not quenched.* But Tom said He was talking about the rubbish heaps outside Jerusalem."

She turned to see out, over the flat fields.

"Too sensible," complained Wyn. "No surprise."

"Oh, yes. The hay barge."

Some days earlier they had seen a barge loaded with hay crossing the sea to Marken. It lay so low in the water that it looked like a floating haystack. Wyn, charmed, had sketched it.

Some boats not boats, thought Wyn. Bits of land. Leaving land. Joining it again. Ferryboats. New York. People standing. Break away from New York. Join New Jersey. Ca seeing that. Not this year. Must paint now, in Paris. *Some day . . . some day she will forsake me again.*

That horror, haunting the horizon of her present happiness, could no longer be endured. She must challenge it, destroy it, or be destroyed by it.

"Ca!"

There was no need to say more. The whole thing was out between them. Neither spoke a word, but a silent battle raged.

You want to leave me. You want to go back to London and Em and those stupid children.

My work. Just as painting is your work.

For you I'm just another Lallie!

No. But without my work I'm only half a person.

Without you, I am only half a person. You are the half of me that can hear. I can't bear it. You shan't go.

I won't go till you tell me to go.

I shall never tell you to go.

Yes, you will. When you are ready.

Why should I?

Because we are friends.

Tears were rolling down Ca's cheeks. She turned, and went through the little doorway, back to the staircase.

Now she goes down and down those dark stairs. Round and round.

So sure that I shall let her go.

At the bottom . . . punished!

A crowd running down there. What is it? A woman fallen from the tower. A dead thing on the stones. Only to jump now. All pain over.

She turned toward the parapet. A little bird had fluttered down there. It was hopping about, as if to bar the way.

Bird! Bird! Light. Soft. Bird and Answer under the trees poor Bird she had so little. White face white pillow the last words we saw *grazie per tutte.*

First time Venice high up big bell shakes us and shakes frightened cling to Answer people stop their ears "Angelus" sunset mountains far away sea far away we see Bird say *grazie* thanking for sunset laughed at her Answer *better than never never saying thank you Wyn.*

Sunset ocean games deck sun goes into sea pops up again. Wonder! Marvel! Down and up *the sun rises up in the west.* That I saw. Paint that? How? Paint coming up not going down? How?

White wheels on black so much I have seen down and up
old man and sky and water *Main sail main top sail* on the steps
she sits always always that old woman *Salute* still sitting in
my picture Freda Pawlett's house the sun popped up again
the boys throw balls against high walls standing up in the flat
all these I have seen the hay sails over the sea butterfly sits
on Answer's foot the great trees stand on one leg talking
she turns and laughs in a doorway in a great white cap the sun
pops up God says *Paint this!* Wyn Bird and Answer painting
a jug Ca's hand comes with a yellow flower making a pattern
on the path . . . a long time ago. . . .

Goodbye Bird. *Grazie per tutte.*

Ca was waiting in the church at the foot of the stairs. Not
until they got out into the sunshine did Wyn see how white
she was. Had she guessed? Did she fear to go out lest she might
find that dreadful little crowd?

They caught a train back to Amsterdam, ate their dinner,
and then, since both were exhausted, went early to their rooms.
Ten minutes later Wyn descended to the bureau. A timetable
told her that the next train for Paris departed at midnight.
She shrank from the ordeal of a twelve-hour journey, involv-
ing two frontiers, since she must depend entirely upon her
slate. In Paris, too, she must look after herself; Annette was
away on holiday. Grimly she packed her bags, paid her bill,
and took herself off. She left a note to be given to Ca in the
morning:

I have gone back to Paris. To my work. You go to London.
To your work. I shall manage. Don't write to me until
I write to you. Thank you for everything.

TWO

She was weak and very hungry. She could not remember
when she had last eaten. There was no bread left. More must
be bought at the bakery across the street. Midday was the
best time for that, when all her neighbors would be indoors

eating their dinners. She did not care to meet them. They stared.

It was long past midday, as she could tell by the shadows on the floor, although her watch and her clocks had stopped long ago. Now they would be out in the street again. She must endure this hunger until dusk, when she could slip along unperceived to the bakery.

Even the baker's wife stared. Had she turned into a monster? Could they not recognize sheer misery creeping along the street? Why should that astonish them? There is plenty of it to be seen in the world by those who have eyes in their heads.

Shifting a little in the chair where she had sat motionless for hours, she glanced at the mirror on the east wall of her studio. She saw confusion, dust, derelict stacks of canvas, a scatter of dirty dishes on a table, and an inert creature peering at her from under matted hair. Some person in a picture had once looked at her like this. She made no attempt to identify it, and fell into a half doze until roused again by hunger. These pangs were intolerable. She could not wait till dusk, but must crawl down and face them in the cruel sunlight.

A sudden giddiness seized her when she got out of her chair. All her limbs were stiff. Painfully she shuffled toward the little hall. Then she remembered her purse, and went back for it, and saw herself advancing in the glass, and saw the name of that picture. "Melancholia." Sitting frozen amid work cast aside.

The floor shook, jarring her feet. Somebody was knocking at the door, and now she must wait until the intruder grew tired of it and went away. The jarring recurred twice before it ceased. After a safe interval she set off again. He was still there when she opened the door.

Kermanshah. A snapshot Ca had. Ca standing in front of a ruin with this tall thin creature. *Donald Fraser*. He said something, but a great mane of hair on his upper lip concealed his words. He proffered a note addressed to Ca.

"Gone away to London," cried Wyn.

At that he gave a horrified stare, just like the baker's wife.

She slammed the door in his face and burst into a violent fit of weeping. How much longer must she wait for food?

The floor jarred again. Why did he go on knocking? Could he hear? She was making those . . . *sobs*. People could hear them. She choked them down, fled to the studio, and sank once more into her chair.

Later she wondered languidly why he had come, and remembered a collection recently brought to Paris which might interest him. He was going to write a book, a translation of the *Tuzuk* of Babur the Mongol. Ca had talked about it, and they had read a French translation which bored them, and reminded them of the Wars of the Roses. Everybody fought everybody else and changed sides once a week. There were exasperating gaps. Babur would break off abruptly in the middle of a crisis, only to resume in the middle of some other crisis two years later.

Ca had said that he wrote his memoirs while riding full tilt on a horse. Fragments probably fell off and got lost. Their French translation was based on a Persian text. Moustache meant to work from the Chagatai Turkish text and to supply notes which would bridge these gaps.

Ca's remembered face saying this was too much. Gone! Gone! Gone! All over, those days of happiness, laughter, and easy talk. Black grief extinguished memory and hope together. Nothing was left now save pain, and pain, while the patches of sunlight shifted on the floor, and the shadows lengthened, and dusk fell.

THREE

Donald Fraser disliked and distrusted women. In his experience they were either dangerous or boring. Often they were both at once. He preferred to live in countries where the sexes are segregated.

Early in life he had been very badly treated by a beautiful but brainless girl. In his own fashion he had remained faithful to her memory. Desirable women were likely to be dishonest and hen-witted. Intellect and integrity were unfeminine qualities. This prejudice was subsequently reinforced by another injury of a different sort. He had meant to translate the *Memoirs* of the Princess Gulbaden. In 1902 a woman did it first.

Upon rare occasions, however, he came across one who neither disturbed nor bored him, and whom he could magnanimously describe as "a good sort." These exceptions made no assault upon his senses, although they were not plain or dowdy. They did not laugh at jokes which he could not see. They did not fidget or chatter. They attached due importance to food. If they read the newspaper (he preferred that they should not), they could do so without mixing up the pages. If they read anything else, they held their tongues about it.

He had been profoundly dismayed by the news that Tom's sister was on her way to Kermanshah. He had, at the Manor House, met Tom's sisters in bulk, and there were too many of them. Tom agreed with him there, but maintained that this one was tolerable. Donald thought that she sounded like a bore, since she had saddled herself for life with the care of the family invalid. Ostentatious self-martyrdom was a typically feminine trait.

Now the invalid had had the sense to bolt, and the martyr was at large. Conversation would prevail at meals. Doors must be opened, and chairs pulled back. Whenever she came in or out (women were always coming in or out), one must get up. She would monopolize the bathroom. She would exclaim over all the most banal aspects of life in Persia, and remain blind to its real charm. In haste Donald removed himself to a hotel.

A fortnight after her arrival he ventured home again, having come to the conclusion that she was a good sort. She came in and out very seldom. She was a good listener. She liked all the right things in Persia. That she took baths was probable, but her claim to the bathroom never interfered with his own private timetable. She held her tongue about what she had read. Only by chance did he discover that she was acquainted with Leyden and Erskine's translation of the *Babur Nama*, nor had she read this for any repulsive unfeminine reason. She took a sisterly interest in everything that concerned Tom, and had followed all his wistful little forays upon the Takla Makan. As a sister should, she believed in that lost city, built by Nestorian Christians, which would reveal an unsuspected civilization when Tom had dug it up. She knew all about the overland silk routes from Cathay to Samarkand, and why Tom's city must be south of the desert, a little beyond Yarkand.

This inoffensive interest she extended to Tom's friend and to that other great book which Tom's friend was going to write. She thought, as she should, that Babur was a greater hero than Akbar, and she even produced an acceptable comment on him. She liked a hero who was so fond of fruit and who could remember, over many years, exactly what melons he had eaten, upon which occasions. His ability to live entirely in the moment, while enjoying a slice of melon, might account for the fortitude which survived so many disasters and disappointments. Donald was struck by this, and gave her credit for thinking of it.

She was such pleasant company that after a while he grew uneasy, fearing that she might be a menace disguised as a good sort. Could he like a woman to this extent without being in love with her? For a day or two he was pensive. Then, at a picnic in the hills, she set his mind at rest. She said suddenly: "If you want to keep in the shade, come and sit very close to me. This little patch is just large enough for two."

Sitting very close to Caroline was quite pleasant, but did nothing to raise his emotional temperature. He might as well have been sitting very close to Tom.

They were both furious when she finally went off to join Wyn Harper who was, by all accounts, a perfect gorgon— ugly, plebeian, a successful artist, therefore unfeminine, and a deaf mute into the bargain. This last was most unfair since it made criticism sound slightly callous. Tom, for once, was in agreement with his family. Sister after sister wrote to him imploring him to use his influence with the rebel, who must be kept in London if the invalid was ever to be rescued from Wiltshire. Tom sent them all picture postcards of the ugliest mosque in Kermanshah, asserting Caroline's right to do as she pleased, but he owned to Donald that she must be cracked.

On his next leave home Donald decided to visit Paris in order to inspect the collection made by the Grammont Mission to Chinese Turkestan, which he hoped to find in the Louvre. He also undertook to visit Caroline, and to report on the degree of servitude imposed by the Gorgon. On this errand, he made his way to Wyn Harper's studio apartment. A person eventually opened the door whom he took to be some kind of subcharwoman until she spoke, or endeavored to speak. Then the door was slammed in his face, and a terrible sobbing broke out on the other side of it. Distracted, he knocked again before taking to his heels. The Gorgon! But worse than any thing that he could ever have imagined— hideous, dirty, more of a beast than a woman. She was shocking.

Downstairs he found the concierge who told him that Miss Knevett had gone back to London, and that Miss Harper was alone in the apartment. He departed to saunter by the river as he and Tom had once sauntered long ago, on a holiday during their undergraduate days. Even then they had discussed interminably the books which they meant to write, since they both meant to make, sometime or other, a signal contribution to scholarship. He could not now quite remember which book it had been. Since then his interest had traveled a century forward in history, while Tom had gone a thousand years back. Tom meditated upon the silk routes; Donald dreamed of Cabul. Actual achievement was further away than it had been when last they dawdled beside the Seine. Consuls and bankers, as they had since discovered, are always kept very busy. One's work interfered with one's life.

It had occurred to them, during Caroline's visit, that they might secure more leisure should she be persuaded to stay and keep house for them. There might be some chance of this if she had now abandoned the Gorgon. He would, in London, seek her out, and plead with her again.

Had she quarreled with the Gorgon? That was unlikely. She did not quarrel with people. Some upheaval among the tiresome Knevetts had probably occasioned this sudden departure. She might intend to return. She must be assured that the Gorgon could get on very well without her. He had called at the studio, and had seen the woman, who looked dreadful, and wept audibly on the other side of the door. What had he done? He had bolted. For all he knew, the poor creature might have hurt herself badly. Since he was a truthful man, he doubted if he could conceal that visit to the studio, and his account of it might send Caroline flying back to Paris. It would not, in any case, convince her that she was more needed in Kermanshah.

For some time he wrestled with these misgivings. Eventually, as dusk fell, he retraced his steps.

Before he reached the house he met the woman shuffling along the street, hatless and unkempt, and caught her arm just as she was about to collapse. They swayed about together. She muttered something that sounded like *Hunkrik. Braduk!* pointing feebly to a little bakery across the street. Thither they tottered. He put her into a chair by a table in the corner and appealed to the proprietress, who shook her head, muttered something about *la pauvre sourde*, and vanished to her kitchen. Donald, feeling like a prize fool, stood over the drooping Gorgon. He hoped that she would not die. He hoped that Caroline, when she heard this story, would give him high marks for chivalry.

Presently the woman returned with a basin of soup. Between them they got their patient to eat a little, and her color improved. The maid, said Madame, was away, and the beautiful English lady was gone too; poor deafs ought not to be left quite alone like this, but Monsieur would now doubtless arrange something. Should she bring an omelette perhaps? Cheese? Coffee?

Wyn Harper finished the soup. When asked if she felt

better, she shook her head and made a gesture of writing. He supplied pencil and paper. She scrawled: *"Can't see what you say. Moustache. You are Donald?"*

He wrote: *"Yes. I'm afraid you are ill."*

"No. Hungry. Maid away. Cooking a bore. Stupid of me."

"How did you recognize me?"

"Picture of you at Kermanshah."

Madame reappeared with an excellent omelette which he was glad to share, since he was growing hungry himself. She also supplied a bottle of wine before returning to her counter to deal with customers.

"Ca gone to London," was the next message that he got. *"She will teach deaf children for the rest of her life."*

At his horrified expression she hooted with laughter.

"I agree," she wrote. *"Boring!"*

He blushed, but could think of no rejoinder. When Madame was bringing the cheese, she wrote: *"Poor Ca. You and Tom want her. I want her. Everybody wants her. She mustn't do what she likes. You came to Paris to see the Grammont Collection?*

This startled him. He replied: *"Yes, but I can't find out where it is. I thought it was in the Louvre. Are you interested?"*

"Not a bit. Ca told me about you and Tom. That collection is in a private house. I can arrange for you to see it. Come tomorrow. I will give you a letter. Thank you for this dinner."

He could make little of all this, but he smiled and nodded. Her looks were reassuring. It really seemed as though hunger might have caused the trouble, and her maid, as she informed him later, would be returning on the morrow. He would be able to give a good account of her, and of himself, to Caroline, without suffering any enormous inconvenience, although there had been some bad moments when they were staggering about in the street, and he had wondered how one got hold of a Sister of Mercy. He now realized that all his French had, in that crisis, deserted him, and that he meant to say, to the first passerby, *"Pouvez-vous attraper une Sœur de Merci pour cette dame, s'il vous plaît?"*

He saw his guest back to her house, and departed, feeling very much pleased with himself.

Having promised to call again next morning, he did so. She had, in the interval, cleaned herself up so thoroughly that he barely recognized her. The promised letter was ready for him, and a written explanation of the circumstances. She had a friend who could introduce him to the present custodian of the Grammont Collection, and procure him a sight of it. Such a statement was now credible. Last night she had looked like something fished out of the Seine. Today her bearing suggested that she was Somebody. He was able to remember that she had lived in Paris for many years, was a painter of repute, and doubtless possessed friends of social standing.

"*How can I thank you?*" he wrote.

"*Not very well unless you shave,*" she replied. "*Let me know if you get there.*"

He did, through her good offices, get there, and spent some interesting hours. Before leaving Paris, he asked her to dine with him in style, as a gesture of gratitude. She chose the restaurant, assuring him that the food would be good, although the clientele was not *chic*. For this he was thankful. A smart restaurant would have daunted him, and he did not much relish being seen in her company, improved though her appearance was.

She seemed to be well known there. Several diners nodded to her. The waiter saved him the trouble of finding out what she wanted to eat; he knew already. Everything was a good deal easier than might have been expected. A lot of the women dining at other tables looked nearly as odd as Wyn. He was sorry, however, that she could not see what he said. Her little slate lay on the table between them, but it was difficult to write and eat.

"*Never mind,*" she told him, when he regretted this. "*Ca says you and Tom don't like to talk when you are eating.*"

This was true, and inevitable chatter was one of his main objections to taking a woman out. Now, perversely, he felt enforced silence to be a hardship. Had it not been for his

moustache he could have told her all about the Grammont
Collection, and she could have nodded from time to time. Since
she was to be deprived of this treat, he ordered a bottle of
Chambertin. The going, however, remained heavy until she
gave a sudden gasp of excitement. A withered, bald-headed
little man had come into the restaurant and was staring about
him in a wistful way.

"*Norris,*" she wrote. "*Ca's brother-in-law. Tom's brother-
in-law. Wife dead. Forget her name. . . .*"

She waved, and the newcomer hastened across to them exclaiming:

"Wyn Harper! I was wondering whether anybody I know
ever comes here now."

She wrote busily on her slate and pushed it at him. He read,
and laughed a little wryly.

"No," he said. "I've been in Japan. Cherry blossom, you
know. . . ."

For a few seconds he rhapsodized over cherry blossom.
Donald's eye fell on the slate which said: "*We thought you
were dead. We have been putting wreaths for years on your
grave in Père-Lachaise.*"

She snatched the slate away, wiped it, and wrote a fresh
command to Donald.

"*Tell him who you are. Tell him to sit with us. He can talk.
We can listen.*"

"Won't you join us?" asked Donald, rather reluctantly. "I
think we all have a friend in common. Miss Caroline Knevett."

A waiter brought a chair. Mark Norris collapsed upon it, and
stared at them.

"Caroline?" he said slowly. "A friend of yours?"

Donald explained their link with her while Wyn wrote another message, "*Where is the Greco Lark?*"

For a moment Mark was at a loss. Then he remembered.

"That picture! Good heavens! I don't . . . it was . . . twelve
years ago. Caroline! A friend of yours, Harper? How is she?
Where is she?"

She wrote, and he looked surprised.

"Charitable work? Caroline? Never! She must have changed. What sort of charitable work?"

At this she motioned Donald to explain. He, overwhelmed with embarrassment, muttered something about invalids.

"Good Lord. Isn't Lallie enough? How is Lallie?"

Wyn's written reply made Mark whistle.

"No! I *don't* believe it." He turned to Donald. "What has really happened to Lallie?"

"Gone off to share a cottage, I believe," said Donald. "With a friend. Another woman."

Mark looked from one to the other, and grinned.

"You more or less bear Wyn out then?" he asked.

"I don't know what she wrote," said Donald uneasily.

"Ah, well. I've left off being surprised at anything. Oh, Harper! I saw a thing of yours. In the States when I was on my way home. In the Reichner Collection. Old chap stooping over a toy boat. Looked like the round pond in Kensington Gardens. Was it?"

Wyn nodded.

"I liked it. I liked no sky and all that sky in the water. I'd like "les Nénuphars" better if he'd put in an old man with a boat. But Caroline! Is she as beautiful as ever?"

Again Wyn unkindly referred the question to Donald, who very much disliked this sort of thing. Mark luckily did not stay for an answer. He ordered some food for himself, and continued: "And as good fun? Lord! That summer . . . '96 it must have been. I never enjoyed myself more. You say she was with you and Tom in Persia? Did you ever enjoy yourselves more?"

Donald said woodenly that it had been very pleasant.

"We went riding," remembered Mark. "We took a boat. I've ridden since. And taken boats. What does she do to one?"

"Just one summer," said Wyn. "Then she goes away."

Both the men jumped. The voice was strangely inhuman but intelligible. She did not seem to be aware that she had spoken. Her eyes were dreamy. She was reliving those happy months.

"How long have she and Harper been friends?" asked Mark.

"All their lives, I think," said Donald. "Miss Harper used to live at Slane St. Mary's."

"Never in my day! I never heard of her."

"Oh, no. She went away, as a child. Lived in Venice after that, I gather."

"Venice? Venice? So that. . . . Good Lord!"

Wyn spoke again, holding up her glass of Chambertin.

"Like this. Ca is like this."

"You're quite right," exclaimed Mark. "Good wine with a meal. Don't you think so?"

He turned to Donald, who protested that this kind of discussion was beyond him.

"She is interested," went on Wyn. "Always. In everything. Like a traveler. Seeing a new country. You show her boring street. What that red? . . . pillar box! oh, beautiful! Quite new for me."

She sketched the stranger, fascinated by a pillar box because he has never seen one before.

"Street not so boring. Ca always a traveler."

Her face changed. She looked at them in amazement: "I speak. You understand."

"Perfectly," Mark assured her. "You speak very well. I never heard you before."

"I speak . . . only if she is there."

"Well . . . she is here, in a way. We are talking about her. We wish she was here."

"If that could bring her!"

Donald remembered Caroline's excuse for hurrying away to join Wyn. "I'm the only person she can talk to." He and Tom had taken this to mean that Caroline was the only person able to understand her. Remembering the uncouth noises that he had heard, when he first went to the studio, he began to guess the truth, and got a faint inkling of all that the poor woman had lost. For a moment he almost found himself blaming Caroline; such a deprivation was too cruel.

"She'll come back," said Mark, who was evidently thinking the same thing.

"Not now. *Les lauriers sont coupés. Parlons d'autre chose.*"

For the rest of the meal Mark inquired after mutual friends in Paris. They were dispersed now, but Wyn had news of some of them, and he had heard of others. Neither he nor Donald took to each other, but they were reconciled to the occasion. Mark had been afraid of a lonely evening. Donald was glad to escape from continual recourse to that slate. With the help of Chambertin the meal went off very gaily. Several of the *habitués* looked across at them in surprise. The sight of Wyn talking was new to them, perhaps.

Over the coffee she drew a swift sketch of the three of them on the back of the menu. They were sitting round their table —Donald upright and insular, Mark voluble, herself excessively Lautrec. She signed it and compelled the others to sign it, declaring that she would post it to Ca in London.

"A surprise," she explained. "She is always surprising us. Our turn now. Mark? Donald? Wyn? Here? How? When?"

CHAPTER 9

Trojan Mothers

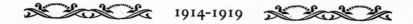

1914-1919

ONE

WHEN WAR BROKE out, all available Knevetts gathered in Victoria Road. Rosemary Preston, summoned by telegram, arrived in a very bad temper, and complained bitterly to Stella as she unpacked her suitcase. A pleasant visit to an old school friend had been cut short for no reason at all.

"All this fuss! Absolutely typical of our family. What am I supposed to do about the war?"

"Mother thought traveling might be difficult. Troop trains."

"All the more reason for staying where I was. Is Aunt B. here? I saw a lot of parcels in the hall which looked very like her."

"Yes. And Aunt F. They're in Mother's room arranging about the war. And Cecily and Eddie are coming to tea."

Rosemary made a face. They liked Eddie Dacre, but Cecily Mycroft was in many ways worse than an aunt. She was no support in youthful rebellions, even though determined to marry a very ineligible young man. Her common sense and prudence were such that nobody could call this attachment romantic. She positively truckled to the older generation in her readiness to wait and to postpone a public engagement.

"Is everybody very much upset about the war?"

"Oh, yes. They're having a high old time. Uncle George says it will all be over in six weeks. We shall go straight through to Berlin. Rosemary! What's that?"

"This? Face powder."

"You don't *use* it?"

"Bella does. It's quite true. It stops one's nose from looking shiny."

"Mother will have a fit."

"Oh, I shan't use it when under the maternal and the auntly eye. Anything for a quiet life."

The box was hidden in a handkerchief drawer.

"I say! When you were at the Wilsons, did you see or hear anything of Aunt Lallie?"

"I did. They took me to call there."

"What? At *that* place? Owl Wood?"

"Why not? The way our family sinks its voice, anybody might think Owl Wood was a brothel."

"Ssh! And you said it wrong. It's broth-el. Like broth. Not a long *o*."

"Anyway I can't see what's so awful about it. Everybody likes them. They've worked a lovely banner for the Mother's Union. It's kept in the church. People call them the ladies of Owl Wood. Like those people . . . you know . . . famous . . . lived in Wales . . . the ladies of . . . ?"

"Llangollen. But . . . did you see the *other one?*"

"Miss Lecky? Of course I did. Nothing wrong with her except she's a bit like a schoolmistress. Like Miss Perkins. The same accent. Remember? 'Naow, gurls! Get ready for Burlington Haouse.' Aunt Lallie looks a lot older, but she's not nearly so annoying. Quite ordinary. Given up all those frills and furbelows, and wears old clothes. They have masses of pets. I can't see why it's supposed to be like Greece."

"Nobody thinks it's like Greece."

"Eddie does. You remember that time *Country Life* had something about the Manor House? Mother sent a copy to everybody in the family, and Sandy had to post them all. He was complaining to Eddie about it, and Eddie said, 'Did you post one to Aunt Lallie in . . . in . . . some Greek place . . . Skyros or something?' Then he saw me, and made a face as if he'd dropped a brick. I suppose Skyros is full of broth-els."

"Sandy is going to enlist."

"What? In the army? Go and fight? What does Mother say?"

"She says he has to. People in our class must set an example."

"If it's all going to be over in six weeks, he'll never get near any fighting. He doesn't know right from left. Somebody will still be shouting at him in a barracks square."

"Eddie is going. I don't know about Gee. Frank is too young, of course. He hasn't left Oxford."

"I can't imagine Eddie drilling. He'll make all the other soldiers laugh."

"Oh, he'll get a commission. Aunt F. rubbed that in. All the Dacres did well in the O.T.C. Not like poor Sandy."

"What does Father think?"

"Oh, he's worried. As usual. Says it's all rot about six weeks."

"After all, Uncle George is more likely to know, isn't he? He was in Parliament, and knows lots of important people."

"That's what Mother says. But I don't believe Father has ever thought much of Uncle George. Oh, and Daph wants to go to the front and be a nurse."

Both sisters laughed, and Rosemary said: "Poor soldiers. As if being wounded wasn't bad enough."

"Aunt F. says she's so thankful she didn't bring Daph out this year. The Season would be over, and if Daph wasn't engaged there won't be any of those country house visits, or Scotland, where you follow it up and try again."

"What do you bet Daph won't have a mysterious lover killed in the war?"

There was a short silence. Stella said, "Don't make jokes about people being killed."

"I know. I was sorry as soon as I'd said it. That's the horrid part about a war. Some people will be killed, I suppose. Bound to be. I only hope they won't be people we know."

Cecily Mycroft burst into the room, tapping at their door as she came.

"Why are you two lurking up here? Come down for goodness' sake. Eddie's here, and he's in a maddening mood. Why are you looking so down in the mouth?"

"The war," said Stella. "People being killed."

"That's not the right attitude. Charlie has enlisted, and we are all very proud. Come along!"

They followed their formidable cousin downstairs.

"What about her Romeo?" whispered Rosemary.

"Flat feet," whispered Stella. "A squint and a rupture."

Eddie was lying on the drawing-room sofa with his eyes shut.

"Now, Eddie," said Cecily. "I'm serious. Have you been?"

He opened one eye, and shut it again murmuring: "Nobody has ever asked me that since I got out of the nursery. Immediately after breakfast. Master Eddie? Have you been? Yes, Nannie."

"I suppose you think you're funny."

"Rosemary does. She's giggling."

"You're merely very silly."

He jumped up, seized Rosemary, and began to dance round the room with her, singing:

> "I'm such a silly when the moon comes out!
> I hardly seem to know what I'm about.
> Skipping! Hopping. . . ."

"Have you been to the Recruiting Office?" yelled Cecily.

"Have I? I wonder! Such a lot of things I was told to do. I made a list, but I lost it. I know I got my hair cut. And bought some braces and some ginger for my Dam at Fortnum's. But . . . the Recruiting Office? No, I don't believe I did."

"Do you realize that the Kaiser says we have a contemptible little mercenary army? He says Englishmen won't fight unless they're paid for it. Do you mean to fight for your country?"

"I thought it was plucky little Belgium I'd been told to fight for.

> "I'm all aquiver when the moonbeams glance.
> That is the moment when I long to dance.
> I can . . . never . . . close a sleepy eye,
> When moon comes creeping up the sky.

"Tell me, sweet Coz, where is my Dam? She bid me be here at four sharp."

"She's upstairs with Mother and Aunt B."

"Aha! When the Last Trump sounds, those three will settle what orders to give to St. Peter."

"Naturally they want to do something," said Cecily.

"Indeed, yes. If they didn't, I should fear that some great natural law had been suspended."

"Your mother is going is offer Connington for a hospital."

"My sainted aunt! With the billiard table for operations?"

"Nonsense. A billiard table wouldn't do."

"Wouldn't it? My dear Cecily, just think! You could have three operations on it at once."

Cecily was growing so furious that Stella interposed: "Which is your sainted aunt? Aunt C.?"

"Oh, no, no! Not by no means. Aunt C. is a female Iago, if you only knew. You should hear what we say of her up at Connington."

"She goes bicycling round London playing with deaf babies," said Rosemary. "I call that pretty saintly."

"How do we know that's what she does? We've never seen her at it."

"My mother," said Cecily, "says that yours makes herself quite ridiculous about all that. There's no mystery about Aunt Carrie. She's frustrated, probably."

"Oh, my! What a lovely long word. Do tell me what it means."

"She couldn't get a husband, so she's taken up good works. That's what most old maids. . . ."

The three mothers, confident and excited, sailed into the room, all talking at once. Sue commanded the girls to go up to the old night nursery and bring down a lot of clothes which she had collected for the Salvation Army, and which would now do nicely for the Belgians. She then asked Eddie to bring a stepladder from the hall cupboard, and to lift down a heavy vase from the top of the bookcase.

"With pleasure," said Eddie. "But do tell me—what has it to do with the war?"

"Nothing. I keep meaning to send it to the Parish White Elephant Sale. It's too heavy for me to lift down, and whenever I remember it there's nobody there. I remembered it just now, along with the Salvation Army things, and you are here."

"Have you *been?*" asked Barbie sharply.

"Yes," said Eddie, and went for the steps.

"That sale is for a new organ," said Sue. "I suppose they'll hold it just the same."

"Better be for the Red Cross now," Barbie told her. "You'll get more things. Insist on that, Sue. You're on the committee."

They turned to watch Eddie as he came in with the steps, climbed them, and removed the heavy, ugly vase from the top of the bookcase. An unwonted silence fell. The flow of advice and admonition was stemmed.

"Eddie looks so young always," sighed Sue as he carried the steps back into the hall.

Flo caught her breath. Barbie made a gesture as though warding off some assailant.

Young?

Immense gulfs of fear and uncertainty yawned all about them. The young, whom we bore, whom we guard, whom we rule? Upon what road do we send them? Sandy? Charlie? Gee? Eddie? Frank? George says . . . but even if George is wrong, they must go.

Then again they all began to talk at once:

"Moo-ma-moo-ma-moo-moo-ma-moo!"
"Yak! Yak! Yakka-kakka-kakka-yakka-yak!"
"Uther-eruther-uther-ruther-ruther?"

TWO

I said, I *said*, we should have to change at Swindon, it's the very worst train we could have, but he was so sure, he is always hopeless over trains, I shouldn't have listened to him I

wouldn't have listened, only I'm so tired, I'm so tired, I ache
all over, I'm too tired, this dreadful day, it's not like me to be
so tired. "Nothing ever seems to tire you, Mrs. Mycroft!
You're wonderful." Well, I said, I always see to it that my
head saves my heels, only seeing our old home look so shabby
and neglected, that was the last straw, Dick might have let it
to people who

Not grief. Not Charlie. I've finished crying, I shall never
stop crying, but three years ago now, I have felt all the things,
I felt them then, I shall always feel them, nothing new today,
it all seemed so unreal somehow, nothing to do with Charlie,
the tablet looks very nice, the service was nice I think, I didn't
seem able to attend much, the clergyman was nice, Dick, such
a shock to see Dick looking so, Dora doesn't, she never has,
the last straw to see him, an old man, coming from Cheltenham, a visitor, not at Home where he ought to be, strangers in
our Home, not Home any more, we just collected to go to
church and went away again, not what I thought, not what I
planned, I thought it would be a comfort.

The old days, such a big family, all of us there, friends from
everywhere, the church full, all the people outside, all the
village mourning, people from Slane Bredy, Ida's mother came
when Clemmie, and now, now, only a handful, as if it wasn't
important, hardly anyone from the village, there must still be
some people who remember us, as if Charlie meant nothing to
them, dead three years ago, one among millions, millions, so
few of us even, I do think Edmund and Molly might have

Tickets! And he's got them, why can't he let me have, I
can't stand watching him fumble, he always loses, oh, I'm so
tired, he would take this train, I knew we should have to
change at

Getting dark, the fields so dreary in the rain, the last straw it
was such a wet, his whole attitude so unreasonable, poor man,
they can't bear sorrow, men, he is broken-hearted, my poor
old man, he worshiped Charlie, I must take care that he doesn't
get a chill, really unreasonable, we must have a tablet somewhere, all the rows and rows of graves with little crosses, miles

and miles of them in a photograph, where else should we put it but in the church at Home? "Grandson of Sir Richard Knevett? I see!" Quite angry. But our family, Domesday Book, poor Flo naturally, tablets for Gee and Eddie at Connington, the Dacres are a family but not so old as, kind of George to come, lumbago, Edmund and Molly really, when they knew that Grace and Tom and Bob couldn't, and so few of the younger ones, Sandy and Frank, the two who didn't, she said Sandy was in Court today but I could see she was ashamed, Flo never even apologized for Frank, that girl he married, she thinks, born five months after it might be his all the same, only things like that didn't happen before. Flo is a fool, she should make the best of it, she wants to break up the, when George dies Frank will inherit now, that girl mistress of Connington, poor Flo, Eddie was her darling, Eddie was so young always.

Cecily might have come back with us, her husband could manage alone for once, if Cecily was here she would be here, I wish she was here, I am her mother, but she is very, they are all so, nowadays, Rosemary and Stella, powder, lipstick, they would never have dared, we never, they don't seem to

Eight of us once, only three now, me and Flo and Sue, all that we have been through, we have won the war, they did not die in vain, Carrie of course, but I am angry with her, I can't forgive, Lallie would have been alive today, all very well to say a lot of people died of it, nobody can persuade me that that creature nursed her properly, if she had been at the flat she would never have caught it, Carrie is impossible, at the funeral, sitting beside that creature, not with us, she has no right to be so happy, enjoying her work so much when

All gone, all changed. Sue says so too, she can't do anything with them, feels she doesn't know anything about them, not like us, we had to fight to get what we wanted, yes, but they don't even fight, they take it, never pay the least attention, one might as well not be there.

But nonsense what he says. The bottom has not fallen out of our world, we have had a terrible war and we have won it, things are naturally upset, but it is nonsense, they can't feel that we are no guides, don't rely any more on anything we ever told them, we are not dinosaurs, men always have to theorize like that, four years can't have completely changed the world, just temporary, settle down, everywhere, people in our class, not the same authority, maids unsettled, so much money in munitions, women at the baby clinic, speaking to one as if, but things will go back to normal, the old life will come back, we have had this dreadful war, and we have won it, and there can never be another, and the old life will come back, but Charlie will never come back. Oh, Charlie! Oh, Charlie!

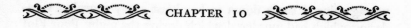 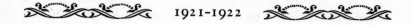

CHAPTER 10

Candidate for a Halo

ONE

"I'M NOT ONE of the Harper coterie myself," said Hugh Beddington, "but I daresay this was a good buy. Poor Kimmons! Most of what he's acquiring for the Barnesfield Gallery will go down to the basement in fifty years' time. This might possibly stay up. . . ."

His voice trailed away. Nobody was listening. Old Dacre, at one end of the table, had gone into a lugubrious coma. Flo, at the other, was glaring at that exasperating girl.

It was too bad, and this was positively his last visit to Connington. No fun could be expected there now. Flo should not invite people if she was going to take no trouble to amuse them. He finished his pheasant in silence, and composed an account of this terrible weekend which might divert Lucy Yates, to whom he was going next.

My dear Lucy, you can't imagine what a morgue that place is now. Oh, yes, I know they lost two boys. So has everyone else. That doesn't oblige Flo to quarrel continually with her daughter. I assure you that's the only form of entertainment offered at Connington—a nonstop bullfight . . . cow-fight! The daughter-in-law? Oh, she gives the place a wide berth. Yes, yes, I know all about that scandal. Who doesn't? But Daphne Dacre! A weedy, pallid, social failure! She only speaks once in twenty-four hours, and then is certain to say the wrong thing. I came down to breakfast every morning wondering which had murdered which during the night. Poor Flo! She's quite given up trying to get the girl married. And the cow-fight is an occupation for her; she might be rather at a loss nowadays without Daphne to snub. I believe the worm has tried to turn—a hat shop, or a bookshop, which went bankrupt. Dacre had to foot the bill, and I imagine Daphne hears about that pretty often. Polly's boy? Oh, nothing in that, believe me. Polly is furious. He's one of a crowd. That girl has been secretly engaged to eleven dead heroes. . . .

Daphne broke the silence with one of her ill-timed remarks.

"I suppose if we had a corpse on our dinner table we'd just go on eating pheasant."

"And who," asked Flo, "does keep a corpse on their dinner table?"

"They always do in the slums," declared Daphne. "When they've only got one room. Till the funeral."

Perfect! A corpse on the dinner table: Lucy would love it.

"I'm glad Barnesfield has bought a Harper," said Flo, ignoring her daughter. "I think I told you, we have a sort of link with her, and one of my sisters knows her very well."

This was an irritating trick which Flo had developed lately. She would suddenly take up a topic which one had abandoned in despair five minutes earlier.

"I don't think you ever told me which sister."

"Caroline, but I doubt if you've ever met her. She goes in for good works. Wyn Harper has taken a studio almost next door to her in London, and they see a good deal of each other."

"Caroline? I think I did meet her once, ages ago. Isn't she very beautiful?"

Flo glanced at him sharply.

"*Very*," said Daphne. "But our family can't see it."

She glared at her mother, who smiled and said: "Can't we? But Hugh . . . when did you meet her? Where?"

"I'm trying to remember. I also have the impression that she is very witty."

For once the mother and daughter seemed to be in agreement. They exclaimed in surprised denial.

Such unusual concord roused the master of the house. He sat up and said: "No, no! Don't make any mistake about that. It was in 1911. She ran third. Doncaster."

Another item for Lucy! One could dine out on the Dacres for months if this went on.

"Aunt Carrie," said Daphne, "has dedicated her whole life to the deaf and dumb. She runs a wonderful school—Seddon House."

"In memory of poor Valerie Seddon's child," put in Flo. "You remember, Hugh? That child nobody was supposed to know about?"

"Absolutely selfless," whined Daphne. "*She* doesn't just live to amuse herself. *She* knows what a tragedy life really is."

"A tragedy," said Flo, "is generally merely a mess. Very inefficient people are fond of insisting that life is tragic. They lose their job, or they go bankrupt, which is tiresome for anybody who has to clear up the mess. But it's rather pretentious to call it a tragedy."

"This sister of yours," said Hugh hastily, "the one I remember; I don't see her as a dedicated, selfless type, I must say."

"Nor do I," said Flo. "But Daphne does."

"Do you remember Mark Norris? A coming man in the nineties, and then snuffed out? I think I met her with him."

"Of course I remember. He is my brother-in-law. He married my sister Kitty, who died."

Hugh had known this but had forgotten it in his anxiety to avert further references to bankruptcy. He said: "Of course! Of course! Went abroad for years. But he's back in London now, isn't he?"

"So I've heard. We've rather lost touch. I believe he scuttled back when he thought the Germans would get into Paris."

"Odd how he's dropped out. At one time he was doing so very well. I'd quite forgotten his existence till I caught sight of him one day in Soho, dining with. . . ."

He broke off, as memory rang up a curtain. Norris had been

dining with a handsome woman, obviously in her forties. That woman, long ago, had been a beautiful girl putting on her gloves in a picture gallery.

"Dining with . . . ?" prompted Flo.

"I'm trying to remember. Somebody I know."

Flo, however, was hot on the scent.

"Man or woman?"

"Man. It's not important. But the sight of him gave me a shock. I suddenly remembered all those ladies in their satins and pearls. Dead as doornails! Not the ladies, of course. The pictures. A portrait won't do nowadays unless the sitter emerges looking half-witted, dowdy, and depraved. Have you seen Lucy's latest portrait, by the way? Quite up to the minute. He's given her a squint and dropsical legs, and she has to pretend that she likes it, poor Lucy."

This won a laugh from Flo, but he was sure that the attack would be renewed later on.

In order to postpone it, he lingered with Dacre over the port as long as ever he could, demanding information upon every possible rural topic. They discussed pheasants, peasants, gates, fences, and the iniquity of pylons for electric cables thrust upon plowland. Dacre placed a decanter for a pylon, took a saltcellar for a tractor, and plowed up and down across the table. He demonstrated the impossibility of a straight furrow when an infernal pylon stood in the middle of the field. Every weed likely to flourish on the unplowed patch, inevitably left at the pylon's base, was named and its habits described. Several long stories were declared to be cut short, although everything said by Sir George was repeated in full, and a good deal of what had been said to him.

Poor Flo was probably sitting by herself with her book, Daphne having retreated to her bower to weep over the eleven dead heroes. Flo's books were a recurring bore. She had always picked one's brains for some comment on them which she could later produce as her own, but she had formerly kept up with the times. Now she never seemed to get hold of a book until everyone else had finished talking about it, and her scandals were as dismal as her literature. What should he tell her about that dinner in Soho? Should he brighten her life by suggesting that her ex-brother-in-law might be having an affair with a middle-aged spinster, given to good works? Should he punish her for being so tedious? He need not decide in a hurry, could he but persuade his host to go on about pylons.

He had not quite decided, when at last they made a move. As they went down a long anteroom toward the drawing room, a furious voice was heard beyond a curtained arch, "You hate her because you've never been able to hurt her."

The cow-fight! Daphne had not fled to her bower.

"Here are the men, at last," said Flo, as they came in. "Now Hugh . . . what do you think of Keynes? *The Economic Consequences of the Peace?*"

"I don't think anything. I don't understand economics."

"Nobody does. But everybody . . . oh, Daphne! Do sit down!"

Daphne was standing in the middle of the room. Her long face was working, and she twisted a handkerchief savagely.

"Was it," she demanded, "or was it not Aunt Carrie you saw dining with Uncle Mark in Soho?"

He took a quick decision, and said in startled surprise: "Oh, no! I've remembered now. It was a journalist. A man called Bunbury."

"There!" cried Daphne, turning on her mother. "Does that satisfy you?"

"Perfectly," said Flo laughing. "Bunbury! I know the importance of being earnest."

"No you don't," said Daphne. "You are never in earnest. I happen to be."

Flo laughed again, and turned to Hugh.

"But you must know what people are saying about Keynes!"

"You're two years late," he said unkindly. "If you'd asked me what they were saying in 1919, I could have told you, but I've forgotten now. How did you manage to be so late for the fair?"

Flo gave him a reproachful look. Daphne smiled, and sat down. The leaden minutes crept past until they could all escape from one another and go to bed.

In the small hours of the night he woke with a start, convinced that somebody had been knocking at his door. He listened. There was undoubtedly some kind of scuffling noise. Groping for the light switch, he called out: "Who's there? What is it?"

Silence fell. When he sat up in bed, it seemed to him that something white was protruding under his door.

The night was cold, and a sensible man would leave investigation till the morning. Exasperated by his own curiosity, he scrambled out of bed. The object was a fat envelope addressed to himself. Within were ten sheets of paper covered with an illegible scrawl on both sides, as he discovered when he was back under the bedclothes. His watch stood at seventeen minutes to three. The girl must have been writing ever since they all went to bed.

He could decipher only a word or two here and there, nor did he try very hard. Aunt Carrie seemed to figure for a page or so, and to provide an excuse for this onslaught. He was implored to believe nothing that Flo said about her—a needless request, since he seldom believed what Flo said about anybody. Aunt Carrie had been culled . . . no, called (the girl never closed her *a*'s) to a dedicated life. So had Daphne, by the look of later pages. Life at Connington was so trivial . . . need for something reul . . . real? . . . and vital . . . thought religion was the unswer. . . .

He flung the crumpled letter on the floor, thanking Heaven that he was to leave Connington next morning. Poor Lucy, whose daughter was reputed to be a nymphomaniac, might cheer up when she heard this, and agree that Flo had brought it on herself.

At breakfast he took his revenge for a ghastly weekend. He gravely thanked Daphne, in her mother's presence, for the interesting letter which he had got from her in the middle of the night. He then quitted Connington, leaving plenty of fresh material for the cow-fight.

TWO

The exposure, the humiliation, her mother's savage ridicule, left Daphne with no alternative save flight. She had been pushing letters under doors in the middle of the night for years. Some people were kind and sympathetic. Others were brisk and bracing. A few ignored her, but nobody had hitherto given her away.

She must abandon Connington and its luxuries in obedience to a Higher Call. Her life must be dedicated to others. She would have been off long ago had Aunt Carrie worked for the blind rather than the deaf, who were less romantic, less touching.

She packed a suitcase. She left a note on her dressing table announcing that she had gone to work at Seddon House. She got herself to the junction unmolested, and, while waiting for a train, she sent a telegram to her Aunt Carrie. Once safe and speeding southward she was able to picture her welcome at the flat.

Aunt Carrie! I've come!

Yes, Daphne! I knew you'd come in the end. I've been waiting for you all these years.

It's been a struggle, giving up everything, but now I'm quite, quite sure.

I know, my dear. I know. I've been through it all. They laughed at me, too. They were unkind. But I found peace. Here is your little room, all ready for you. And tomorrow I'll take you to the children. *Your* children. Oh, we need you so much! To have a young thing like you working with us will make all the difference!

Wonderful Daphne Dacre! Those children are different creatures since she came to Seddon House. She lives with her aunt—quite a remarkable woman, too, in her way. (Spinsters take to good works because they can't get husbands.) The world's reproach. They have chosen the better part. Nuns in a little convent.

In this euphoria she exulted until she had rung her Aunt Carrie's bell, and Ida opened the door.

She had forgotten Ida, now a target for family disapproval, spoiled by Carrie, and giving herself insufferable airs because her cousin had taken Mark Norris's former studio.

"Hullo, Ida! Did my telegram arrive?"

"Yes, Miss Daphne. But Miss Carrie didn't open it, not till she came in half an hour ago. It's a bit difficult. We've got no room empty. There's gentlemen everywhere. . . ."

The drawing-room door opened, emitting a reek of pipe smoke and a rumble of male voices. Aunt Carrie appeared. She seldom kissed people, but she gave Daphne a friendly tap on the shoulder, and said: "Come and take your things off in my room. Leave your suitcase in the hall for the moment."

They went down the corridor to that room with a view from Westminster to Richmond. Daphne, crestfallen, asked if her arrival was inconvenient.

"Not really. We can manage. You see Tom and Donald Fraser and Mark Morris are all staying here. But we've settled what to do. After supper Donald will move out to a little hotel in Hammersmith, and you can have his room."

"Uncle Tom? I thought he was in Persia."

"He's just arrived, and Donald came down from Scotland to meet him. Mark is here for only a couple of nights. He's in the middle of moving from a flat in Highgate to another in Putney. When he goes, Donald can come back."

"I hadn't realized . . . Uncle Mark . . . I thought the Family never saw anything of him nowadays."

"I do. We've always been friends."

A shout came down the corridor.

"Caroline! How many bottles?"

"Do you like beer?" asked Aunt Carrie. "Tom is going out to get some."

"No," said Daphne faintly.

"Enough for four of us," called Aunt Carrie through the door.

Turning back she said, "You look very tired."

"I am," admitted Daphne, whose head was going round. "I . . . I've been through rather a lot lately, Aunt Carrie."

"I don't believe you feel up to dinner with all of us. Why not lie down on my bed and let Ida bring you a tray?"

"Oh, Aunt Carrie, I'd much rather. If it isn't a bother."

"Not a bit. Only . . . please don't call me Aunt Carrie. I'd rather you didn't. Say Caroline. I must go now. I'll come in after supper, and drink coffee with you."

Beer? thought Daphne, lying down on the bed. And Mark Norris actually staying in the flat? Even with Uncle Tom as chaperon, this was going rather far. Aunt Carrie . . . *Caroline* . . . could know nothing of the tales told at Connington. Some discreet hint ought, perhaps, to be dropped.

Presently Ida appeared. She dumped a tray beside the bed and departed without a word.

One could hardly, at the moment, describe this flat as a convent. The Family considered it absurdly large for one woman, but the criticism was only muttered, since "a bed with Carrie" was useful for anyone coming up to London. Uncle John was dead, and Aunt Sue had settled in Folkestone; there was nowhere else to go.

Remembering this, Daphne could not but be thankful that the flat was, at the moment, full of uncles rather than aunts. Her own arrival might have caused much more comment and inquiry. She must lose no time in establishing herself as the mainstay of Seddon House before Aunt Barbie or Cecily or Stella turned up. Later, perhaps, she might persuade Caroline to move. A flat just large enough for the two of them and Ida would be pleasanter.

To conciliate Ida a little might be as well. When she came for the tray she received an apology for this sudden invasion.

"Not more sudden than usual, Miss Daphne. Sometimes we don't even get a telegraph. They just turn up. Mrs. Edmund, she's the only one that ever writes beforehand to know if it's convenient. And I can't make up that bed for you. Not till I've done the dishes. But Mr. Donald has moved his things, and I've put the clean sheets ready, so, if you're in a hurry . . . ?"

Ida paused suggestively. Daphne graciously assured her that there was no hurry. She could wait until Ida had time to make up the bed.

"And how is Wyn?"

"Miss Harper? She's very well, thank you."

"I've been hearing about her lately from an art critic who admires her work."

"A lot do."

"It's wonderful, isn't it? But so sad she can never talk."

"Oh, she can talk all right, Miss Daphne."

"Only on her fingers. The time I met her, she had to talk on her fingers, and Miss Carrie translated for her."

"She can talk like a person to anybody she likes. If she talks on her fingers that means she can't be bothered."

Caroline, coming in with the coffee tray, heard this, and looked rather stern.

"Now, Ida! You mustn't say that. You know quite well that Wyn can't talk to a lot of people whom she likes very much. Miss Maxwell, for instance."

"That's natural. She says herself she can't but think of Miss Maxwell as Teacher, even after all these years. She remembers that she has to try, and when she starts trying it's no good."

"I know. But it mustn't be said that Wyn won't talk to people because she doesn't like them. Often it's not true, and it makes her sound so disagreeable."

"Well! She never goes out of her way to be agreeable."

At a look from Caroline, Ida scuttled out of the room. Daphne crept farther under the quilt. "Aunt Carrie in a freezing rage." Rosemary and Stella had referred to these episodes, and Daphne now understood what they meant. She accepted a cup of coffee, and waited until the room had grown a little warmer before explaining her arrival.

"Please, Caroline, I want to stay with you and work with

you. Do let me. I want to dedicate my whole life to those poor little children."

Caroline put down her cup and stared.

"Really? I never knew you were interested."

"Oh, I am. I am. I've always wanted to. But I didn't know if I ought to leave home. I mean . . . with Gee and Eddie gone, and Frank and Wendy never coming near the place, it all seems so dismal. We don't even have so very many people to stay now. They tire Father. I felt I was the only one left . . . but this is what I've always really wanted to do. To give up the world."

"Give up the world? You don't have to do that. Quite the opposite. You want to give the world to the children."

"Oh, you know what I mean. I want a different sort of life. Not what the Family . . . you've been through it all. You've had to fight them. You know what Mother can be? If only you'll help me, and let me stay here."

"Stay here, certainly, if you want to train in London. But, if I were you, I'd go to Manchester. There's a very good course there now."

"Train?" asked Daphne startled. "You mean learn to talk on my fingers? I'm sure I could pick up all that very quickly if I could start right away at Seddon House."

"Seddon House? You want to work there? I'm afraid they never take untrained people."

"But surely . . . your niece . . . wouldn't that make a difference?"

"No, I don't think so."

"Wouldn't Miss Spender make an exception?"

"I don't think she would have. Anyway, she's retired now. Miss Dyson is our principal and she has no use for untrained people. She's a splendid person. Very fierce."

This word astonished Daphne so much that Caroline had to explain: "We need fierce people. To fight for our children. They've just taken two years off their education. The Minister says that less must be spent on handicapped children; they cost too much."

"How dreadful!" said Daphne vaguely. "But why didn't they make you principal? You've always run Seddon House, really."

"Me? How can you think so?"

To think so was a tribal reflex. Caroline, whatever her shortcomings, was a Knevett, and therefore must be running any activity in which she was concerned. Daphne might believe herself to be a rebel, but her views on a point like this were orthodox.

"I never ran anything in my life," declared Caroline with some warmth. "I shouldn't know how to. I'm only one of their traveling teachers. So is Miss Maxwell, though she's always talking about retiring. We drive about London and play with very little children who can't get to any nursery school. Seddon House has a group of us, and we have people now working in most large towns. We call it playing. It's games which help to make up for not hearing. We used to bicycle, but now we've got cars, which is much better. I can often pick up a child or two from houses that have no gardens, and take them along to one where there's a nice garden, and they can play."

The idea of this appealed to Daphne. To arrive as an angel of mercy in this house, and that would be more agreeable than taking orders from Miss Dyson.

"How do you get to hear about them?" she asked.

"Doctors and baby clinics and health visitors know about us. If they hear of a case, and think the parents would like one of us, they tell them about it, and notify us."

"How grateful the parents must be!"

"Well . . . one has to go carefully. They don't always understand. They think we ought to be able gradually to teach the child to hear, not to get on without hearing. They can't see the point of our games."

"I think I should love it. I can drive a car."

"Seddon House sends nobody who hasn't been fully trained, and hasn't spent some time in an ordinary Montessori school."

"Really, I think that's rather narrow-minded. Teaching is

a gift. Either you have it, or you haven't. And playing with babies can't be so very difficult."

"You've got to know as much as if you were going to teach them afterward in school. Whenever we can, as soon as a child gets to be about five, we get into touch with the school to which it will eventually go. We find out what the teacher will want. No two teachers think exactly alike. Some like oral preparation. Some like manual. We try to keep clear of any disputes about methods. We want simply to slide the child easily into the school life it is going to have—to save it from any sudden change, or feeling lost or bewildered. We have to be very careful not to annoy the teachers. They are apt to be suspicious of people who haven't had proper training. Quite rightly."

"But this training . . . should I have to pay for it?"

"Oh, yes. But your father will pay, won't he? If he knows your heart is set on it?"

Daphne burst into tears.

"No, he won't. No, he won't. Mother won't let him. You know what she is. Oh, I did think you'd help me!"

"So I will. In any way that I can."

"He had to pay before. All those bills for the bookshop. When Mysie Ferrars and I tried to start that bookshop. And I left a note behind to say I was going to work at Seddon House."

"Hush. Everything will be all right."

"How can it? How can it?"

"I don't know. But things do come right. I've found that. If one is patient and waits."

"I can't go back. I'd sooner kill myself."

"I never said you had to go back. Stay here, and we'll see what can be done."

"I said I was going to work at Seddon House."

"You don't have to tell the world you aren't working at Seddon House. Not at once, anyway."

"They'll find out."

"We may have thought of something before they do."

"I can't ask for money. I can't."

"You would, if you had absolutely made up your mind.
You wouldn't care what anyone said. You'd get your training,
whatever it cost you. If you feel like this, then perhaps Seddon
House isn't exactly the right thing."

"To do something worthwhile . . . wasting my whole life
. . . so miserable . . . wish I was dead. . . . Let me go to Seddon
House. Ask them! Beg them! I could be a scullery maid . . .
wash the dishes. . . . I wouldn't mind what I did, so long as
I could say I was there."

"No. You'd only be in the way."

"Oh, you're cruel! You're cruel!"

There was a tap at the door and Daphne hid her blubbered
face under the quilt. She heard Ida say: "That bed's made up
and a hot bottle in. And the gentlemen want to know if you've
quite deserted them, Miss Carrie."

When she peered out again, Caroline was mashing up a
couple of aspirins in a glass of warm water.

"Drink this. And tomorrow we'll think."

THREE

The studio where the "Greco Lark" had been painted was
now shut off from the rest of the house. It was let, with three
bedrooms, a kitchen, and a bathroom, as a separate dwelling
known as 25a Buckleberry Road. Wyn lived there with
Annette, and traffic with the flat was as frequent as it had been
in the old days.

Mark often dropped in before or after a visit to Caroline,
since he belonged to that small group of people with whom
Wyn could, as Ida put it, "talk like a person." Why he should
be thus favored he did not know. Wyn, when asked, told him
that it was because he had once rescued her from a whole
evening tête-à-tête in Paris with Donald Fraser. He did not
believe this, but was flattered by the distinction, since she
could talk like a person to no other painter. Not that they
were often in agreement. Mark, after long stagnation, had

begun to paint a little. Any picture by Wyn provoked in him a strong desire to paint something else, quite different. He would never, as he well knew, recapture his lost status, but he had begun to work for pleasure, which was more than could be said for his labors in the days of Lady Bumblebee.

One day, some six weeks after his removal to a new flat in Putney, he encountered Ida on the doorstep of Wyn's studio. She carried a bowl of clotted cream, part of a generous tin sent from Devonshire by Mrs. Edmund.

"You've come to see my portrait?" she asked.

"Why! Is Wyn painting you?"

"Nearly finished."

"Is it like you?"

"Too like by half."

Annette opened the door. They gave her the cream, and went along to the studio where Wyn was working on a large picture which ran through every shade of white.

Ida sat solidly at her kitchen table in the flat. She was enjoying the complete repose achieved by all good servants when they sit down to their elevenses. A lifetime of labor lay behind and before her. At this moment every muscle was at ease.

The day was cold. In a dozen ways the eye conveyed its chill to the nerves. Harsh winter light shone through a window where chimney stacks cut across a gray-white sky. The scrubbed deal table was yellow-white. The starched planes of Ida's apron were a blue-white. Warmth was gathered into the cup which she held, whence strength and life flowed pleasantly down into her sturdy body.

"The tea has come out nice," conceded Ida. "Anybody can see it's good tea, properly made."

"A great compliment," said Wyn.

"I agree," said Mark. "And there has never been such a symphony in white since Oudry painted a dead duck."

A riot of multicolored vegetables would, he thought, be his choice when he painted Ida. Quite different!

This white monstrosity should have, he suggested, a fancy name. Wyn unexpectedly agreed.

"Yes. To mean something very old. Ca found. In Latin."

She produced from the pocket of her painting overall a slip of paper on which was written, in a scholarly hand:

Non magnis opibus jucunde corpora curant.

LUCRETIUS. II. 31.

"Having no great possessions they cheerfully tend their bodies."

"How did Caroline get hold of this?" he asked.

Wyn told him that an old man, grandfather to one of Ca's pupils, had produced it when told about the picture. He was very fond of Ca, and gave her sherry whenever she went to the house.

"I see. A very old institution. As old as hard work. Adam probably had elevenses when he knocked off work for a bit, in Eden. But isn't it rather a mouthful?"

"Only first three words."

"*Non magnis opibus?* It'll look classy in the catalog of your exhibition."

They all laughed. Wyn's exhibition hung fire. It was time that she should have one, but she could not bring herself to face the hard work and the publicity involved.

"If it was called something like that," said Ida hopefully, "they mightn't know it was supposed to be me. I'd just as soon they didn't."

"What Wyn wants," said Mark, "is a dogs-body. Somebody who will do all the donkey work—drive her about, answer the telephone, arrange sittings, write letters, make civil faces at people, and fix up that exhibition. She can't always be sending for Caroline and Miss Maxwell. She should have a regular minion, to whom she can twiddle her fingers, and say: For God's sake throw this woman out before I throw up. And the minion would say: Oh, Lady Fish-face! Miss Harper is terribly sorry, but she has an important engagement."

"Nobody like that," said Wyn.

"No," agreed Ida. "Ladies who can talk manual aren't that sort. Too set on doing good. What Wyn says on her

fingers sometimes would give them a fit. She does need somebody like you said, but it's got to be somebody that isn't too
particular."

"If only Caroline would give her mind to it! How is she
by the way? It's been weeks since I saw her."

"Well, she's got a bit much on her plate, if you ask me,
sir. She's taken on a lot of cases for Miss Maxwell who's had
pleurisy. And on top of that there's Miss Daphne."

"D'you mean to say that girl hasn't gone yet?"

"No, Mr. Norris. Looks like she's a fixture."

"Caroline is too softhearted."

"No," said Wyn. "Hardhearted. She makes Daphne take
lessons with Miss Spender."

She became doleful Daphne gaping helplessly. Then she
was dour Elsie flicking insult at lightning speed.

"Yes," said Ida. "Miss Spender, she hates being retired and
now she's laid up with a varicose vein. Can't get about. So
Miss Carrie said she could do a job teaching Miss Daphne to
talk manual. Every morning she packs Miss Daphne off. Every
night Miss Daphne comes back howling she can't stand no
more of it. But Miss Carrie says it's either that or go back to
Connington."

"Positively sadistic," said Mark. "And how unlike Caroline!
What is she up to? Is it a device for discouraging nieces who
turn up unexpectedly? Not a bad idea . . . but drastic!"

"Why, Miss Daphne wanted a job at Seddon House. Of
course they'd never take her there! But Miss Carrie says that
if she works very hard, and learns as quick as she can, talking
manual, she might get a job with grown-up people that don't
want teaching, only somebody useful that could understand
their language. In a club, or to go shopping with them, or
something. Not much of a job, but better than dying on her
feet, year after year, up at Connington. Miss Flo badgers the
poor thing to death."

"Something in that," agreed Mark. "I wouldn't be Flo's
daughter for a million pounds. Has she managed to learn
anything?"

"Oh, yes. Miss Carrie says she's learned a lot. She's trying hard, and Miss Spender pushes her, and she's quicker than you might think, to look at her."

"Well, I never expected to feel sorry for Daphne Dacre. But if it comes to a choice between Miss Spender and Flo . . . Harper! Did you ever meet Flo?"

Wyn nodded, and became Flo. She grew tall and slender. Her stained overall acquired style. She examined the picture on the easel and nodded, as though endorsing the only correct critical opinion. Then she threw him a most disconcerting glance. What could be amiss? Had he a smut on his nose? Were all buttons securely fastened?

"Exactly!" he cried, with a guffaw. "That's what she can do to you. She's a devil, and why anybody puts up with her, I can't think. That poor girl was doomed from birth. Past all help, even Caroline's."

"Oh, no," said Ida. "Miss Carrie says something is sure to turn up, if only she'll wait."

"I've heard that before. Caroline has a bee in her bonnet about waiting. And, with all respect to her, it's bosh. There's no reason at all why anything should turn up for anybody! Pure chance! A man can wait all his life, and never quite discover what he wants to do or to be."

"Not if Miss Carrie is around."

"You think she makes things turn up?"

"I don't think she knows beforehand what it's going to be. But, when she's got a finger in the pie, it does."

"Hmph! A sort of midwife for destiny?"

Wyn, who had been watching them closely, now said, "What that thing we do to food?"

She patted her stomach.

"Digest?" hazarded Mark.

"Yes. Good wine with a meal. Digest better. Grow strong. Life is a nasty meal. Makes us sick. Weak. Nicer when she is there. We digest. Grow strong. Find out what we can do."

"I see what you mean, Harper. Or you might say she supplies a propitious climate. The prisoner inside us begins to sprout. No use for Daphne to wait at Connington. Waiting under Caroline's wing is something else. . . ."

"Yes," said Ida, "and she isn't always wanting people to change, and be something different. Only to find what suits them naturally, so to speak. Miss Lecky and poor Miss Lallie! Everybody sniffed at them, and their pets and their hobbies and their funny ways. But they were happy. And Miss Lallie, she studied Miss Lecky as she never had anybody else, and versey vicer. It suited them. I daresay if Miss Daphne does find something, it will annoy a lot of people. But Miss Carrie doesn't criticize. Even if she praises anybody for anything, it's for some funny reason."

"That's true too," agreed Mark. "She's not given to praise. She defends people if they're attacked, but that's not the same thing. Harper! Have you ever heard her praise anybody?"

After a pause for reflection Wyn said, "Beddington."

"*Beddington?* Hugh Beddington? Heavens above! Why?"

"She says he is a clever critic."

"The whole human race to choose from and she selects Beddington! The scrapings of the barrel! But Daphne, my dears . . . what could turn up for Daphne which would annoy us all most?"

He pondered and exclaimed: "I know. Your dogs-body!"

At Wyn's expression they both burst out laughing.

"She's much too silly," protested Ida. "I'm sure Miss Carrie never thought of such a thing."

"No, but I have. And I think it might answer very well. She's learning to twiddle her fingers. I believe she can drive what Connington still calls a "motor." And she's been brought up to talk to Lady Fish-face. She wouldn't dare be silly with Wyn. Which of us would? Come to that, not everybody would put up with Wyn's craggy temper. Daphne would have to—or else. I call it an ideal arrangement."

"Anything would be ideal that got her out of the flat," agreed Ida.

"Yes. It would take her off Caroline's back. It would be a good deed. Did you ever do a good deed, Harper? Isn't it time you did one? Just a little tiny good deed?"

"Not tiny," said Wyn. "She is a long white worm."

"She never had your advantages, my dear."

At that he got a suspicious glance. What advantages?

"Yes," said Ida. "You needn't get thinking she's had a better chance than you, Wyn, for all she can hear. She never had a teacher like Miss Maxwell. You! You knew what you wanted to do, and were let go after it. Nobody held you back, or laughed at you. Lady Dacre, she's a masterpiece at making people feel small—making them look silly. Miss Daphne is only what her mother has made of her. If she wants to make herself over, so to speak, why not?"

"You'll be a pig," said Mark, "if you don't lend a hand to the poor white worm. And it's time that you patronized the Family a little. The Knevetts have been trying very hard to patronize you for years and years."

Wyn's scowl vanished. She became a Knevett. She tramped across the studio, kicking everything out of her way, and pulled up in front of Ida, demanding: "How is *Winsome?*"

"Doing nicely thank you, ma'am," piped Mark. "Young Daphne is working for her now, and seems to give satisfaction."

"You two!" cried Ida. "As if it was serious! Not but what I wouldn't enjoy saying it."

FOUR

Sheer terror kept Daphne at the flat for week after miserable week. To go home a failure, spurned by Seddon House, would be intolerable. All the aunts and all the cousins would hear the story, and cackle over it. Word had doubtless gone out to them, although no direct comment on her exploit had come from Connington. She tried to convince herself that the most shameful item, that letter pushed under the door, would not be published, but she could not be certain. Her mother was capable of any cruelty, any betrayal.

Cousins had lately grown more formidable than aunts. The triple domination of the elder Knevett sisters had been weakened by the postwar eclipse of Barbie Mycroft. Charlie's death and the waywardness of her daughters had been too much for her. She could do nothing with this changed world save survey it with a resentful, bewildered, heartbroken glare. Sue Preston's mooing, unsupported by Barbie's yakking, could be disregarded.

In childhood Daphne had always looked down upon her cousins since Connington sneered at them. This was no longer possible. The Prestons and the Mycrofts and Pamela Davenport, having staged successful rebellions, were all married. They were not afraid of their mothers, nor had they run up bills for bankrupt bookshops. Their contemptuous pity, laced with ridicule, was hard to bear. Yet none of them was actually unkind to her save Cecily, whose temper had been soured by disappointment. In the face of maternal opposition she had, in the end, married her ineligible young man. Now she supported him, since he seemed to be incapable of self-support. Work of one kind or another was at intervals found for him by the Mycrofts; no employer could endure his inefficiency for long, and Cecily kept a roof over their heads by teaching in a very inferior school. Conscious of a tribal "I told you so," she plodded through life, dowdy and truculent, making sure that the follies and failures of her contemporaries should be duly brought to light.

Caroline was adamant. As the price of support, Daphne must repair every day to awful old Miss Spender for instruction in the manual alphabet, hundreds upon hundreds of signs, and a very confusing, topsy-turvy grammatical construction. She also learned that only fantastic conceit could have induced her to suppose that any deaf mute would ever have the slightest use for her. For no one save Caroline would Miss Spender have undertaken so futile and thankless a task, and what good Caroline expected to come of it, Heaven alone knew. *My nephew will put the policeman's bloaters into the pillar box on Ash Wednesday.* Surely, after two months of instruction, so simple a statement as that need not be repeated?

Every night Daphne came home in hysterics. Every night she found fresh strength in Caroline's applause. She was not slow or stupid. She was learning with remarkable speed. In two months she had covered ground which might have taken most people six months. She could not have a better teacher, nor was it nonsense to talk about bloaters in pillar boxes. She must be prepared to recognize unlikely and unexpected communications. She must converse with all sorts of people upon all sorts of subjects. Miss Spender was guarding against too narrow a field of topic and idiom by saying these startling things.

It was, besides, far better to be out of the flat all day. She would have no defense against inquisitive relations, turning up uninvited, unless Caroline was there to protect her. This was indeed a spur to effort. Her heart was in her mouth whenever she got home first and heard the doorbell ring.

It rang one day when she was in her bedroom, practicing signs in front of the glass. Then came the din of Wyn Harper's horrid voice, talking to Ida. Presently Ida looked in to ask if she knew whether Caroline would be late that afternoon.

"If she's gone to Sydenham, she won't be back before suppertime. Poor Wyn's in a fix. Got people coming, a princess or something, not a real princess, foreign, wants to buy a picture. And she's all alone. Annette's gone to the dentist. I've rung Miss Maxwell, and I can't get no answer. There's just nobody to help Wyn out. I was wondering . . . Miss Daphne . . . couldn't you?"

"Me? What would she want?"

"Just to bring those ladies in, you know, and be there, and tell them what Wyn says. It's so awkward with only that slate. I'd go myself, only I just can't get to learn finger talk. I've tried. If she's got Annette, or Miss Carrie, or Miss Maxwell, they can say what she's said on her hands. Well . . . sort of. It wouldn't do always to say exactly what Wyn's said, specially if they say something stupid about her pictures. You can talk on your hands now, a bit? Wouldn't you have a try?"

Daphne did not feel able to refuse, although she was terrified of Wyn Harper, whose eye told her that she was a poor white worm. She went reluctantly into the drawing room. At the sight of her, Wyn's face changed. The upper lip became very long. She glowered accusingly at Daphne's legs. With great manual rapidity she expressed her moral disapproval of silk stockings. How could a young woman with such frivolous legs propose to do anything useful with her hands?

She looked so exactly like Elsie Spender that Daphne was quite frightened, but managed, after a while, to giggle.

"Why do you go?" demanded Wyn, changing her face again, but still flicking her hands very fast. "Tell on your fingers."

Something in her eye forbade any claptrap about a dedicated life. Daphne explained that she wanted a job, and that Caroline had recommended this ordeal as the best way of getting one. Wyn nodded, as if satisfied, and informed her that she seemed to have learned a good deal in a short time.

Could she, ventured Daphne, be of any use this afternoon?

She got another nod. Wyn became a ladylike young person, ushering in visitors, standing by discreetly, helping to put one canvas after another on an easel, relaying information, slipping off to answer the telephone, and showing the visitors out.

"I could try," said Daphne. "But please don't go too fast. I'm very slow still, I'm afraid. And if I don't know a sign, spell it. But I'll do my. . . ."

She broke off, appalled. There was a fresh clamor in the hall. Another voice was talking to Ida. A tribal voice. Whether they yakked or mooed, they all had inflections in common.

"Why frightened?" signed Wyn.

Daphne could only gasp and shiver, waiting for the ax to fall. These weeks of labor had been fruitless. *They* had caught up with her. Which of them was it?

The door was flung open, and in marched Cecily saying: "It doesn't matter. I'm in no hurry. I can wait till she gets back. And if you could rise to a cup of tea, Ida, I'd be grateful."

Ida's distressed face was visible for a moment before the door was firmly shut in it.

"Why, Daph! Ida said you were out!"

Cecily glanced for a moment at Wyn, identified her as Ida's cousin, and gave her a brief nod before sitting down. She had much of her mother's peremptory manner, but did not otherwise look like a Knevett. Thickset and sallow, she charged every situation with a slightly lowered head, as though intending to butt somebody. As usual, she wore shabby tweeds, and a felt hat was pulled carelessly over her lank straight hair.

"I'm glad I've caught you," she said. "I'm in town for the day, and I came on purpose to get news of you. Everybody is longing to know. How are you getting on at Seddon House?"

"I . . . I. . . ."

Daphne and Caroline had settled what she was to say if anyone asked her this, but panic had driven all recollection of it out of her head. Cecily smiled knowingly.

"Not quite as delightful as you expected? We're all surprised that you're still there. We thought you'd have run home in a week. But really, you know, Daph, you seem to have been making a terrible fool of yourself lately. You mayn't know it, but going on as you do, pushing letters under people's doors in the middle of the night, is a well-known symptom of hysteria."

The worst! The worst had happened. They knew. Everybody knew. There was no escape. None.

"It's kinder in the long run to tell you. . . ."

Cecily broke off to stare at Wyn, who had uttered a kind of growling shriek, and was rapidly flicking her hands.

"What on earth is the matter with her? Can she understand? Is she talking? Why does she put her hands to her head like that? It makes her look like a cow."

"It . . . it's the sign for a cow," quavered Daphne.

Wyn's command was repeated.

"Tell this cow to jump out of the window."

"A cow? What cow? She must be mad."

"You work for me," continued Wyn. "Secretary."

Witless Daphne could only gape.

"Telephone. Drive car. Write letters. Talk to cows. For me. Not Seddon House. Work for me. Tell her. Quick."

"I . . . I don't go to Seddon House. I'm . . . helping Miss Harper."

"Miss . . . ? Oh? Helping her? How?"

"Telephone. . . ."

"Oh. I see. I thought she was pretending to telephone just now. But do you understand deaf-and-dumb language? When did you learn?"

"S-since I came. And . . . I can drive her car, if she wants."

"Well, that's very kind of you. But it's the first we've any of us heard of it. We thought you were at Seddon House."

"Not kind," instructed Wyn. "I pay you. Tell her."

"She pays me," gasped Daphne.

"What? Money? How much?"

After turning to Wyn for information Daphne reported that she was earning six pounds a week.

"*Six pounds?* But that's ridiculous! That's more than. . . ."

Cecily flushed furiously, and so did Daphne. Five pounds a week, so the Family had ascertained, was all that poor Cecily got at that horrid little school. Daphne began to feel uncomfortable. She had many faults, but pleasure over the humiliation of others was not one of them.

"Tell her we go," commanded Wyn. "Say cows are coming to my house."

"I'm afraid we must go now, Cecily. A princess is coming to see Miss Harper's pictures, and I have to be there."

"A princess? It looked as if she was talking about cows again. What is all this? I insist. You must explain."

Wyn had taken Daphne's arm and was marching her out of the room. She now dropped it, and looked at the girl steadily: "Stand up to her," said her eyes. "If you do, I'll help you. If you can't, you're no use to me or anyone else."

"Really, Cecily, it's no business of yours. Tell everybody anything you like, and get out of the way."

"I don't believe a word of what you've been saying. You invented it on the spur of the moment. You were never very truthful. I shall ask Ida."

Cecily lowered her head and charged out of the room. Daphne tried to faint, but was shaken back to life by her new employer.

"She'll find out it isn't true!"

"We decide what is true. Come."

They went into the hall in time to hear Ida say: "Oh, yes, Wyn's been looking around for a secretary now for quite a while. She can afford it. And Miss Daphne can talk manual ever so well. She's had the best teacher in England. And there's nothing unnatural if Wyn talked about cows. She often calls a person a cow if she's taken against them."

FIVE

A couple called Price, living at Kingston, had been put in touch with Seddon House. Christine drove down to see them on the day when Wyn's exhibition was to open with a Private View. The interview saddened her so much that she scarcely had spirits for a gay afternoon.

These scenes broke her heart, although she should have got used to them by now. The shock, the bewilderment, the despair, were always the same. The Prices were still stunned and incredulous, still hoping for some miraculous reprieve, and they recoiled from her advice as from some kind of capitulation. The child of so many hopes would some day be cured of this disability. It was unthinkable that he must live out his allotted span thus burdened. Something should be done to his ears. When they were set right, no flummery would be needed in the way of games which should develop all the remaining faculties. "Doctors did not know everything." In many cases "it all came right after seven years." Such a disaster could not possibly have arisen from German measles, from which Mrs. Price had suffered during her pregnancy.

It was a case for Ca, thought Christine. If the Prices could be induced to accept any help at all, Ca would have some chance of success, since she was good with intransigent parents. She could win their confidence by behaving as though their child was perfectly normal. She would prattle away to him as once, long ago, she had prattled to Wyn. Should any sign-talk grow up, it would seem to spring from some natural and happy collaboration. She could provoke such engaging responses that parents were disposed to join in the fun. If the baby laughed so much, when feeling her nose and throat as she talked, they could themselves provide similar entertainment. Obstinacy or apparent slow-wittedness she could explain in a way which did credit to the child's intelligence. For any Arthur she could produce a wasp, if only her help was sought in time.

At the moment, all help was likely to be rejected. Pictures of children at Seddon House, digging in the sand heap or feeding their pets were "very nice for poor little things like that, but our Colin isn't like that."

Education, a wider knowledge of medical facts, were the only remedy in such cases, and Christine felt an increasing bitterness against all those whose support in this field might have been valuable, and who had withheld it. She was coming to share Elsie's view of Wyn, and she no longer took the pride which she had once expected to take in this, the most brilliant of her pupils. She had taught Wyn Harper—to do very well for herself.

The name of so successful an artist would have been a boon in the campaign for better educational facilities. It would have silenced those who maintained that poor little Colin Price belonged to an expendable section of the community. Wyn still refused to join the Association. She had taken all that she could from anybody willing to help her, and had given nothing in return. As a complete member of the human family, giving as well as taking, Myra had done more credit to her teacher.

Christine now saw very little of Wyn, since Wyn no longer needed an interpreter. Daphne Dacre undertook all that sort of thing very competently. Had it not been for Ca and Ida, Christine might have ignored the Private View. She could not hurt their feelings, and must pay tribute to Ida's hat, of which she had already heard tidings. It was even more impressive than that bought for the first tea party at Blount's Hotel. According to Ida, it was a "black satting clotch."

As for Ca, criticism of Wyn was impatiently brushed aside. It was much more difficult, she said, to sympathize with Daphne Dacre than with the children at Seddon House. Wyn's tolerance in that quarter showed that she had a kind heart. To be sure, the girl had learned to make herself useful, had undertaken all the labor of arranging the exhibition, but plenty of secretaries could have done this without tormenting their employer with recurrent fits of hysteria. Wyn had put up with her for eighteen months, had boxed her ears once or twice, but had never thrown her out. Daphne had been rescued from hideous social isolation, her self-respect had been established, and her freedom from the past secured. As "Miss Harper's wonderful secretary" she gave herself airs, of course, and was inclined to patronize her aunt, but what did that matter?

"And nobody in the world," Ca would protest, "could have been more generous than Wyn was to me when she made me come back to London to work with you and Elsie. I knew she would be very miserable all alone in Paris. I very nearly went back. And then she sent me a picture of herself and Mark and Donald all having dinner together, just to let me know she was getting on all right. It's a pity she's not interested in Seddon House. But everybody has their own way of managing."

This was Ca's plea for anyone condemned on moral grounds, nor was it reserved for those whom she loved; she advanced it on behalf of people with whom she could not get on at all. Her sister Flo's way of managing involved, she owned, a total disregard for truth, but it might, in certain circumstances, merit vindication. She would not scruple to seek Flo's support should she ever wish to conceal the truth. Nor would she agree that it is always wrong to conceal the truth. Right and wrong were still words at which she boggled. She seemed to regard all human affairs as a haphazard, unforeseen emergency, and her fellow creatures as snowbound, or shipwrecked, scrambling through abnormal conditions as best they might. Until rescued, they must be allowed a wide latitude in their ways of managing. Her serenity, her capacity for enjoying herself and applauding the pleasures of her neighbors, struck Christine as springing from a very grim kind of stoicism. Elsie, who had grown extremely fond of her, once summed it up for both of them, "She's a very, very good woman, but she has no morals."

The Private View was in Bond Street, and a ghost from the past was clambering slowly out of a taxi. That streaming beard, that flapping cloak, had vanished from Christine's life when the move to Venice was made. He must be very old, and had probably forgotten her long ago.

After a short, sharp peer he seized her hand exclaiming: "Miss Em! Well, well! Another old pupil. Not that *you* look a day older! A sight for sore eyes."

"How nice of you to come."

"Thought I might as well, when I got her card. Don't get up to town very often nowadays. Live at Leighton Buzzard. Ever been there? Don't go. She sent her card, y'know. Thought I'd see what she's bin up to. How's the other one? The other little dear?"

"Myra?"

"Umhm! Myra. She was the gal for me. What? Gone? Oh, I'm sorry. When?"

"A long time ago now. In . . . in 1906."

"Dear, dear! Gone! I've never forgotten her. Yes, yes. They slip off, that sort. 'Unwatched the garden bough shall sway —the tender blossom flutter down.' Yes. A tender blossom. Couldn't draw for toffee, but I never told her so."

"No. You were always so kind, and she enjoyed it so much."

"Ho! This one here, too sharp by half. Asked one day why I scolded her all the time, when she could paint, and never a black look for the blossom, who couldn't. I told her. I told her straight. I said: Because she's a little dear and you, my girl, are not."

"Poor Wyn!"

"Poor Wyn, my foot. She never wanted to be a little dear. Had other fish to fry. And by all accounts, she's fried 'em. Well . . . let's go in."

The gallery was full of people talking at the tops of their

voices. Daphne had exhibited something of her mother's talent for organizing a social occasion, and it was not easy to get a glimpse of the pictures on the walls.

"You may well stare," said Elsie, colliding with Christine in the doorway. "They sent me a card, but I wouldn't have come in a hundred years, only I didn't want to hurt Caroline's feelings. Horrible bleak pictures and such ugly colors, when you can get near them. Modern, I suppose."

"I'm not sure that they are," said Christine. "They say Wyn is the last of the Impressionists. Very modern pictures are like jigsaw puzzles that haven't been put together."

"Daft. Pictures ought to be beautiful. And she's not here herself, you know. The Dacre creature is receiving everybody as if it was her show. Oh, yes, and poor old Ida! She's stranded with nobody to talk to. Dacre is too high and mighty to bother with her, I suppose, though she's Wyn's nearest relative, and personally I'd rather she was hostess. And there's a ghastly picture of her up on the end wall. It's got a Latin name in the catalog, but you can see it's Ida. A lot of people buzzing over it. I think she's afraid they'll recognize her. She's got her cooking apron on. In the picture, I mean. That Wyn of yours never considered anybody's feelings. Well, I'm off. Caroline has seen me here, so there's nothing to keep me. Goodbye."

Ida was cowering under the clotch as though she hoped it would extinguish her. She whispered to Christine that there was sherry and everything in the little room behind. Miss Daphne was there. Lord Seddon had been, and so had Miss Grace, but nobody else from the Family, although they had all received cards.

"So few of them live in London," suggested Christine.

"Oh, they'd have come up fast enough if it was anything they could talk big about. But they don't like Miss Daphne working for Wyn. Miss Grace, she don't mind, because she's really in Society, more than any of them, even Miss Flo. Well, her mother-in-law was a Lady in Waiting."

Christine was sorry to have missed the elusive Grace, who was seldom mentioned without a footnote indicating this august mother-in-law. She seemed to exist in a region far above and beyond the Knevett world, was never quoted, and figured in few anecdotes.

"And there's all the critics here," continued Ida, "that say about Art in the papers. That's why they've got the sherry. Oh, Miss Lecky! Well, this is a surprise! Ever so well, thank you. This is Miss Maxwell, that's a great friend of Miss Carrie's."

A yellow withered ghost extended a claw. Christine took it, and suggested that they had once met in Elsie Spender's house.

"Did we? I forget. I'm here because Wyn Harper is Carrie's friend, and Carrie's sister Lallie was *my* great friend."

Miss Lecky's voice, as Christine remembered it on the wasp occasion, had been harsh. Now it sounded like the rustle of wind in dry reeds. She turned her dim eyes from Christine to Ida, as if imploring them to remember Lallie whom she alone had loved, and she alone had mourned.

"I never met her," said Christine. "But Caroline often talks about her. And she has some lovely embroidery you both did for her."

"The tablecloth? Oh yes, we had fun making that. Just white chain stitch and we made it up as we went along. I think it has every wild flower in Wiltshire. Where is she? Where's Carrie?"

"She's here somewhere," said Ida. "And have you looked at the pictures, Miss Lecky?"

"The pictures? Oh, yes, I must look at the pictures, mustn't I?"

The little wraith floated off as though blown by a puff of wind.

"Poor thing," said Ida. "She's never got over Miss Lallie dying. Took all the life out of her. Miss Carrie, she went straight off to Owl Wood, and brought her back to the flat till she'd got over the shock a bit. And went with her to the funeral. *They* didn't like that."

"What is she doing now?"

"Runs a home for lost cats or something. She comes round to the flat every so often, so as to talk and talk about Miss Lallie. But you mustn't stop here keeping me company all afternoon, Miss Maxwell. You'll want to see the pictures. And mind you get some sherry. Wyn would want you to."

Reflecting that Ida would really have made a very good hostess, Christine fought her way toward a wall. She was rewarded by a spectacle of sunbaked boulders assembled in a geometric pattern. The quiver of intense heat was conveyed by a very slight infraction of outline. This made her smile, for it recalled an incident in Wyn's childhood. On a very hot day she had sketched a hillside near Trentstoke, and had then covered her picture with wavering horizontal lines. Subsequently she had flown into a fine rage over the iniquitous difficulty of painting what she saw. Those quivering lines were there, but when she put them in she spoiled her work. Now, after thirty years, she had solved that problem.

The next canvas showed boys playing a ball game against the high walls of an ancient town standing up in flat country.

"Aigues Mortes," said a voice at her elbow. "It's a kind of fives they play down there. Arrpairr seems to have painted a good deal in Provence."

The voice was familiar. It belonged both to the past and to a middle-aged man talking to a woman with long limp clothes and long limp hair and a wide felt hat with a high crown. Christine had seen pictures of women like this, but had never met one. She looked cross, which was wrong. The women in the pictures were too primitive to be cross.

"After all I've heard about Harper," she grumbled, "I'm disappointed she hasn't showed up. I wanted to see her writing on her little slate."

"Oh, I daresay she's less bonhomous than she was in the Cruchot days. I wonder if she does funny turns any more."

His eye fell upon Christine. They gaped, remembering occasions but unable to recall names.

"Bill Taylor," he said. "You were Miss . . . Miss . . . ?"

"Maxwell. You used to take her to parties."

He introduced the cross woman as his wife, and told her that Hal was dead and buried in Flanders, a fate which had overtaken a good percentage of the class *chez* Cruchot. He himself was doing pretty well. He sometimes sold a picture, and he boiled the pot by illustrating children's books.

"One can't hope to get far nowadays," muttered his wife, "unless one's deaf or something."

At that he turned on her.

"That's not fair. Harper has never made capital out of that. We always admired her for it. She's done her best to avoid any publicity. Many people don't know even. I bet that's why she's not here. She's determined to be judged on the same terms as the rest of us."

They wrangled for a time over it while Christine reflected upon this aspect of Wyn's refusal to take the limelight, and wondered if her own irritation had been quite justified. She could understand better Wyn's motive for avoiding publicity, at least until her reputation was perfectly secure. She must be known as a good painter before she could afford to be known as a deaf painter.

"Do you admire her work?" she asked Bill.

He hesitated, and then said: "I do and I don't. It's very able. But there's something cockeyed about it, to my mind. Well, now . . . there's one the other side of the room: "Sunset in Mid-Atlantic." It makes you jump. What's wrong? It's not a sunset. Red sun on the edge of the sea. But everything in the picture suggests it's coming up, not going down. The slant of the deck, the pitch of the waves, they all send your eye *up* when you come back to the sun. She knows, she must know, what she's done. Why do it? If she ever saw a sunset like that, I'm a Dutchman."

"But she did," said Christine. "We both did. Coming back from America. The sun set and then it came up again. We both nearly jumped out of our skins."

"*What?*"

"The sea looked flat, you see, but it wasn't. The liner ran

up to the top of a long swell and caught the sun again for a minute. We realized that afterwards."

Mrs. Bill yawned, and he took her away with an apologetic farewell. He deserved a nicer wife. Christine felt sorry for him, remembering the sanguine good-natured student in Paris.

Working her way along the wall she next encountered Ca talking to Mark Norris and a man who looked like Somebody, and who was eyeing his companions with furtive curiosity.

"Isn't this a beano?" exclaimed Mark. "I never saw so many nobs to the square inch. Young Daphne has certainly roped them in. My Private Views were slum parties in comparison."

"It's a good deal fuller than it was last time we were all three here," said the stranger. "I realize now! We came to an Impressionist Exhibition in the nineties. Lots of lovely Sisleys and Renoirs, and only a dozen people looking at them. And you," bowing to Ca, "lost your gloves."

"I only hope Daphne hasn't overdone it. What are you going to say tomorrow, Beddington?"

"Tactile values. I'm a Berensen boy. Harper is strong on them. I must allow that."

"Tactile values?" queried Ca.

"Paints hot to look hot. Cold to look cold. Water to look wet. Rough, smooth, hard, soft, all that sort of thing. . . ."

They moved on to scrutinize a cluster of tall trees on a hilltop, which faintly suggested a group of stately people standing in consultation.

"Ah," said Beddington. "Kimmons bought that for Barnesfield last year."

"Why should they look so like people?" mused Mark.

"I suppose," said Ca, "that you knew the difference between trees and people a long time before you drew either?"

"Why, yes. I imagine so."

"With Wyn it's the other way round. She drew them before she had grasped the difference. She drew quite well when she was six. She once told me that she went on thinking trees were a kind of people till she was eight or nine. She saw things and drew them before she knew what they were, quite. That's why a lot of her pictures are a little odd. Even after she knew, she went on seeing them a little differently."

There was a pause while they digested this.

"Offers qualities rather than definitions," decided Beddington.

"Sounds classy," said Mark. "I won't pinch it till you've come up with it in print."

Beddington sidled away, and Mark chuckled.

"Never ventured on a piece of original criticism in his life. Merely says what's safe, in a chatty, highbrow way. Flo is the only person who takes him seriously."

"I do," said Ca. "He explained to me once why some girls in a picture would never get sunburned. He was very good about it. But we must go and find Ida, Mark, and bring her along to have some sherry."

They went off, and Christine stood gazing at the trees, and thinking of a child who found an acorn and put it in a cradle.

"It's quite romantic," said a woman behind her. "She had this ambition, even as a child. She does everything for Wyn Harper, you know. Devotes her whole life to her."

"Rather a pretty girl," said another voice. "It must be a dreary job, I should think."

"Oh, it makes her perfectly happy. Louise went there once, to the studio, and she says it's touching to see them together —this girl talking for the poor thing, and explaining what she wants to say. It's a sort of vocation, really. Wyn Harper would be quite lost without that wonderful Miss Dacre. Owes everything to her. Everybody says so. Some people are like that. Saints. They just naturally are saints."

Very slowly Christine edged her way toward the little room. There she caught a glimpse of Daphne looking happy and triumphant in a little gold hat which stood up all round her head exactly like a halo.

 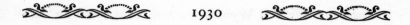
The Wholebine Monkey

MORE THAN HALF of Ida's life had been spent in London, but she wished to end her days in Slane Forest and to go there before she was too old to enjoy her leisure. In due course, her retirement was arranged. A pleasant couple in one of the new bungalows at Slane Bredy were looking for a lodger. Their front room could be furnished as a bed-sitting room where Ida might have all her own bits and pieces.

"Caroline will drive her down there next week," reported Daphne to Wyn. "She seemed to want you to come too, but I sat firmly on that idea."

She said this a little smugly, since she enjoyed interpreting her employer to Caroline and Ida. The chance to do so did not often come her way. Despite nine years of selfless devotion, she had not been promoted to that choice group in which Wyn talked like a person. Nor could she interpret the gargles very well, lacking the long practice enjoyed by Miss Maxwell and Annette. It was humiliating to depend upon hands, but no proof that she did not really understand Wyn better than anybody else. Ida was receiving a generous annuity from her famous cousin, and should not make further demands.

A question was now flicked at her, "Why sit on it?"

"You've never been back to the forest since you left it, have you? And never will go."

"Ca think I shall go?"

"No," admitted Daphne. "She told Ida you wouldn't."

"Say why?"

"They don't realize how painful one's childhood memories can be. I do."

"What did Ca say?"

"Oh . . . she said . . . she said you were frightened."

"Frightened!"

The word offended Wyn so much that she taxed Ca with it when next they met.

"But you are frightened," said Ca. "You are frightened of remembering."

"I remember. Without going back."

"Only one thing. When they pulled us apart in the lane. And you remember that all wrong. You say that hundreds of people all dressed in black came on purpose to watch. There were only three: Fitzy and Lallie and Grace. And they didn't come on purpose. We were just walking past and you rushed out."

"You remember wrong. There was a great crowd."

"No. You make too much of it. You insist there was this great crowd because you want to think it more important than it was."

"Not important. Finished. Over. We were too strong. They couldn't part us."

"I know. It's finished. And I think it really made more difference to my life than to yours. But if you went back there you might remember . . . oh . . . something else. I don't know what. But you don't want to remember it because it isn't finished. So it frightens you."

"You want me to go?"

"No. Perhaps you manage better if you do forget."

"Rubbish. Frightened! I shall go. Next week. With you and Ida. Room for me in your car?"

"Yes. But not for Daphne. We've sent off most of Ida's things by rail, but she'll have a lot of odd bundles, if I know her."

"Daphne! Take a holiday from Daphne. Nice day with you and Ida."

Nothing could frighten Wyn any more. She was sure of that. She had proved her strength, and had been equal to all trials. The acquisition of Daphne as a factotum had immensely increased her self-confidence, since she had the silly creature completely under her thumb, and could use her without depending on her.

"All right," said Ca. "It will be rather nice. Ida wants to give us a tea party in her new home with her mother's good china and her grandmother's silver spoons."

On a mild autumn day they all three drove westward. Ida was left to unpack, and to make friends with her hosts, while the other two took a short drive in the forest.

The great tree trunks stirred Wyn to a sudden excited curiosity. Among them she had been born—sister to Dainty and Ruby, cousin to Ida. During those six forgotten years, she had discovered her vocation. Like a duckling that has taken to the water, she had left the forest knowing one end of a pencil from the other. None of her kin had felt such an impulse, nor did she believe that her deafness had anything to do with it. Some mysterious ingredient, dominant in her, was missing in them.

After a couple of miles they came to a bleak little box of a schoolhouse built midway between Slane Bredy and Slane St. Mary's so as to accommodate the children from both villages. Thither had the little Harpers trudged in all weathers, bread and cheese in their pockets, the damp seeping through their broken boots. Ida, better shod, and carrying a more plentiful lunch, had been taught there too.

"Not me!" said Wyn, when Ca pointed this out.

Had she been born twenty years later she would have sat there, learning nothing perhaps, but forced to attend, since her presence would enrich the school by five pounds a year.

"Born too soon for Miss Dyson," she crowed.

Improvements upon this unsatisfactory arrangement had been secured in consequence of a campaign untiringly fought by Miss Dyson and her allies. Wyn was perfectly well aware of this, but, in order to annoy Ca and Em, she chose to blame the principal of Seddon House for all slow progress.

Elsie Spender had merely been rude whenever they chanced to meet. Miss Dyson was far more disconcerting. The woman was impassively good-mannered, and it was impossible to shut her up. She continued to send, unasked, annual reports of the activities of the Association, although Wyn resolutely refused to join it. She had written to know if Wyn would give evidence before a Royal Commission, should a fresh one be secured. Deaf mutes were no longer automatically classed with imbeciles, which signalized a great advance in the public attitude toward them and their problems. Their evidence would now, almost certainly, be accepted, and testimony from a distinguished artist would strengthen their cause.

To this Wyn made no reply. Miss Dyson, not a whit abashed, persisted in the campaign. Her last request had been quite outrageous. It seemed that a group of deaf adults had taken up painting as a hobby. Wyn must be aware of the very great pleasure which this activity could bring into the lives of people whose pleasures were restricted; any help or encouragement from her would provide an immense stimulant, and she might be able to explain some things to the students as nobody else could.

Daphne had been instructed to write on her behalf explaining that she disliked amateurs of any sort, and thought it a mistake to encourage them.

"So who taught you to spell?" asked Ca, driving away from the school.

"Em."

"Did she really? Sure you weren't born knowing?"

Sarcasm from Ca was rare, and Wyn laughed.

"Glad we came," she said. "Beautiful, this forest. I forgot that."

"I suppose it is. I never thought so. Sue used to say how dreadful to live in London, after the forest. I like London. I'd just as soon live there."

Wyn remembered that she had once commented on that to Mark. Ca, she said, cared nothing for beauty, and did not mind where she lived. Mark had replied with a quotation which she could not exactly recall . . . *wonder . . . the human face . . . no music save the happy-noted voice. . . .*

They were driving down a steep hill to a cluster of cottages.

"Where this?"

"Don't you know?"

"Oh. . . . Oh. . . ."

A mean little public house. A stream crossing the road with a footbridge beside it. Smoke going up in the still air, and the smell of burning wood. On every side mounting walls of foliage, yellow oak, flaming beech, and dark green splashes of holly.

"Changed much?"

"Not a bit, as far as I can see. No new bungalows."

"Where your big house?"

"A bit farther on."

They splashed through the stream, and came to a squat church.

"Dead Knevetts," said Wyn, craning up to peep over the churchyard wall. "Wicked Sir Harry there?"

"Only a very little bit of him. It was rather horrid. The rest was eaten."

"I didn't see that. Thought you said eaten."

"I did say eaten. Rats. They had a law then, though they didn't often use it. They could stop a man being buried till his debts were paid. Everybody hated Sir Harry so much, that's what they did. The servants ran off and left him on the bed where he'd died. The house was empty for some months —till my grandfather came back from Madeira."

"What a horror!"

"Just like the forest," declared Ca. "All forests are horrible. Even in fairy stories. Full of witches and dragons and robbers. And children taken there and left to die."

"Rubbish. Nothing wrong with this forest, except Knevetts."

"I think it's the other way round. Knevetts would have managed better if they'd lived somewhere else."

"Never hurt Ida. Her home. She loves it. My home too."

Ca reflected on this, and said: "No. I don't think it's your home. But you're right about Ida. She's . . . a very old sort of person, and I expect it suits her just as it suits the trees. But it doesn't suit us. We don't belong to it, and it doesn't belong to us. Edmund always said we took it all away from other people. It was church land till the Reformation, and then we somehow grabbed it. And we grabbed a lot more of the free forest in the eighteenth century, when rich people seized so much of the common land. But we never turned into proper squires. We just lived here like the dragons and the wolves in fairy stories. That's what Edmund said."

Their next pause was at a pair of stone gateposts flanking a weedy drive. The tumbledown house at the end now belonged to Edmund's son, who lived in Kenya. It was let to a retired clergyman. He took, as pupils, a dozen boys who had been expelled from public schools.

"They can't get up to very much mischief here," explained Ca. "Although I believe they set it on fire every now and then."

These details delighted Wyn. She stored them up as a weapon against Daphne, who was inclined, when in a sentimental mood, to talk about her mother's unique and beautiful home.

"Domesday Book?" she inquired.

"All a myth, so Edmund said. He got so tired of it that at last he went and looked up Domesday Book. Not a Knevett anywhere. Now look on the other side of the road at that field going uphill. That used to be the old kitchen garden where we played. It's all been plowed up now."

"Don't remember that. Where did I live?"

"If you want to see that, you must walk. It's up a narrow lane, and there's no room to turn a car."

They got out. After trudging for a hundred yards up a rutted lane, they came to a ruin—a chimney wall standing above a stone enclosure full of nettles.

"That used used to be your house."

"Here?" asked Wyn, looking up and down the lane.

"Yes. Here."

"Where we are standing now?"

"More or less. But I can't tell you where this huge crowd was, that you say came too."

There had been no huge crowd. This was not the place. Yet Wyn was sure that she had seen one, perhaps on some other occasion.

"Not here," she agreed. "In the road. At the church."

"Some funeral, perhaps. And you got it mixed up. There were always lots of funerals, and everybody went. It was the only fun they had. The black dresses made you think of a crowd."

Still Wyn lingered, fascinated, wondering if this were all.

Then, like a tiger, memory rushed from its lair and pounced. She gasped, and sank down upon the shattered doorstep.

"Wyn! Are you ill?"

"No. I remember."

"Come away!"

She was hauled to her feet. They crept back along that dreadful lane, and got into the car.

"There's a new road," said Ca. "It used to be only a track. It goes up to a nice view. It was always a good place to go to. I'll take you there."

She reached into the back of the car for a rug to put over Wyn, who was shivering. Then she drove uphill until they reached a clearing in the woods whence they could see out to the Welsh hills. There they stopped, and sat in silence.

"I was in a dark place," said Wyn at last. "A long, long time. Under a bed, I think. I knew . . . I knew enough to know I was lost. . . ."

She paused seeking words for an anguish too atrocious to be described. It had once been hers, and could overtake her again.

"Helpless. Quite alone. I knew I was me. I felt. I was alive. But I was a dead person. Part of me . . . there ever since. I made my life on top of it. I forgot that prisoner down there. Still there. Always there. Always alone."

Ca was staring out over the plain below. Her face, seen in profile, was remote and stern.

You are not the only prisoner in that dark place.

She had not said it, but she was thinking it, since she spent her life hauling prisoners out of the dark.

"Don't sit there thinking, Ca. Speak. Help me."

"You could do something to help the others. It would do you no harm, even if it did you no good."

"Don't like babies."

"No. And they don't like you much."

"Spitty little things. What then?"

"There's to be some kind of Committee of Inquiry."

"Go there? Say: Uck! Uck!"

"No. Use hands, as so many others have to do."

"Take dear Daphne?"

"No. They'd have a really intelligent person interpreting."

"Say what? Please, we are very clever. Very useful. Make a law. Then all Ca's babies will be clever and useful."

"Don't be a donkey. Yours is an important case because you might have talked very well if you'd been managed better. Em thinks so. She thinks it was all her fault for driving you on too fast."

"Em thinks I'm a lousy cow."

"No. She understands rather better than she did. She sees that you couldn't have people saying: How wonderful of a deaf person to paint! You had to be judged like everybody else. But she thinks that you are so well established now that it wouldn't matter. And you needn't always be so rude about Seddon House."

"Tell all about Em's mistakes?"

"Yes. If your case could be discussed and understood, then other teachers might not make the same mistake. She's getting old now, Em. She's seventy-four. She's afraid she'll be dead before this committee gets to work, and she won't be able to tell them what she knows. You'd never have got out of the dark if it hadn't been for her."

"Umph."

Wyn was aware of a certain relief, but the prospect of a victorious Dyson was repulsive. She would be drilled, no doubt, by some kind of Dyson, along with a crowd of boring strangers. Dyson would see to it that they were asked the right questions, and that they gave the right answers. To patronize a sketching class for amateurs could hardly be worse.

Unconsciously she simpered, putting on the kindly face which would be expected of her when examining their horrid pictures. Ca shook a little. She was laughing.

"You," she explained. "Even if you won't take an interest in that class, you might at least make a funny turn of it for me and Mark. What you would look like if you were taking an interest, I mean. You should have seen your face just now."

"I should tell those people where to put those pictures."

"What did your Mr. Gordon say to Myra?"

"Can't remember. Too long ago."

Three of them sat in a row in the schoolroom at Belgrave Square. God whirled in. Wyn trembled. Em looked nervous. Myra, all confidence, proferred a sketch made at Trentstoke— a lopsided cottage and some trees like cabbages. For this she got a lollipop, while Em and Wyn were told where to put their pictures.

"Poor Mr. God! Gone to heaven. Daphne saw in the paper. You like these hills?"

Ca was gazing at them again with a hungry intensity.

"When I was very unhappy," she said, "when I lived down there, I used to come up here and look at them. I thought, if I only had wings, I would fly away, fly away, to somewhere else. I used to feel I almost could if I wanted it enough."

"You had to stay here longer than I did."

"Yes. But it was never so bad after I got your first letter. I saw then how things can change and alter. Even then I never foresaw what a happy life I was going to have in the end. Thanks to you."

"Because I sent you back to Em?"

"Oh, long before. I owe it all to you. Without you I might never have found out what I must do. For years I was miserable and bewildered, as if I was making some dreadful mistake all the time, and I couldn't find out what it was. Then, one day, I saw Elsie make a sign to a little boy, the sign for a house we made up long before. Then I knew. I'd always thought of it as something only for very clever people, like Em, or very good people like Elsie. It had never occurred to me that I might be able to do it; that it was really very like us playing in the old kitchen garden. You have made my life, right from the very beginning."

'— "And you have made mine."

"I never meant to," protested Ca, looking apologetic.

Wyn laughed.

"No. You hate good works. But now you are happy? You don't want to fly away any more, when you see those hills?"

Ca gave her a quick look, and said nothing. If she could, she would be off, thought Wyn in a sudden panic. Keep her here. Make her happy. Do what she wants.

"All right. Perhaps I buy a long beard, like Mr. God, to hide my face. When I look at their pictures."

"Oh, Wyn. I never said look at any pictures. Only . . . speak up to that Committee, if they ask you."

"No. Buy a long beard. Go the whole . . . sow."

"Hog."

"Sow. Joke. Time for tea with Ida."

They drove back to Slane Bredy. The great tree trunks slid past. The sense of oppression lifted. The lost hamlet was left behind with all its legacy of anguish.

They found Ida unpacked and ready to preside over her new tea table. Her mother's good china was all washed and shining. The rattail spoons were polished. There were cakes and scones and cucumber sandwiches. Two flower groups, painted by Wyn, hung on the walls, and a photograph of Ca dominated the mantelpiece.

Her new quarters seemed to please her, although she declared that it was too soon to say. Mrs. Jackson talked like a sensible person. Everything in the bungalow was very nice except that chiming doorbell, which was a bit affected.

Within two hours she had collected an amazing amount of local information. The parson was unpopular; supposed to be a Roman. He preserved in the Ladies' Chapel. The old smithy was gone, and a lot of petrol pumps put up instead. There was a bus service to Severnton on market days. The postmistress was an old schoolmate. A lot of the same families lived in the same houses, but some very funny people lived in the Brents' old house. He was writing a book, and so she had to do Teas. The Women's Institute had quarreled with the clergyman over the parish hall trestle tables, which he kept locked up in his garage. Ida had not yet heard all the ins and outs of that, but she would do. The new people at the Free Forester had taken away the Wholebine Monkey. Wasn't that a shame?

Wyn and Ca looked blank at this and Ida explained.

"The old inn sign. The one your grandpa painted, Wyn. They've got a new one doesn't look half so nice. I ran out to have a look. More like a poster, if you know what I mean."

"My grandpa? The blacksmith?"

"Oh, he was only your stepgrandpa. Your real grandpa, he was a painter."

"What?" cried both her guests.

"Painted a lot of inn signs round about in Severnshire. Must be getting on for a hundred years ago, though."

"I never heard this before," said Wyn.

"I daresay it never came up before. We had no call to remember him. He was a bad lot. Drank and that. But a lovely painter, when he was sober. Come to think of it, that's probably where you get it from. Grandma, she supped sorrow with the spoon of grief. Didn't last long though. He fell out of a gig and broke his neck, day after your mother was born. And before the year was out Grandma married my grandpa. He was a blacksmith, and he'd always been sweet on her. Your mother and mine were only half-sisters, for all there wasn't but eighteen months between them."

"I remember that old sign," said Ca. "I thought the street looked different somehow."

"Doesn't look the same at all. It was famous, that sign. A

gentleman riding through once, he was so taken with it he wanted to buy it. Joe Cranton, that owned the Forester then, he wouldn't part with it. The gentleman asked who done it. When he heard he said: Ah, that fellow? A Wholebine Monkey. Said he'd seen some more signs your grandpa done. It made people laugh because there wasn't no monkey, only a forester boy in his olden-time clothes. But the name stuck, down here. Anybody would say: I'm off to the Monkey. Or it might be: Down at the Monkey last night there was language."

"I can't see," complained Wyn. "I can't see that name. Fingers, Ca!"

Ca spelt out an alternative which had occurred to her, "*Holbein Manqué.*"

"Oh. Oh, yes. My grandpa! Then. . . ."

"Don't suppose they say that any more now," said Ida, sipping her tea. "Quite forgotten by now. Times change, even in the forest."

CHAPTER 12

Recall

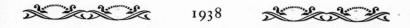

ONE

TO FILL IN the time before breakfast had become a problem for Flo. She invariably woke at five, but she could not demand breakfast before eight lest Emily and Clara should rebel and give notice. They were surly and lazy and inclined to bully her, since they knew that good servants were scarce in Bath. Should they walk out, she would be quite helpless. No friends or relations would hasten to look after the old thing until a new staff had been engaged; so far as they knew, she had none.

Once awake, she must be doing something. A tea tray and a small bustle with an electric kettle filled out ten minutes.

And then?

Formerly she would have caught up with her correspondence. She had always been an early waker and, as everyone agreed, a most amusing letter writer. Long before breakfast, she would be sitting up in bed scribbling away to innumerable friends and to all those members of the Family with whom she happened to be, at the moment, upon speaking terms.

People died so. One by one they slipped away beyond the reach of the postman. The few survivors were not the most congenial. They were not those upon whom she could rely to welcome or to recount a diverting scandal.

The Family had dwindled. Brothers and their wives had

[221]

never counted for much with her; of her seven sisters, five were gone now. Clemmie, Kitty, Lallie, Barbie, and Sue! Never again would she mystify them, outwit them, succor them, or pump them for news of one another. Grace, to whom she had been so generous, who would never have married Davenport had it not been for that Season, was, at the moment, in a fit of the sulks. It would blow over. These little tiffs never lasted. She had merely thought it a pity that poor Grace should be the only person in London unaware of the rumors concerning Pamela's husband. If false, they should be contradicted at once. If true, a psychiatrist might be able to do something. Sisterly concern had compelled her to drop a diplomatic hint, for which she got scant gratitude.

"Thank you, Flo. I'm not sure that you always mean as well as you say you do, and this is the last time that I shall ever speak to you."

That had been said three years ago. The tiff had lasted in a very silly way.

Carrie wrote, of course, on the first Sunday in the month, but her letters were tedious—they recorded the blameless activities of great-nephews and -nieces. Yet, lacking them, Flo would scarcely have known where everybody now was, or how employed.

Carrie and her men! That was a joke, had anybody survived with whom to share a joke. Credited in former days with two possible lovers, she now lived serenely with both. Tom, as a fourth, provided a respectable front, but who could ever have foreseen such an establishment when that flat was originally selected for the girls? After years of occasional visits, those three had now settled there for good and all. Nor was there any woman in the place save Carrie. They had imported a sallow creature in a fez who had worked for Tom and Donald in Persia. It was too funny, and a triumph over all those who had refused to believe in Carrie's double life, but everyone who might have chuckled or exclaimed had now gone across the Styx. In the eyes of the younger generation, a woman of sixty-three had reached *l'age canonique,* and could offer no material for speculation.

Eddie would have laughed. Eddie would have written letters. So, perhaps, would Gee. But they were young still and
buried somewhere and up in Heaven. *They were not.*

Letters from Frank had almost ceased in consequence of an
occurrence which even Flo could not manage to describe as
a tiff—a drama in which somebody flew into a rage while she
waited, amused, until they came round again. She had, herself,
flown into a rage, and had told him what she thought of his
wife.

Had she controlled herself and waited she would, sooner or
later, have routed her foe. Frank had been caught. He might
eventually have welcomed his mother's help in freeing himself.
He could have been led to perceive, more and more clearly,
just how bad a bargain he had made. On a hundred small occasions, adroitly staged, Wendy's inferiority could have been
exposed. By losing her temper, Flo had ruined all. She had
given the woman an excuse for refusing to stay at Connington
where so many little traps were laid for the unwary.

When George died, the young couple took possession. Flo
retreated to a dower house nearby whence she hoped to carry
on the campaign. These hopes were vain. Connington was
always fortified by Wendy's vulgar friends who treated the
dowager as a standing joke. After a stormy year or two, she
retreated to Bath where a circle of old friends awaited her.
These proceeded to die, or to go away, or to take umbrage for
silly reasons.

The old are captious. They fly into a rage upon some provocation which, twenty years earlier, they would have laughed
off. They will not tolerate each other's foibles, while demanding the widest latitude for their own. They grumble continually. They are bores.

Poor Hugh Beddington had pointed that out once. He had
vowed that on his sixty-fifth birthday a self-denying ordinance
should come into force as regards malice and spite. Thenceforth he meant to be very good-natured, as a provision against
his declining years, since he had observed that ill-natured old
people seldom dine out. Poor Hugh! He had not stuck to his
vow. He continued to be spiteful and malicious. And then he

was not there any more. Why not? Nobody took the trouble to find out, although there were rumors of a slight stroke. One forgot about him, for some years, until one read his obituary notices.

Daphne, stubbornly dutiful, wrote from time to time. Her letters might have been designed to infuriate Flo. In Wyn Harper's employment she met important people concerning whom good stories would have been welcome. She told none, and she ignored her mother's questions. She could write of nothing save Miss Dyson, and Wyn's interview with a Committee of Inquiry, and a Slade scholarship for some boy in Wyn's art class. Had she been actually working at Seddon House, her letters could hardly have bored Flo more.

Five o'clock! Three hours to breakfast! Letters! I must get on with my letters.

To whom?

There was, luckily, the silver and the furniture. Emily did not take proper care of them; she was a slut who would not have lasted a week at Connington, even as an under-housemaid. Flo had her own little box of polishing materials. When she had drunk her tea she could put on her dressing gown and creep stealthily about the house, defying the silence of the morning. She had nice things. She had removed many treasures from the dower house, hoping for a battle with Wendy. There was none, since Wendy did not know nice things when she saw them. She was putting in a cocktail bar at Connington, and it was all one to her what that old trout took from her shack across the park.

In and out of the rooms Flo would bustle, muttering to herself, and rubbing away. Walnut, mahogany, brass handles, ornate key plates, inkstands, candlesticks . . . until Emily's heavy foot on the stairs sent her scuttling back to bed. She was, when it came to the point, rather frightened of Emily.

Then she was officially "called." She had a second cup of tea. She dressed. She went downstairs. She ate her breakfast.

And then?

Some of the day could be occupied with the newspaper.

Who was dead? What ought one to think about Fascism, supposing one was asked? What would George have thought?
George had been disposed to approve of Mussolini. People like
the Italians, he said, deserved somebody like that. It was tiresome not to be able to tell people what George thought, although his political career had ended for good and all in 1906,
and he had thought that the war would be over in six weeks.

Next came a short, unfriendly interview with Clara, known
as "ordering," in which Clara told her what she should eat.
When was over, she took her morning walk down to the
library, where she changed her book. She had always been a
great reader.

After lunch, and a short siesta, she sat in her drawing room,
awaiting callers. It was always possible that somebody might
call. Such residents as she now knew never seemed to do so,
but a friend visiting Bath might wish to look her up. She must
still have many friends, although she could not always locate
them. If they came she was ready for them. A handsome old
lady sat in a room full of nice, well-polished things, ready to
amuse and to be amused. She had met so many interesting
people in her time, and could tell such diverting anecdotes that
her acquaintance must still be something of a privilege.

For a couple of hours she would wait expectantly. Then
she would settle to read the day's book, turning the pages
rapidly in search of a quotable sentence. Bridge might have
helped her through this part of the day, but she scorned it as
the resource of women who had no conversation.

At eight she dined. By ten o'clock she had always turned
over all the pages in her book. She could take her sleeping pill,
and climb into bed. Such an early retirement had its drawback:
if she took her sleeping pill at eleven, she might not wake
quite so early in the morning. By ten o'clock, however, she
had always finished her book.

These books would have lasted longer had somebody else
been there. For a few months she had tried the experiment of
a paid companion, who should sit with her and make little
noises whenever she wished to comment on her book. The plan

had failed because the silly woman had not understood her function. She did not confine herself to attentive exclamations. She talked. She gave her own opinions. She was a crashing bore. When snubbed, she smiled with tolerant good humor, as though her employer were ninety and senile.

"Are you sure you have your latchkey?" she would ask, if Flo went out alone. "Are you sure you can get as far as the chemist's?"

She was sent packing.

Spasms of helpless rage often shook the monotony of Flo's life. To be so disregarded, ineffective, and unimportant was intolerable. Any form of antagonism would be preferable. She did not ask for love; she had never loved anyone much except Eddie. So long as she could feel that she was doing something to somebody, she was perfectly able and willing for a fight. Barbie and Sue, she suspected, had felt the same kind of frustration in their later years. Their children were kind and considerate, but Flo's sisters had died bewailing their lost empire.

To make somebody jump would be a relief. Once it had been easy. She had but to invent a myth about passion flower fruit, and the whole house was in an uproar. How could she do it now?

She could publish her memoirs perhaps. Everybody seemed to be doing this. More often than not, her day's book had been written by some silly woman or other. If Helen Palgrave and Lucy Yates could do it, Flo Dacre could do it twice as well. The process was simple. The title must be a quotation evoking time and memory. *All Our Yesterdays* would be suitable, but she had better make quite sure of the source and the context. The first chapter, dealing with childhood, must be quaint. There must be an impressive landscape background, and an ancestral home was always an asset. Then one grew up, and the anecdotes could begin. These might make a lot of people jump. Grace's mother-in-law might have been a Lady in Waiting, but Flo knew some very funny stories about her. They must be told gracefully, of course, but they need lose nothing of their sting. Nor could the dead sue one for libel. If their descendants wished to be spared, they should have recognized one's existence. They should have called when they came to Bath.

The scheme was so attractive that Flo had already made two false starts. She had written and torn up an account of the Knevetts, beginning with Domesday Book. Something more intimate was needed, she thought, and she had composed nine words of it: "The Forest! It was always there. My earliest memory . . ." was of biting Barbie, but she had better not say so. Memoirs were hard work, much harder than one would think when reading Lucy Yates. The book must have a first chapter, although everybody would skip it. Or could one be very original and begin boldly with a description of Mallie Stornaway absent-mindedly lighting a cigarette in church?

On a morning when she was aching to make somebody jump, two letters lay beside her breakfast plate. One was from Carrie, although this was not the first Monday in the month. The other was from Frank, who never wrote save on business matters. With a sniff she tore open the envelope and read it.

> My dear Mother,
>
> Christopher, as you may remember, comes of age on the 28th. We are having a sort of tenants' beano in the afternoon and a dance here in the evening. It would be so nice if you could be here. We very much hope you will come.
>
> Yours affectionately,
> Frank.

It was some time before her thoughts fell into any kind of sequence. Billows of fury seemed to be swirling her round the room. She sat holding the letter while her egg, always boiled too hard, grew cold.

So they wanted her back, did they?

After years of neglect, she was coolly invited to forget the past.

Why?

Because her absence, on so public an occasion, might cause comment.

Indeed it might cause comment. Did Frank really suppose that none of his neighbors could do sums? "Born five months after the marriage." Plenty of people must have whispered and surmised, hushed up though the scandal had been. Who could be sure that Christopher was really his son? There were plentiful grounds for doubt. She had made her own inquiries into Wendy's past. Frank had been but one of many.

George shared her suspicions, but forbade her to utter them. One does not, he insisted, foul one's own nest. The child had been born in wedlock, and must be accepted as the heir of Connington. She had promised George, on his deathbed, never to breathe a word of their doubts to any living soul. Nor had she, save to Barbie and Sue. Even when she lost her temper, she had refrained from making that accusation against Wendy.

But now? Now?

That promise did not, surely, oblige her to attend these farcical celebrations. No, no! Not at all. One could be absent. One need say nothing, but one could be conspicuously absent.

Not moldering away at Bath. That would give them an excuse for talking about age and decrepitude. No. In the neighborhood. Lively as ever.

Buxton! At Buxton a week or so before the party. Seizing the opportunity to call on old neighbors. "How young and well you look, Flo! You'll be at Connington next week, of course? We shall all be there." . . . "We-ell, no! I don't think so. They did ask me, but . . . no, I think I'll go back to Bath."

No more need be said. Word would go round the county. Christopher would come of age amid a storm of whispers and conjectures. Flo wouldn't go. She obviously couldn't bring herself to be there. It does look as if *she* thinks. . . .

Emily came in to clear the breakfast table, saw the untouched egg, scowled, and withdrew. Flo had not noticed her at all.

All very well for you, George. You're up in Heaven. I'm here, and I haven't spoken to a soul for weeks and weeks—not a single soul except Emily and Clara and the girl at the library. An outrageous thing to do? I'm going to be outrageous. I'm not dead yet. They seem to forget that. They deserve it. They deserve it.

Still formulating this plan, she ate her cold hard egg. What had she to lose by it? Their affection? Their confidence? They felt none, and let her know it. They should jump! At length her eye feel upon Carrie's letter. She opened it.

My dear Flo,

I have a great favor to ask of you. I'm in a difficulty, and I think you are the only person who can help me.

I have been ill for some time. The doctor says that I shall not get better, but he can't say how quick it will be. I seem to be getting worse very fast now.

This is tiresome because people must guess soon, and it will be a worry, and will spoil the great rejoicings over Wyn Harper. We are all so pleased and happy about it. Ida is coming up from Slane Bredy to go with Daphne to Buckingham Palace to see the ceremony. And there is to be a great party that afternoon at Seddon House. All Wyn's friends are going and her art pupils. It will spoil it all for a lot of people if they are upset about me, and I'm not sure that I can last out until after the Great Day.

You are so very clever at keeping a secret and getting people to think what you want them to think. Can I come to you until the rejoicings are over, and will you help me to keep it all very quiet? It will be a nuisance for you to have somebody ill in your house, but it need only be until after Wyn has been "done" as Ida puts it. Then you can push me out into a nursing home.

I hope it is not too much to ask. I'm still able to get about, but I'd like to come as soon as possible, please, Flo? I could go to Grace, but I'm afraid she would tell everybody.

Yours affectionately,
Caroline.

In the kitchen the bell pealed.

"Now what's she want?" speculated Clara.

"Nothing," said Emily. "Only to keep me on the run. I went in there once. She hadn't touched a thing. Just sat there glaring at nothing, like she does."

She finished her tea. Again the bell rang.

"All right, all right," she told it, wiping her mouth. "I'll go when I'm ready. Not before."

When at last she went upstairs, Lady Dacre met her, waving a letter and looking as pleased as Punch.

"Emily! I want the spare room got ready. My sister is coming to stay."

"Yes, m'lady."

"Air the bed well. My sister has been ill. We must take great care of her. I'm not sure about the mattress. I may have to get a new one."

The spare room had never been occupied before. Emily looked glum. She had not bargained for guests, and would draw the line at an invalid.

"She may want a nurse. We must see."

Emily said that nurses give a lot of trouble in the house. The implied threat was disregarded, and she was instructed to Hoover the spare room before she did anything else. A message was sent to Clara. There would be no ordering today. She could settle the meals as she liked (as if she ever did anything else!).

"I must go out at once. I must send a telegram to my sister."

Off went Flo. Having dispatched her telegram, she trotted home to write a confirming letter. Of course Carrie could come, as soon as ever she liked. Together they would bamboozle everybody, although the whole scare was probably a mare's nest. The doctors in Bath were excellent, and would soon set everything right.

It was such rapture to be back again in the world—needed, consulted, giving orders, doing something to somebody. By ignoring certain sinister implications in that letter, she was really able to feel as pleased as Punch. With careful nursing

Carrie would certainly recover. She must do so, or this pleasant little intrigue would lose all its savor. It must eventually become: That awful fright we had over Carrie when I managed so cleverly.

The spare room mattress was undeniably lumpy. After lunch she went out and bought a luxurious new one. She also, when changing her book, took out an extra subscription, in case Carrie might like to have a book too. It would be a blessing not to read in silence any more. They would sit together, reading their books, and when Flo wished to comment on her book, Carrie would make attentive little noises. She had always been courteous about that sort of thing, whatever her faults might have been. At five in the morning, when one woke up, there would be something to do. One could run in to see if Carrie was awake, and if she too would like a cup of tea. The long silence was ending.

A wire came announcing Carrie's arrival on the next day but one. There was much to be done first. Flo bought an adjustable bed table, a backrest, air cushions, and other sickroom appliances. She was so busy that she found herself obliged to postpone her campaign against Wendy. Her answer to Frank's invitation was hasty but genial. She could not be certain, at the moment, of getting to Connington by the twenty-eighth. Carrie was coming to her. Carrie had been unwell, and needed nursing. It sounded like arthritis. She might not be able to leave Carrie. She would let them know.

The wages of Emily and Clara were suddenly and substantially raised, in view of the extra work caused by an invalid in the house. They still grumbled loudly, but had really grown quite curious to see the sister who could inspire such eccentricity. Their employer seemed so different, looked so different, that they could not make it out at all. In the past she had been a stingy housekeeper. Delicacies of all kinds were now being ordered in profusion.

Finally she called upon the vicar. People who thought that they were going to die sometimes demanded a parson, even though they were quite mistaken, and got better. Flo herself went to the abbey on Sundays, it was something to do, but she had not hitherto made the acquaintance of her parish priest. He seemed to be a sensible, inoffensive creature, and promised to come if summoned. She hoped that it would not be necessary. Religion was embarrassing.

On the following day, having made every possible provision for mind, body, and soul, she set out to meet her guest at the railway station. Already she had pictured to herself a pale confused Carrie, with pleading eyes and feeble gait, crawling out of the train and unable to secure a porter. So prepared was she to welcome and to reassure an invalid that she did not immediately recognize a tall, gaunt, bent woman limping purposefully down the platform, followed by a porter carrying a suitcase.

Nothing remained of Carrie save the puzzled brown eyes and the tranquil voice.

"I've got here," she announced with some triumph.

And took Flo's proferred arm as though admitting that to get there was probably the final effort. Henceforth she must lean upon others.

All worn away, quite worn away, thought Flo as they drove off in the car she had ordered. Hardly here at all. Those idiot men! Haven't they eyes in their heads? If Ida had still been at the flat she'd have seen it. Soon now! Very soon. . . .

Her own eyes filled with tears, and she looked out of the window. It would be selfish to cry. Had Carrie wanted lamentation she would have gone to Grace. She wanted an ally, She had always chosen how she would live. Now she chose how she would die.

"Is that the abbey?" she asked.

Flo murmured yes, unable to check her tears. Then, fearing that this averted face might seem hostile, she stretched out a groping hand. Carrie took it in a bony claw which was still firm and warm.

She used to have beautiful hands, remembered Flo. Once . . . putting on her gloves . . . she kept me waiting. Annoyed me. But I thought then what lovely hands she had. Oh yes, my sister had beautiful hands.

TWO

Mark lay stretched upon his bed, and had just fallen into a doze when Tom roused him to say that old Ida was in the drawing room, and they would be cads if they did not gather to hear about yesterday's grand doings at Buckingham Palace. She was extremely disappointed that Caroline should have missed it all.

Mark groaned inwardly, feeling that he had already heard quite enough about Wyn's exaltation. He was glad that the old battleax should have done so well, but he thought her work overrated. All successful work was overrated. His admiration was reserved for a few obscure toilers never likely to appear in any Honours List. Should one of them, by some freak of fortune, shoot into fame, his appreciation cooled. He began to fear that the fellow had gone off, except upon those chilly days when he suspected that his own judgment might be completely warped by jealousy. He had, perhaps, forfeited all right to criticize since he had been for so long a *maître sans œuvre*.

"Do we get tea for her?" he asked, remembering that their Persian slave was out.

"No. She's going back to the studio for tea. Donald is bringing port. Ida fancies it, and we thought it would meet the occasion."

They found Ida looking critically round the room. It was neater than it had been in the days of the Aunt Heap. There was no clutter of feminine employments. The workbaskets had vanished, and the half-finished jigsaw puzzles of which Lallie had been so fond.

"Where's that big blue picture used to hang over the mantelpiece?" asked Ida. "The one their cousins painted."

"Gone to an exhibition," said Tom. "Eighteenth century watercolors. A lot of our pictures have gone, including one which everybody now allows to be a Constable."

"I always thought it was," said Mark. "But I didn't say so. If I had, it would have been snatched away from Caroline. I wonder nobody tries to snatch it now."

"Nobody interested enough to snatch," said Tom. "And where could it go? To the Manor House? Standing empty with part of the roof taken off to save taxes?"

"But Miss Carrie? How is she? Have you heard?"

"Not from her. Flo sent me a line to say that she had arrived all right."

"But what is it? What's she got?"

"Flo was a bit vague, but we gather it's arthritis."

"Oh, that arthritis! It's dreadful. But they can do a lot for it these days. Only it gave me such a turn to come up and not find her here. To think of her away when Wyn was done!"

Donald came in with the port which he poured out and handed round. They toasted Wyn. Then Tom said: "Now, Ida! Tell us all about it."

"Oh, it was wonderful! Buckingham Palace! And that's a funny thing. Poor Miss Maxwell . . . oh, it is a shame she didn't live to see this day, she'd have been so proud . . . she told me once, she remembered when Wyn was a little thing she said she'd take me to see the Queen. And Miss Maxwell thought, poor child, pathetic to think a thing like that. But it's all come true, only it was the King. Buckingham Palace! I never thought I'd get inside there! Well, we went in a taxi. Wyn and Miss Daphne and I. Wyn said might as well go in a bus, why not? but we made her take a taxi. And when we got there, she had to go off with a very nice gentleman who came and took her. Miss Daphne, she wanted to go too. Thought Wyn couldn't manage. If *she'd* had her way, she'd have gone in and got done herself, I do believe. But Wyn said she could manage. She had on a dark green costume.

So then we went all along through the Palace, and the pictures, old masters, but we couldn't stop to look at them, there was this big room and a band playing "Men of Harlech" and seats for Miss Daphne and I and everybody. A lovely band. And there was a platform and a table with all the medals and that put ready, and a young fellow handed them all to His Majesty in the right order. Oh, it was very well arranged! I suppose they're used to it. And all the people looking so pleased. Come to see their friends done. All sorts of people. There was a fireman done. He'd been very brave. I don't know what, quite, but it was in the papers, he'd rescued a lot of people, and he got a medal. And just behind us there was his wife and these little children, so excited to see their daddy talking to His Majesty. Quite a long talk they had. But that wasn't till later. First His Majesty came in, and we all arose. And he put some ribbons round some gentlemen's necks. And the band played "The Road to the Isles." Lovely music all the time. We were sitting down again, of course. And then some more gentlemen were made into knights. Miss Daphne, she timed it, and she said three knights a minute.

And then a lot of people got medals. That was when the fireman was done, and you could see that His Majesty said something very nice to him, because his ears went quite red. And those children! I turned round to smile at them, they had on these white gloves, and their mother had told them to be sure and keep them clean, so they had their little hands stuck straight out in front of them, for all they were so excited. I mean you could see she'd brought them up very nice.

And then, *then*, it was the ladies' turn. And the band struck up that lovely tune, "The Beautiful Blue Danube." Romantic, you know, as a compliment to the ladies. Oh, I do think it was a shame Wyn couldn't hear that lovely tune. In they come, one after another, to be made into Dames and get medals and all. Wyn looked very nice and she curtsied beautifully. She looked as nice as any of them. They weren't so young, and ladies who have done something special aren't always what you might call oil paintings. There was one come in a wheel-chair.

His Majesty smiled at Wyn, ever so kindly, but he didn't say anything. I expect they'd told him it might be awkward for her. And when it was over we all arose again, and he went out. So we found Wyn, and all went home in another taxi. And the flowers! And the telegrams!"

Ida paused for breath as the doorbell rang. Tom went off to answer it.

"So many little chores crop up when Caroline is away," lamented Mark. "We don't realize how she coddles us."

"Time you coddled her a bit! I'd never heard a word about her being so poorly. They said at Seddon House that she hasn't been at all the thing for a long while. They were worried."

"So were we," said Donald. "On the day when she went off to Bath, she looked so ill that we wanted, one of us, to go with her. But she wouldn't hear of it. You know how obstinate she can be."

"Oh, yes. She's always one to do things in her own way."

"A very odd way," said Mark. "Bath may be a good idea, but Lady Dacre is the last hostess I'd select if I were out of sorts."

Tom returned.

"A man to read the electric meter. He says he knows where it is. I don't."

Ida laughed.

"In the kitchen cupboard. A nice pickle you'd all be in if you wanted to turn off at the main, any reason. I remember when that meter was put in. When we first come here we didn't have the electricity. Gas. And a coal range in the kitchen and coal fires in all the rooms. Coal sheds seven floors down. Jane and I had to haul the scuttles up. But we thought it all quite up-to-date. It was, then."

"Was the party at Seddon House nice?" asked Tom.

"Not so nice as the Palace. Well, we missed Miss Carrie so much. Everybody said so. Wyn's great friend. And Miss Daphne was a bit trying. They don't like her there. Never did. She puts on such airs. But a lot of it was very nice. They had a lovely tea for the older children, and a lot of people from the Association came, and some of Wyn's pupils from her painting class, and they'd put up decorations, and made a sort of throne for Wyn. Oh, and they've got a very nice picture of Miss Maxwell, that Wyn painted. And another one that Lord Seddon gave them. Miss Myra when she was a little girl. That old drawing master did it. Sweetly pretty."

"They ought to have one of Caroline," said Donald.

"Wyn never could paint her. She tried often."

"I tried once," said Mark. "She's a difficult subject. I never finished it, and now it's gone the way of all things. I've an idea it might have been a good picture. I don't know. . . ."

"If only it had survived," muttered Donald, "you'd know."

Antagonism, always latent between these two, flickered up. Tom scowled at them, and asked Ida if there had been speeches at Seddon House.

"Oh, yes. A gentleman. Some great doctor. He said all the reasons why we should honor Dame Wyn. Her pictures and all the work she's been doing these last years for deaf people. Only he didn't say deaf. He said hard of hearing. It sounds nicer. And how little help a child like her got sixty years ago compared to now. And how it's getting better all the time, with science and everything, so we must never be content. There'll always be something more. And about the Oracles."

"The Oracles?" cried her audience.

"Electrics. I think a gentleman in America invented them, but perhaps that was something else. Sort of artificial ears, by what I can make out. It seems there's hardly any born that can't hear at all. There's just a little tiny bit of hearing left, but it dies away if it isn't encouraged. And just to know what sound is, he said, makes all the difference to their speaking. Wyn might be able to hear a thing or two, if she'd had these Oracles when she was little, but it's too late now."

"Have they got them at Seddon House?" asked Mark.

"Not yet. But they will do. Miss Dyson said about that, when she made her speech, and about how the war put everything back twenty years, and how they're catching up now at last and all the improvements they hope to get in another couple of years. Nineteen forty! London's going to be fine for the children in 1940.

"So then it was Wyn's turn to make reply. She got a young fellow to do it for her. He's in one of her painting classes. It was a nice idea, but he spoke a bit too soft. I expect they'd learnt him to speak soft, and he didn't know how much louder he had to speak in that big room. So we couldn't make it out very well, only he finished by saying that truth and beauty are the same things and that's the only earthly thing we need to know. I'd have thought we had to know a bit more than that, but we all clapped and cheered.

"Oh, yes, and the children cheered too! They'd been practicing specially for weeks. And when Miss Dyson said: Hip! Hip! they all yelled *Hurray* along with us. Only they got so excited they wouldn't stop. They loved it so. They'd never done anything like that before. And, of course, they did make rather a peculiar sort of noise, more like a monkey house. So at last Miss Dyson had to take them somewhere else. And we could hear them still at it, cheering hard, when we drove off. Oh, yes. It would have been a lovely party, only Miss Daphne was so aggravating. I heard her talking to that doctor. She wouldn't dare say it in front of Wyn, or she'd get a flea in her ear. But she does behind Wyn's back, and it's not so."

"Does she claim to have taught Wyn to paint?" asked Tom.

"For two pins she would! She says it's all thanks to the Family that Wyn has risen up like this. She says they all took an interest from the very first, and saw how bright she was. And when Uncle left the forest they wrote to Lord Seddon about Wyn, and asked him to take her by the hand. So that's how Miss Maxwell came to teach her. It's not so. Nobody took an interest, only Miss Carrie, and, what's more, they tried to stop that. It was the very opposite of what Miss Daphne says. She's clever, and she's useful to Wyn in lots of ways, but she only does it for the sake of the credit she gets. That's all she thinks of."

"She's certainly a most annoying girl," agreed Donald.

"It's not exactly her fault," said Mark. "She was brought up to think that credit is very important, and then she was starved of it. She needs to feel that she's making an impression, in order to be sure that she's alive at all, poor girl. We may growl at her for demanding her daily dose of credit, but is she so very much worse than the rest of us? I might still be painting, if I didn't care a hoot what anybody thought of my work.

And you two," he nodded at Tom and Donald, "might each have written a book."

He was growing very tired of being the only *maître sans œuvre* in the flat. They would never write those books, and it was absurd of them to talk as though they still meant to do so. He would have taunted them before had he not been frightened of Caroline; malice of any sort was liable to put her into a freezing rage. She had better hurry back from Bath, he thought, or they would all begin to bicker. They were three disappointed old men, but they generally managed to forget it.

They ignored him. Tom went to answer a fresh ring at the door, and Donald asked Ida about life at Slane Bredy.

"Oh, there's plenty going on. And a bus to Severnton twice a day. Seems to make the forest ever so much smaller, somehow. And there's the Institute. I was put off that at first by a hymn they keep singing, but I've got used to it. Bring me my bow! It says. Bring me my arrows! Bring me this, bring me that! Put me in mind of Sir Richard, hunting mornings, yelling for his boots. But they have nice parties, and interesting people come to speak. We could have done with something like that in the old days. And now we've got our own trestle tables."

Tom came back, and stood in the doorway looking at them.

He looks his age, thought Mark. We all do. But he's aged a lot lately. I hadn't realized . . . he looks ten years older than he did . . . when he came and hauled me in here . . . half an hour ago. Something has happened!

Ida thought so too. She got to her feet and cried: "Oh, Mr. Tom! What is it? What's happened?"

They waited until Tom had found his voice.

"A telegram," he said at last, "from Flo."